Prai... ...ylor's
Ain't Love Grand?

"...love will have its way in this charming tale of opposites attracting." –**Book List**

"Dana Taylor writes with sparkling wit and snappy dialogue, crafting characters who whose warmth and humor will steal your heart. A bright new star in the publishing world, Ms. Taylor is on her way to the top of the best-seller charts!" –**Merline Lovelace**, Best selling author of *Untamed*

"...a fresh voice, an impeccable sense of comedic timing, vivid narrative, and fascinating characters. First-time novelist, Dana Taylor, has honed her craft well and earned a respectable place within the genre." –**ForeWord Magazine**

"...a strong message involving having faith and God, and the courage and love that he instills in life. Dana Taylor's story is an uplifting, romantic adventure of small town life and love in Oklahoma." –**Romance Junkies**

"...a fabulous new author who has written a laugh-out-loud romance... This is comedy at its best. ...a wonderful story that you surely will not want to miss." –**Romance Reviews Today**

"Ms. Taylor has created a unique leading lady with real personality and wit....an altogether refreshing approach...Kudos to the author for daring to be different AND kudos to the publisher for knowing a good thing when they see it!" –**BN.com Review**

THAT DEVIL MOON

DANA TAYLOR

Karoline —
Enjoy a little
mystic fun!
Dana Taylor

Echelon Press

This is a work of fiction. Names, characters, places, and incidents are products of the author's imagination or are used fictitiously and are not to be construed as real. Any resemblance to actual events, locales, organizations, or persons, living or dead, is entirely coincidental.

Echelon Press
712 Briarwood Lane
Hurst, TX 76053

ISBN: 1-59080-344-2
www.echelonpress.com

First Echelon Press paperback printing: January 2005

Cover Artist: Nathalie Moore
Editor: Kat Thompson

Printed in LaVergne, TN, USA

Dear Reader,

I hope you enjoy my mystical tale of Beaver Cove, Arkansas. Writing is a journey that is only completed when stories meet readers. In this case, it became a collaborative effort when I ran the "Devil Moon Cake Contest" on my website. Try the winning entry from Deborah Oakes–it is to die for!

I'd like to thank Echelon Press for encouraging authors to write beyond the usual. Maddie and Phil showed up one Sunday morning in my subconscious, caught in the spell of that Devil Moon. I wrote the opening scene as the sun rose. From the beginning, the characters' personalities came through loud and clear. Day after day, I sat down and wrote out the scenes as they unfolded, without knowing exactly what would happen next. The creative process was exhilarating and a bit frightening. In the end a story emerged that touches on divorce, drug abuse, sexuality and, ultimately, redemption–all in a *fun* way. I greatly appreciate Echelon allowing the story to go forward in its own quirky fashion.

If you like what you read, please spread the WOM (word-of-mouth). Independently published books are little jewels buried in a mountain of literary debris. Only readers telling other readers will pull them out of the heap.

Visit www.echelonpress.com for more special manuscripts. And, please, drop by my website, www.danataylor.net, to say hello and keep up with all the happenings that are *Definitely Dana*.

Sincerely,
Dana Taylor

Dedication

Special thanks to the many who helped along the way–Karen Syed, Kat Thompson, Susan Sipal, Sherry Aman, Sara Taylor and the girls at the virtual Writer's Playground. But this book would not be in existence without a particular cyber angel. Her daily e-mails demanding "what happens next?," hours of editing, and constant encouragement kept me spinning a story that took me totally by surprise.

This book simply must be dedicated to Carla Hughes.

Prologue

Sweet Moon, I thank thee for thy sunny beams;
For thy gracious, golden, glittering gleams

A Midsummer's Night Dream

It was hormone hell Saturday. She'd felt it building all week. The time when the gentle streams of chemicals in her blood turned into a raging flood of estrogen, swelling her breasts, swirling her emotions.

After a small bottle of wine, a large chocolate bar (with nuts), a piece of cake, and three Loretta Young movies, Madeleine Woodbridge Harris was still wide awake and edgy. She hit the remote, bringing silence into her cozy living room, crossed the carpet, and looked through the picture window toward the lake. Dousing the lights, she stared at the glistening water reflecting the enormous summer moon.

It beckoned seductively, "Come to me..."

Drumming her fingers on the windowsill, she said out loud, "Jeez, I'm turning into some kind of hormonal she-wolf, drawn by the full moon."

Then again, she thought, a swim might relieve some of the tension, take away the gnawing sadness.

Once outside, she grabbed Grammy's beach quilt that hung on the porch swing next to the back door. Grammy had quilts for all occasions and circumstances, made from every scrap assortment imaginable.

Even now with Grammy gone a year, Maddie could hear that Arkansas twang. "Little sister, things is made to be used. Don't be making my quilts into museum pieces when I'm gone. You make 'em part of your life."

So, hugging the beach quilt, a little tipsy from the wine, she padded across the meadow, a willowy figure seeking relief on a hot Ozark night. Clear lake water lapped the bank, still warm from the long summer day. Hidden spots of paradise dotted these hills she now called home. She'd come from up north during Grammy's last days and never wanted to leave.

Flinging the quilt on the coarse sand, she stripped off her blouse, shorts, and shoes. Her breasts seemed to take on a life of their own, pulsing and swollen. Aching in constriction, she released the bra clasp at her sternum. *Ah, free at last.* The panties went next and lastly the clip that confined her silky honey blond hair. Tumbling soft curls tangled across white shoulders.

Arms raised, she reached for the moon. Woozy-wine thoughts floated by. *Free from clothes, free from rules. Just a few moments of freedom...*

The warm evening breeze kissed her skin as she walked to the water's edge. Cool liquid on hot skin. Simmering desire swirled around her like hovering fog on the lake. She was Eve, Lady Godiva, and Delilah all rolled into one. Basic, elemental woman.

The moon smiled at her, whispering again, "Come to me." She sank into the pebbly water seeking the arms of a phantom lover.

Phil Wilcox was having a shitty night. A rambunctious party going on in the apartment across the pool, spilled out into the main courtyard. His teeth gnashed at the splashing, music, and laughing. Sitting in his leather recliner in the dark, with only the illumination of the ever-undulating mood lamp, he tapped his fist on the armrest. His sparsely furnished bachelor pad offered little diversion. He hadn't bothered to hook up cable yet, and local TV at this hour consisted of infomercials and loud Southern preachers.

Resentment poured through him as he relived the phone conversation with his ex-wife from seven hours earlier.

"She isn't coming, Phil," Pam said in the little girly voice he used to find so endearing that now churned his stomach.

"Why the hell not?"

"Don't get pissy with me or I'll hang up. She has a slumber birthday party for her best friend. These things are very important to eleven year olds."

Phil bit back his irritation. "Why didn't you tell me about this before now?"

"Oh, I'm sure I did."

"I'm sure you did not!" He tried to take a reasonable tone. "Okay, so are we making the visitation up next weekend?"

"Can't. I've got my family reunion next weekend. You wouldn't want her to miss that, would you? I really gotta go, Phil."

He hung up and thought about calling his lawyer. Again. But the damn court system didn't give a rat's ass about his lost visitation. He'd been through it too many times.

Another long night of paying for past sins yawned before him. At least he wasn't ten years younger when he would have screamed obscenities into the phone and gone out and gotten drunk.

Now it was three-fucking-o'clock in the morning and he felt as restless as a caged bear. In the old days he would have been in a pleasant, boozy haze by now. Probably passed out on the couch. Nights like this he missed the good old, bad old days.

A riotous female shriek pierced through his walls, followed by the sound of a big, loud splash. The goddamn party was going to go on all night. He stood and ran his fingers across his short-cropped hair.

He shrugged and mumbled, "What the hell, might as well go fishing."

Phil steered his beloved 1981 Buick Skylark Convertible up the curving mountain road. At least Pam hadn't gotten *that* in the divorce settlement. He turned onto a dirt road that led to the lake. He liked to explore, find new places to throw his line. A buddy had told him about Lake Luna, nestled ten miles from town in the hills. He stopped his car, thinking he could see water beyond the brush and trees. Getting out, he heard the slapping of small waves. Close, definitely close.

Looking up, he marveled at the brightness of the moon, made out the dark craters on the surface. Damned, if it didn't resemble a wizened face. White light circled the orb, then arced into space. He stood mesmerized, hypnotized. Thought he heard someone whisper his name, beckoning.

He shook his head. "Get a grip, Wilcox. Next, you'll be talking to the Man in the Moon."

He opened his trunk and grabbed his rod and tackle box. Inhaling the pungent, lakeside air, he spied reflected light on water through the bushes. His feet crunched twigs and leaves as he pushed through branches, drawn to the surface of glistening silver on black.

Oh man, he needed this bad. One night away from complaints, responsibility, and guilt. He wore guilt like an invisible cloak. Invisible, but heavy as iron chains.

Maybe he could stare at that huge moon and get lost in it, forget his sins–just for a few minutes. Phil blinked. A shaft of moonbeams glowed like a laser, showing him the way. Optical illusion, no doubt. Still, he followed, the smallest glimmer of excitement warming his belly.

Beyond his vantage point, Maddie had risen out of the water, the liquid sluicing down her slender body as she padded up the bank. The beauty of the night, the melancholy breezy rustle of the leaves brought an ache to her entire being. Alcohol erased all her inhibitions, plunging her into a wave of drowning emotion.

A schizophrenic conversation whirled in her mind.

"Oh, God I'm lonely. I want to wrap my arms around someone warm and wonderful."

"Don't be silly. You don't need anyone. You're a self-reliant woman. It's just your hormones."

"Shut up! I'm tired of always blaming my hormones for feeling bad. This ache in the pit of my stomach is more than hormones. I want more, I want someone..."

"Oh, just go onto bed. I hate it when you whine."

A rising tide of tears rose in her throat. "I hate it, too. I can't help it."

"Fine, cry all you want. Nobody's watching."

Sitting on Grammy's quilt, she pulled her legs up and hugged her knees. She stopped the mental gyrations and gave into the emotion. Big, salty drops washed down her cheeks. Her eyes squeezed tight; her throat choked, holding back racking sobs. Squeaks bubbled from her diaphragm.

Drip, drip, drip. Not nearly there yet. A few crocodile tears weren't going to do it.

Oh, Lord, I'm going into a full-blown crying jag.

She laid back on the cottony surface, flinging one arm over her eyes. High-pitched mewling followed the erratic contractions of her lungs. She gave in entirely, moaning like a wounded animal.

She sobbed, she wailed.

Wash it all away. Wipe away the humiliation. Forget the betrayal.

Her shoulders heaved in full-bodied crying frenzy. Riding the teary tide, she peaked and rode the wave down to the shallows. Quieter tears trickled.

Rational thoughts splintered into cutting fragments and then dissolved entirely. Her brain dozed as her body still wept, curled into a fetal position. Blanketed in moonlight, blue air warmed her, offering slight comfort. Still the longing remained, the bone-deep longing for love, for connection.

Phil heard the eerie, thin wailing. The hair rose on the back of his neck. He remembered the tales from his childhood of "haunts", the lost souls that wandered the earth in perpetual limbo.

He followed the sound. It was real, not his imagination. Was it a cat? No, it really sounded like crying. Female crying. Hell, he'd heard that enough during his marriage to recognize it all right.

Brush in his path thinned out as he reached the rockier edge to the lake. Then there were only jagged ledges to navigate as he rounded a bend and came upon her–a pale form in the moonlight, curled on a blanket by the water.

Hair fanned out above her head. Turned away from him, her naked shoulders and back curved down to the rise of hips and a white, beautifully formed bottom.

Christ, Phil knew he should just turn around and look for another fishing spot. But he couldn't go away, couldn't stop moving toward her. Drawn…pulled by an irresistible force. He paused for a moment and quietly put the rod and box down, then continued on the path, attracted by a fascination he didn't stop to analyze.

The sounds she made broke his heart. When he'd heard crying like this before it had been through a locked door. He dimly remembered standing in the hall, slapping at the wood, too drunk to put it together or be any help at all. But tonight he was stone-cold sober.

He dropped to his knees before her shaking body. His fingers reached and touched a smooth shoulder. Loneliness and despair radiated from her, emotions he recognized only too well. He wanted to help. Put an end to the pain–if only for a few stolen moments. Scooping her up against his chest, he fully edged down on the quilt. Holding, helping, healing. That's all he meant to do.

Maddie drifted in some personal nether world. Half asleep, she saw a kaleidoscope of Thomas moments. The teasing beginning, the happy middle, and the betrayal of the end. She gasped, feeling herself suddenly against a warm chest, wrapped in security. Dreaming Thomas had returned to her, she lifted her arms and clasped them around his neck, pressing her face against his shoulder.

Thomas? No, not Thomas. Better than Thomas, warmer. A dream man, then. Exactly what she needed. Some times an overactive imagination paid off. Oh, yes, this is what she wanted, longed for. Lord, Dream Man smelled really good, too. Tasted good. Felt good.

She let loose–an explosion of estrogen and emotion. *Come on, Dream Man, fly me to the moon.*

Her need engulfed Phil. She kissed his neck, entwined her limbs about him. She smelled of sweet wine, chocolate, the lake and woman. He'd only meant to offer comfort, but she dragged him into her tilting, sensual universe.

He struggled against the temptation. Against the rush of desire.

Oh man. *Oh man, oh man.*

She trailed a line of kisses down his neck and found the material of his shirt displeasing. Buttons flew as she ripped his shirt apart. Hot hands darted over him. He tried to still them. Honest to God, he did.

Never opening her eyes, she nestled against the curly hair on his chest. He savored the feminine scent tickling his nose. *Okay, sweetheart, we'd better call it quits.*

Before he could pull away, she shoved him flat on his back. Phil found himself covered by a ravenous Moon Goddess. She nuzzled his pecs, making the blood rush to his groin.

Oh, Jeez, when was the last time he'd felt this great? Just another second and he'd put an end to it.

She rose over him; silky hair concealed her face. His eyes lit on a trio of small moles on her white throat. Glimmering light glowed around her milky skin, making it all seem like a dream. How could he resist the bountiful breast poised so close to his mouth? When he encircled her with his lips, the Moon Goddess moaned and writhed.

Then her hand found him, caressing, arousing.

Oh God. Oh, Jeez. Oh, man.

Phil Wilcox gave up the struggle of conscience and accepted the gift. One night of ethereal oblivion, a magic carpet ride to the stars.

On the handcrafted squares of Grammy's quilt, they entered their personal world of sizzling sensuality. Nobody else existed–only the Dream Man and the Moon Goddess. Cocooned in moonbeams, silvery light sparkled around them, swirling, spinning.

A face on the giant orb in the shimmering sky appeared

and grinned. Oh, how he enjoyed bringing these mortals together...That ole Devil Moon.

Chapter One

I used to be Snow White, but then I drifted.

Mae West

Maddie was roused by the predawn chill and the lumpy sand poking her under Grammy's quilt. Finding herself wrapped in one side, she stretched and unfurled herself from the blanket, still luxuriating in the afterglow of that fabulous dream. Then she heard a noise, a sort of buzz saw snoring, manly noise. Opening one eyelid and then the other, she viewed a shoulder. Traveling her vision upward, she saw a thick neck and a masculine head above the shoulder.

Oh my God, a voice whispered in her mind. *OH MY GOD!* That same voice screamed in her brain.

Eyes wide open, dreadfully, fully awake, she sat up, focusing in the dwindling moonlight. She noted the discarded clothes, the fishing rod and tackle box. Giggly hysteria threatened to overtake her.

He's caught himself a big one all right.

Then she returned her gaze to the masculine figure beside her. Though turned away from her, she took a quick inspection of him in the dim light. Most of his face was buried in Grammy's quilt. Short buzz-cut hair, thick arms, and a muscular back. She didn't see a lot of flab. Nice buns. He reminded her of a teddy bear.

He made a smacking, snorting sound and she panicked at the thought of him waking up. What had she done? Feeling the languid hum in her solar plexus, she *knew* what she'd done. Maddie-madness had struck again.

The whole event made her cringe with embarrassment. *Run, escape, fly away.* She grabbed her clothes and pulled them on. She dashed up the incline toward the safety of her cabin. Looking back, she wished she could take the quilt without disturbing him. Impossible. He lay sprawled all over it. Another buzzing of his lips sent her running. She'd come back for it later. After he left.

Squawking crows awakened Phil. For a moment he wondered where he was and why he wasn't in his small bedroom. Then he remembered. The enlarged moon, the weeping woman, being engulfed by need and desire. Sitting up, he ran his fingers through his short hair, feeling the prickle of the ends across his fingers. Looking around, he grabbed his clothes and quickly pulled them on. His eyes searched the horizon for the mysterious nymph. He shook his head wondering if he'd hallucinated the whole thing, but then he glanced down at the quilt.

Hallucinations didn't leave blankets behind.

The woman probably felt embarrassed. He certainly felt a twinge of chagrin. He thought he was well past the age of one-night stands, remembering the days when women made themselves readily available at post-game celebrations. That kind of meaningless encounter turned him off nowadays.

But somehow last night wasn't meaningless. Echoes of passion reverberated in his mind. She'd been soft and cool, intense and hot all at the same time. Warmth infused his chest as he pictured her outline in the moonlight, the swell of her hips. She'd been a sweet, sweet gift. Mercy granted to a lowdown sinner such as himself.

Perhaps he should go knocking door to door, blanket in hand and apologize for his rash behavior. Or perhaps thank the lady for a really great trip to the moon. He recalled nothing of her face, only those three luscious dots on her throat and the rest was all sensual memory.

Though desire to meet her nudged him, in the end he decided to leave well enough alone and move on down the road. The lady obviously had issues and God knew he dragged around enough of his own baggage. They were two people who'd met each other's needs on a lonely, hot summer night. Why spoil the memory of a fabulous encounter?

He gathered up his tackle box and fishing pole, then spied the homey quilt on the ground. *What the hell.* Impulsively, he threw it over his arm, a souvenir of a secret sweet memory he could roll around in his mind when the bitterness in his life became overwhelming.

Heading to his car through the wooded path he softly whistled, *It Was Just One of Those Things.*

Maddie stood in the shower, using all the hot water, washing the night away. She had really gone bonkers. She could blame the wine, blame the hormones. Blame the Man on the Moon.

Don't be ridiculous. You've got no one to blame but yourself. A Harris takes full responsibility.

Stepping out and wrapping herself in a fluffy white towel, she tried to get her head on straight. She was Madeleine Harris, a stiff-necked, upright paragon of moral sanctity. Her mother was a Woodbridge, of the Boston Woodbridges, whose only lapse in protocol had been to fall in love with an Arkansas backwoods boy. Beau Harris had claimed his highbrow bride, then taken Boston by storm with his devastating charm and savvy business sense. What would her parents say if they knew of last night's escapade?

She patted herself and bent over to catch her slick hair in a turban-towel twist. She stood upright and gazed at herself in the mirror. Blue eyes stared back with a hint of alarm. Was that a love bite on her throat? Yes, right beneath the trio of moles.

Oh, heavens to Betsy and great day in the morning!

Last night she'd really gone over the edge. What would the school say, if they knew? Madeleine Harris, prim and proper assistant principal at Beaver Cove High, baying at the moon and getting laid by a wandering fisherman. And, oh Lord, what would all those girls she lectured in Female Health call her if she confessed she'd had unprotected sex with a total stranger...A skank. Not just a skank, a *stupid* skank. The list of STD's went through her mind–herpes, gonorrhea, syphilis...AIDS.

She exited her steamy, tastefully decorated bathroom and entered her bedroom. The knap of the new carpet comforted her bare feet. She inhaled deeply, trying to center herself. *Serenity now.* Not working. The taupe walls and peaceful landscapes failed to calm her jitters.

Maddie swore she would go see that herbalist Randy always talked about. There must be something growing in a rainforest somewhere to keep her from going on these wild hormonal tangents. She needed to get under control, keep all her loose threads bound up. She sat on her flowered quilt bedspread, inert, tempted to just roll up into a ball and die right then and there.

Then Grammy materialized at the foot of her bed. "No use frettin'. He didn't look too diseased to me. Looked damn good to these old eyes. Get off your ass and quit feeling sorry for yourself."

Not again. Maddie threw an arm over her eyes, fell back on the mattress, and groaned. Surely these conversations with Grammy were normal, just a role-playing thing.

"I am *not* going crazy," she muttered.

But then, schizophrenics heard voices, saw people that weren't there, didn't they? Maybe she was like that fellow in *A Beautiful Mind.*

She peeked toward the specter at the foot of the bed. A gray-headed figure clad in a floral day dress wavered before her, lips pursed in true Grammy-irritation.

Oh, this isn't looking good.

"Go away," Maddie hissed.

Mercifully, Grammy disappeared when the phone rang. Maddie reached across her nightstand and eased up against her many decorative pillows.

"Hello?"

"Maddie, my dove, how are you this bright Sabbath morning?"

Ah...Randy, her best friend and light-in-the-heels drama teacher at the school. He could make her laugh with his sweet, naughty ways. An image of his merry brown eyes under the shock of wavy dark hair cheered her.

She really needed a shot of Randy about now. "Forgive me, Father, for I have sinned. How would you like to take me out to breakfast?"

"*Ooo*, a confessional! I can hardly wait. Get on your best bonnet and Father Randy will be there in half an hour."

Maddie sighed as she hung up. Thank God for Randy. The one person who knew all her foibles and loved her anyway. Of course, she kept Randy's secrets under lock and key in her mind. That's what lifelong friends were for.

She heaved her bones off the bed, decided she'd get organized, go to another town and take blood tests, deal with whatever the consequences of her actions might be. Then her mind tripped on that word again, "test." Grimly, she realized she'd have to add "pregnancy test" to her list.

Oh, that damned Devil Moon.

Maddie and Randy drove to their favorite greasy spoon, the Hillbilly Heaven Café, nestled in the rocky Arkansas hillside. Randy always expected the stuffed animal heads on the wall to start talking like Mr. Ed. And he winced at the bad art for sale on the walls. Still, he wouldn't trade this hole-in-the-wall for the finest New York bistro. He loved the strong coffee served in sturdy mugs and the vinyl tables topped with vases of tacky plastic flowers.

They huddled in their favorite booth, speaking softly. Randy listened to Maddie's disjointed tale of her erotic escapade, patting her hand when she entered into self-berating. *My, my she'd been quite the free spirit.* Personal peccadilloes came as such a shock in the harsh morning light. Randy well understood the power of sexual urges and emotional overload. He'd had his share of morning-after regrets. Still, she was coming down too hard on herself.

"You know what you had, don't you?" he whispered.

"Temporary insanity?"

"Well, that, too. But I'm thinking of Erica Jong's 'zipless fuck' from *Fear of Flying*."

Her blue eyes widened. "My God, you're right. That's exactly what it was. But I'm not the kind of person who goes to bars and picks up strangers. I was in my own back yard!"

He smiled at his Maddie, dressed in her pert matching short set, her sleek blond hair perfectly combed. Those startling blue eyes of hers could really nail you to the wall or shine with happiness. The straight nose tilted high when she chose to put on her Mother Superior act; the mouth smiled with beguile or thinned to a grim line, as befitted her mood. And whether she liked it not, Maddie was a moody miss.

"Listen, doll face, you need to cut yourself a little slack. You don't have to play Perfect Assistant Principal twenty-four seven. You're human. You got a little drunk and had a tumble on the grass. It's fortunate this guy wasn't some psycho-slasher. He didn't hurt you, did he?"

"Oh no." Her eyes softened. "If it had really been a dream, it would have been the best dream I ever had." She lifted her cup and flushed as she sipped.

He whistled softly. "I get it. Well, goody for you. It was a short, but satisfying romance. Which is more than I can say."

Maddie lifted an eyebrow. "So how is your mystery man in Little Rock? Are you ready to tell me about him yet?"

A knot formed in Randy's stomach. "There's nothing to tell. We've gone our separate ways."

"What was wrong with this one? Too loud? Too quiet? Too anal? Too casual?"

"Too perfect. I couldn't find anything wrong." He fiddled nervously with the spoon on the table. "Scared the hell out of me. I ran."

Maddie lowered her coffee cup. "Aren't we a fine pair? Both running away from perfect men. At least you know the identity of your perfect man."

Randy placed on hand on his chest and struck an orators pose. "*And therefore is Love said to be a child, because in choice he is so oft beguiled.*"

Maddie drummed her fingers. "You and your quotations. That's got to be Shakespeare. *A Midsummer's Night Dream?*"

He nodded. "You have to get up early in the morning to fool Maddie Harris."

"Maddie Harris is pretty good at making a fool of herself." She sighed. "At least we have each other. And you always have your mother."

Randy rolled his eyes. "O lawsy, isn't that the truth? Don't let me forget. I've got to pick up a box of Depends before we head back up the hill."

"You're a good son." She spread butter on her wheat toast and nibbled. "When we were little and I visited over the summer at Grammy's, you were always next door taking care of Mother Bailey instead of running around with your friends. I remember watching you cook dinner for her when you were twelve and I was eight."

"I've progressed from box dinners to gourmet cooking since then. My soufflés are to die for." Speaking of which, his eggs were getting cold. He dug in.

"I know she takes you for granted, but there aren't many men who would arrange their lives around an invalid mother like you have."

"As Noel Coward put it, *My mother has an umbilical cord made of piano wire*." God, it sucked to be a stereotype. Gay man with dominant mother and no father figure. This is Your Life, Randy Bailey.

"Well, I think Beaver Cove is darned lucky that a man with your talent is sticking around here throwing your energy into its high school drama department. I know this wasn't exactly your dream, but the kids in this town are a lot better off because of you." She spread marmalade on his toast, just the way he liked it. "I'm certainly glad I have you to run to when I come undone."

He accepted the toast from her graceful hand. "Listen, dear heart, move on. You're not the first girl to take a tumble in the moonlight after a few glasses of wine. Just don't make a habit of it. You're lucky this fisherman wasn't a throat slasher. Bolt yourself inside your house the next time you hear the call of the wild. Or better yet, call me and we'll watch the late, late show together. I always can use an excuse to escape Mother."

"It's a deal." She squeezed his fingers.

Randy covered his hand over Maddie's and went into an Irish accent. "Now, my child, go and be sinnin' no more. Say three *Hail Mary's*, take two aspirin and call me in the mornin'."

Maddie smiled. "Thank you, Father. Oh, Randy, what would I do without you?"

"You'd muddle through, but life would be dull, wouldn't it?" He leaned back in the booth. "Certainly, school wouldn't be half as fun without me there to rescue you from unwanted suitors like Phineas Manchester."

Maddie made a face. "Ugh. Don't remind me." School was starting in two weeks and that meant the beginning of meetings and preparation. "Have you gotten the new seats for the theater yet?"

"No. Promises, promises, all I hear are promises, promises. McCall told me he had it in the budget and was just waiting for the okay, but I haven't heard more."

"Have you pressed him?"

Randy lowered his head, a lock of hair falling over his forehead. "Ah, Maddie, you know I'm kind of scared of McCall."

Maddie's eyes snapped, the Woodbridge starch coming back into her sails. "Well, I'm not. The budget meeting is next week. I'll find out where your new seats are or my name isn't Madeleine Woodbridge Harris."

Randy winked at her and did his best Bette Davis imitation. "*Fasten your seat belts, it's going to be a bumpy night.*"

Chapter Two

Men seldom make passes
At girls who wear glasses

Dorothy Parker

The following week Phil Wilcox pulled out of the McDonald's drive-through with his usual *Egg McMuffin* and black coffee. He pushed aside the leavings of last night's dinner from Taco Bueno to make room for breakfast. His morning drive to the school took about twenty minutes from leaving his apartment complex, making the detour for food and pulling into his parking place marked "Coach" at Beaver Cove High.

His cell phone beeped the most annoying tune in its repertoire. Seemed only fitting to assign that one to the most annoying person in his life–ex-wife Pam.

He hit the green button and drove with one hand. "Yeah?"

"Listen, I know it isn't quite the fifteenth yet, but could I have the support check now? I'm a little short."

Right, same old song and dance. He wondered how much support his daughter, Melissa, saw from the money he shelled out every month. Pam always looked dressed to kill, while Melissa looked like a Salvation Army reject.

"I guess I could drop a check by after my meeting. Is Melissa going to be there? I could take her out for lunch."

"Your visitation isn't until Saturday, Phil. She doesn't have to see you until then."

Phil gritted his teeth. While he'd been salvaging his life as an assistant coach in the NFL, Pam had been systematically working a number on Melissa. He'd looked it up on the

Internet–Parental Alienation. Pam had done her best to poison his daughter's mind against him.

Pam continued in her singsong voice. "Don't think just because you've waltzed back into town with this lame high school coaching job, that you can barge into our lives."

"Believe me, Pam, I have no interest in barging into your life. I just want to see my daughter before she's a grown woman." He squeezed the phone a little tighter. "You know, I don't *have* to pay you until the fifteen."

She issued a put-upon sigh. "Fine. I don't appreciate black mail, Phil. Maybe you can say hello to her when you bring the money."

"Fine."

"Fine."

He clicked off and threw the phone across the seat. Nobody frosted him faster than Pam. But, hell, he knew he deserved it. He adjusted his back, still a constant ache from the career-ending football injuries. He'd really blown it. Self-pity had led to self-medication followed by self-destruction. It all slipped away–the career, the marriage, the soaring ego, leaving him stripped to the bone financially, emotionally, and spiritually. Three years in AA had forced him to see his culpability.

God, if only he could break through the wall of Melissa's resentment. Those accusing eleven-year-old eyes bored into his soul. *Loser-alcoholic-has-been.* He hoped–hell, he *prayed,* to that Higher Power to give him back his daughter.

Taking this coaching job in his old hometown seemed like an answer to those prayers. No more traveling, no more missed visitations. He'd even force himself to be nice to Pam.

Of course, when he first arrived at the school and saw the crappy equipment, he raised hell with McCall and quickly got some positive response. He had a good feeling about the upcoming school year, even looked forward to teaching history.

He turned a corner and saw a billboard for the Lake Luna Motel. A big moon and a large mouth bass invited potential vacationers. His night at Lake Luna flashed to mind. The Moon Goddess. He couldn't really recall her face, but those three beauty marks on her throat stuck in his mind. Magical moonlight moments. He hadn't gone back to the lake, not wanting to actually meet the lady and ruin the perfect illusion. The impulsively grabbed quilt still rested in his trunk. He meant to anonymously return it soon.

As Phil sipped his coffee, Maddie zipped along in her Camry down the hilly roads on her way to school and into the valley where Beaver Cove proper resided. The town of 30,000 enjoyed the overflow prosperity of being close to the corporate headquarters of both Wal-Mart and Tyson foods. She passed countless long chicken houses that dotted the Arkansas countryside. Little chicken farms had grown into major commercial concerns, feathering local nests, so to speak.

That's why it really steamed her when she dwelled on the budgetary problems of the school. The townspeople needed to rally 'round and give the students of Beaver Cover High the kind of facilities she remembered from her Bostonian school days. There just wasn't an appreciation of culture in Beaver Cove that went beyond country western music and banjo picking.

As Maddie pulled up to a stoplight, she flipped down the visor and took a quick inspection in the mirror. She smiled approval of her best assistant principal power outfit–dark suit, trademark scarf about her neck topped by a French twist hairstyle. Dark-rimmed eyeglasses cranked up her no-nonsense persona a couple of notches.

She didn't notice the light turn green until the guy behind her laid on his horn. Waving a small "sorry," she sped toward school.

Phil mentally grumped at women drivers. He'd watched the blonde primping in her mirror, oblivious to the flow of traffic around her, then gave her a wake up "beep." Once again moving forward, he dug into his breakfast bag for the egg sandwich. Generally an adept old pro at driving and fast food manipulation, he dropped the hot muffin in his lap.

"Shit," he muttered, momentarily looking down to pick up the pieces of bread, egg, and ham strewn across his lap.

At that moment Maddie saw she was about to miss the turn into Java Pete's and she really needed a latte to get her through the meeting. Without turning on her blinkers, she tapped her brakes and commenced a quick right into the parking lot.

Phil looked up and saw the Camry coming to a sudden slow. He swerved and hit his brakes, but not soon enough. His vintage Skylark bashed the fender and taillight of her cream Camry. A sickening crunch of metal and plastic signaled to both of them the beginning of a bad day.

Maddie jumped out of her car. Phil remained behind his steering wheel counting to ten and counting to ten again–a temper-controlling device he'd been taught in AA. Maddie had not been taught any such coping skill.

She stood in her high heels and snug suit inspecting the effects of the collision. Her beautiful Camry–wounded, forever damaged. She knew it would never be the same. The body shop might say they could match the color, but she'd always notice the difference.

As she made small moaning noises and flapped her hands, she heard a deep male voice with an Arkansas drawl comment, "Doesn't look too bad."

Maddie glanced over her shoulder at the Skylark's owner–a big bruiser, obviously a sports fan with his Braves ball cap, Cowboys T-shirt, and Rangers sweat pants. Maddie surveyed this fashion plate and watched his mouth thin at her blatant assessment. She had to give him points for his clean-shaven square chin and intelligent looking brown eyes.

"Look, lady, if I've passed your inspection, we'd better get these cars off the road and exchange insurance information before we cause another accident."

Maddie glimpsed the growing line of cars in the other lane. "Of course, let's just pull into this parking lot."

Once out of the stream of traffic, Maddie opened her glove compartment, immediately finding the current insurance card in its shiny plastic holder. The Queen of Organization, she had a motto: a place for everything and everything in its place. She also adored lists. Sometimes she made lists of the lists she needed to write.

Getting out of her car and walking to Phil's driver side, she watched him fumbling through his glove compartment crammed with papers. As he read each one, he mumbled an obscenity, crumpled it, and threw it on the passenger side floor, where it joined an assortment of trash from various fast food meals.

Maddie shook her head at the disorder of the vehicle and said, "You know this accident is your fault. You rear-ended me."

Phil finally found the elusive slip of paper and uttered, "Ah!" as he got out of the car. Looking Maddie square in the eye he told her, "That's true, but I think there's a law about using your turn signal."

Maddie gave him her best school marm expression. "I believe there's also a law against tailgating."

"I was not tailgating you, lady."

"I beg to differ. First you impatiently honked at me, and then you followed me much too closely. You should always leave at least one car length between you and the next car. I've taught Driver's Ed. I know what I'm talking about."

Phil made a low growling noise and shot her the penetrating look he usually reserved for opponents through the facemask of a football helmet. "I don't have all day to receive driving tips from you Miss..." he looked down at the offered insurance card, "Harris. Let's just exchange the information and get the hell out of here."

Maddie drew herself up to her full five feet seven. "Fine. I'll get a pad of paper."

She wrote a meticulous list, in duplicate, of necessary information: tag numbers, VIN numbers, phone numbers, addresses.

Phil leaned against his car and studied her. She was packaged all right in her basic black suit with the yellow scarf tied around her neck and the matching blouse peeking through the jacket. With arms crossed, he tried to give her a defining word in his mind–officious, uptight, high-strung, anal. She could be a real pain in the ass, he was sure. But that was true of all women in his experience.

Maddie stood tapping her foot while worrying one end of the pen in her mouth. "Let's see, am I forgetting anything?"

"I don't know what it could be. I've given you everything but my mother's maiden name and the locations of my vaccination scars."

"No, I'm sure there's something...Well, anyway, Mr. Wilcox, my insurance company will be in touch with your insurance company."

Phil moved toward his car door. "I can hardly wait." Without an attempt at a polite goodbye, he grabbed his list and got back into his car.

Maddie appeared momentarily nonplussed at his rudeness, then slipped into her Camry. Her car blocked Phil's exit and he sat watching her go through her getting-ready-to-drive routine. After a quick look in the mirror, she adjusted her seat belt, observed the gauges on her dashboard, and shifted her skirt in place. Phil's patience wore out and he laid on the horn again.

Maddie jumped and glared at the uncouth baboon in her rear view mirror. She pulled out of the parking lot and headed for school. Phil veered around her and tried to put as much distance between himself and the cream Camry as possible.

Unfortunately, traffic remained heavy and they stayed neck and neck with each other. Maddie started to get very nervous. Each time she took a turn, he took the same one. The man was a stalker! Dear God, what should she do? Well, she just wouldn't stand for it. She'd taken self-defense classes. Surely those karate moves would come back to her.

Meanwhile in the Skylark, Phil had turned on his radio and cranked up a country station, totally oblivious to Maddie's presence in the other lane. Football practice and designing plays occupied his mind as he wolfed down his remaining breakfast.

Turning into the school, he parked in the space marked *Coach*, cut the engine and took a minute to gather his briefcase. He jerked as a startling banging on his window caught his attention. Amazed to see the punctilious blonde mouthing off at him, he got out of the car and tried to catch her drift.

"You've got exactly ten seconds to leave the premises, Mr. Wilcox, or I'll call the authorities. I don't appreciate your attempt at intimidation!"

"What the f–, what are you taking about?"

"What am I talking about? I'm talking about you following me to my place of employment. It's called stalking, Mr. Wilcox, and I'll not stand for it." She wagged a manicured finger in his face. "Don't forget, I have your tag number. I have your VIN number."

Phil glanced around and saw Maddie's car parked in the space marked *Harris*.

He shook his head. "Well, I'll be damned. It just so happens I work here, sweetheart."

Maddie took a step backward, blinking her blue eyes behind the dark-rimmed glasses. "What?"

"You heard me. I think 'place of employment' is the one thing you forgot to put on your list. I'm the new football coach for Beaver Cove High."

Phil watched the color rise in her cheeks. Blondes really can't hide a blush, he thought. For a moment he found it kind of cute and then he remembered her prickly personality.

"I've got a meeting, Miss Harris." He slammed his door and started striding toward the administration building.

Maddie fumbled for words. "Oh, I'm sorry, I just assumed..."

Phil turned and looked her up and down. "Thought you'd like to know, you've got a run in your hose."

She focused on her legs, saw the light streak against the dark nylon and groaned, "Oh, darn!"

He turned away and chuckled. *Oh yeah, it's going to be fun to pull her chain.*

* * *

Of course Maddie ended up the last one to arrive for the budget meeting. Heading toward the old three-story school building, she barely noticed the familiar cracking concrete steps that led up to the heavy glass doors. Yanking on a handle, she made a sharp left toward the teachers lounge. Her heels pounded loud clicking noises that reverberated down the cinderblock-lined hallway. The smell of fresh paint assailed her nostrils, making her dimly aware of the sparkling new coat of pale green color on the walls.

Pushing on the door marked *Teachers Only*, she smiled wanly as all heads swiveled toward her. The lounge was divided into two sections, one containing an old couch and comfortable overstuffed chairs; the other held a long conference table where teachers could grade papers. The windowless room featured a large mural of Lake Luna, complete with a shining moon reflecting on water. The budget committee sat convened around the table.

Doug McCall, the burly, gray haired principal, held court at one end. The department heads had their appointed chairs denoting pecking order by their proximity to McCall. She immediately noted Phil Wilcox sat to the principal's left, while the chair to Doug's right remained empty for her. She passed Randy who sat between Phyllis Green, the Home Ec teacher, and Phineas Manchester, the self-important head of the English department.

"Nice of you to join us, Miss Harris," McCall said with his Alabama accent, eyes staring over the reading glasses perched on his nose.

Maddie smoothed her skirt as she slid into a chair. "I had a little mishap this morning. I'm sorry I'm late."

She exchanged a quick glance with Phil, whose mouth appeared to be suppressing a grin. Maddie unzipped her briefcase and opened up the traveling office on the table.

"I was just going over changes in the budget," McCall said as he handed her a printout.

His voiced droned on about science textbooks, school lunches, the new copy machine, and athletic equipment.

Maddie studied the line-by-line entries, finding few surprises. Athletic equipment did seem higher than usual. Then she searched for the new theater chairs. She couldn't find them.

She tapped her finger on the table. "Excuse me, but I don't see the new seats for the theater."

She glanced at Randy who gazed down doodling on a pad of paper, avoiding all eye contact.

"No, Miss Harris," McCall said, "if you'd been on time, you'd have heard we have to put that off for a year."

"What? We've sold wrapping paper, fresh fruit, and over-priced candles as fundraisers. I've gotten soaked in car washes for two years to buy those chairs. What happened to the money?" Maddie demanded.

"We had an emergency come up and those funds were needed elsewhere."

"Emergency? What kind of emergency? I don't remember any fires."

McCall crossed his arms. "When Mr. Wilcox arrived and saw the state of the athletic equipment, he immediately called it to my attention and I had to appropriate the theater funds."

Maddie shot Phil a slit-eyed stare. "Oh, I see. We need new towels, balls, and punching bags for the big boys to play with, so let's just rob the drama department."

Phil spoke up. "May I say something?"

Maddie gave a wave of her hand. "By all means."

He stood up and addressed the room. "I'm Phil Wilcox, your new football coach. I understand it's been a while since Beaver Cove had much of a team. When I got here two weeks ago, a quick appraisal of the athletic equipment revealed you had real problems. Safety problems. If I'm going to get these kids in shape, I've gotta make sure the practice uniforms and equipment are going to prevent as many injuries as possible." He shot Maddie a quelling glance. "That seems to me to be a higher priority than some parents getting their butts pinched while they're watching *A Midsummer's Night's Dream* at the next school play."

Well, of course, when he put it that way, what could she

say? Let the jocks get hurt? Still, it really frosted her that the money had been stolen from Randy's department. She didn't see the library or science departments losing any of their new computers.

"Any more questions?" Phil asked pointedly at her.

She shook her head, really hating his arrogance. This guy bugged her big time.

The meeting ground on with each speaker taking a turn. Maddie had several issues to cover and carried them off with her usual competent efficiency. Yet, every time she made eye contact with Phil, she experienced a prick of warm awareness. He sat with his jock, macho smugness. She longed to bring him down a peg or two. Fortunately, she kept her cool and no one sensed her fancy emotional footwork, or so she hoped.

Phil wondered what she'd look like without the stiff suit, glasses and taut hairstyle. There could be a babe under the uptight facade. In the old days, he only went for the obvious bimbos, who waved T and A in everyone's face. Not that he went for this school marm, but he had a feeling there was more to her than met the eye. And what met the eye wasn't bad.

When the meeting broke up, people chatted and caught up on the events of the summer. Phyllis Green made a beeline for Phil. Broad in the beam from eating too many students' fritters and tuna pinwheels, her biological clock ticked at a furious rate. She honed in on any potential candidate for the groom's spot on the wedding cake of her dreams. Phil found himself trapped by the cloying woman with the bowl hair cut.

Maddie smiled as she packed her briefcase, seeing Phil hemmed in by the husband-hungry kitchen queen. But she soon found herself fending off her own familiar unwanted suitor, Phineas Manchester.

The tall, thin professor moved into her personal space. "Madeleine, you've had an excellent summer break, I assume? I've called you several times, but never found you home."

Maddie mentally thanked the inventor of caller I.D. with all her heart.

"Oh, I've been in and out. You know how it is. How's the

dissertation going, Mr. Manchester?"

"I wish you'd call me Phineas." The way his tongue waggled to the tips of his crooked, discolored teeth gave her the creeps. "It's coming along. Comparing the works of Chaucer and Stephen King is a major undertaking." Lord, what was that aftershave–Old Fish?

He leaned closer. "You know, we never have had that dinner you've promised me."

Mercifully, Randy startled the whole room with a huge cry of pain. Maddie sighed with relief. Randy to the rescue from Phineas Manchester again. It was a game they played. Whenever Phineas had her trapped, Randy staged a diversion. Today he enacted "old war injury." Of course, Randy had never been in a war, or served in the military.

Maddie backed away. "Excuse me, Mr. Manchester, I have to help Mr. Bailey. We'll talk later."

Maddie grabbed her briefcase, dashed to the groaning Randy's side saying, "Put your arm around me. I've got your medicine in my office."

Randy hooked an arm around her and supported his back with the other. "I just get these terrible, sudden spasms. I should have never jumped out of all those airplanes!"

"I know, I know. Just lean on me." She led him out the door.

Phil watched the scene as the pair made their dramatic exit and thought it was the biggest display of bullshit he had ever seen in his life.

Maddie pulled open the blinds in her office and pushed up a window for fresh air as Randy took a seat in one of the chairs before her desk. She'd personally painted the walls a high-gloss eggshell. Landscapes chosen for their psychologically calming effect graced the walls.

She kicked off her shoes, chuckling at him. "I thought your 'war injury' came from putting out oil well fires in Desert Storm."

"Oh, that's right, I forgot." He swung one leg over the arm

of the chair. "Well, you know how improvisation works. Pretend I had to jump out of an airplane to get to the fires. Anyway, what's up with you, Miss Blush and Flustered?"

"I don't know what you're talking about." Maddie sat primly in her leather desk chair.

Randy crossed his arms and said, "Gimme a break."

She sighed. "Oh, all right. It's that new coach–Wilcox. We had a fender bender this morning and then I falsely accused him of being a stalker. He made me feel like a complete idiot. Then he gets all your money for the new seats. And did you see the smirk on his face? I just wanted to smack him one."

Randy played one-handed catch with a coin. "You *have* had a busy morning. Don't feel too badly about the seats. We'll get them eventually. At least I got the full funding for the musical and materials for sets."

Maddie straightened the items on her already perfectly neat desk. "Good. Hopefully I won't have to cross paths with the coach very often."

Randy laughed. "Don't count on it. Before you arrived the chaperones for the Moonlight Madness Dance were announced. You and the Incredible Hunk are definitely on the list."

Maddie buried her face in her hands. "Don't tell me who else is assigned."

"That's right, your ardent admirer, Phineas Manchester and Phyllis Green, the gruesome gourmet."

Sinking her head down on the desk and groaning, she heard Randy's Bogart rendition from Casablanca, "*Of all the gin joints in all the towns in all the world, she walks into mine*."

Chapter Three

In youth, it was a way I had
To do my best to please,
And change, with every passing lad,
To suit his theories

But now I know the things I know,
And do the things I do;
And if you do not like me so,
To hell, my love, with you!

Dorothy Parker

Back in her snug little cabin that evening, Maddie gratefully took off her business clothes and slipped into comfortable slacks and a soft mock neck cotton top. She gazed around the bedroom. Respectful redecorating had kept her busy over the summer. Grammy's crammed plates and pictures on the walls had given way to a few dramatic watercolors over freshly painted buff walls. One of Grammy's more artistic quilts hung behind the bed. Another hung on a quilt stand in the corner. What a challenge to keep the best of her grandmother's touches, while making the space personally her own.

She wandered into the bathroom and pulled the pins and clips out of her hair, freeing it from its pent-up style. Maddie brushed it out and shook her head, enjoying the feeling of liberation. She swiveled her neck to release tension.

The three dots on her throat caught her attention. She lightly traced her fingers over them. How Thomas had brought that area of her body alive, her first erogenous zone. She remembered lying on a posh leather couch as he paid special attention to her throat, ear lobes, the lids of her closed eyes before he moved to other more obvious body parts.

Thomas…that smooth, urbane, college professor son of a bitch.

Maddie clutched the rim of the marble sink and moved closer to the mirror. Did her past show? Was she turning into one of those classic black and white photos of wrinkled old women who wore every event and misfortune of their lives in the lines of their faces?

The surface of the mirror began to waver like a rock hitting a glassy pool. Grammy's face now stared back at Maddie. "What in tarnation did that scoundrel do to you anyway?"

Maddie didn't fight the hallucination. Her private talks with Grammy didn't really hurt anyone did they? Her subconscious needed some way to deal with her emotional baggage.

Her mind wandered to the day she met Thomas. They shared an umbrella to the Boston College English building. Her first day of teaching at the college level. As a tenured professor, he impressed her with his confident, worldly wit. He made her laugh and helped her through the first tenuous weeks.

Being impressed with her Woodbridge pedigree and Harris fame, he wined and dined her like a regular Prince Charming. Then he bedded her with equal elegance.

Her mother liked him. "I think Thomas is simply wonderful. He's just the intelligent, polished kind of man I've always hoped you'd find. Did you know he's related to British royalty?"

Beau Harris thought he was a phony from the get-go. "That guy is a stiff. If you call him 'Tom' he gets a sour look on his face and says 'my name is *Thomas*'. Do I insist everyone calls me 'Beauregard'? Hell no."

But, he was outnumbered when Maddie and Amanda both went ecstatic over wedding plans. Thomas Smithton and Madeleine Harris were engaged in a big public announcement at the annual New Year's Eve bash. Their party took up the entire society page. The plans for the wedding, the showers, the honeymoon went on and on. Maddie bought special wedding planner software for her computer to keep it all straight.

The bloom went a little off the bud two months into the engagement. Thomas became short tempered and moody; lovemaking turned perfunctory on Saturday nights. Maddie tried all the harder to please him, agree with him. She bought him presents. Small criticisms of her hair, her body, her taste started to eat away her self-esteem in tiny bites. He had to know all her plans, her complete agenda of everyday. If he seemed a bit controlling, that just showed how much he cared. Shining moments of fun and passion became suddenly ruined by his peevish fits of temper. She chalked his moodiness up to work-related stress and doggedly kept on her rose-colored glasses.

Reality crashed the morning she opened up the Boston Buzz, a gossip rag that had been mysteriously dropped on her doorstep. As she sat down at the small glass dining table in her brownstone apartment and dipped her tea bag in the steaming mug of hot water, she blinked the sleep out of her eyes to focus on the front-page pictures. An electric shock ran through her body as she recognized the love of her life, Thomas Smithton, in a large photograph, surrounded by six smaller pictures of pretty girls. College age girls. Maddie's picture was inserted in a box headlined "The Fiancée."

"Groom-to-be Exposed as College Casanova

Looks like love is on the rocks for well-known Boston socialite Madeleine Woodbridge Harris and her college professor beau, Thomas Smithton. According to a class-action lawsuit filed by pre-law student, Samantha Collins, Smithton has been diddling pretty freshman girls for years. He seduced the wrong girl this time. Collins alleges the silver-haired professor gives private lessons not mentioned in any class literature. Poor, poor Madeleine. And just a month before the big-blowout wedding. Wonder if she can get a refund on the reception hall?"

Recalling that last meeting in Thomas' office, Maddie wondered how many crow's feet began on that fateful day.

Holding the newspaper in her hand, Maddie had confronted her lover. "Please, Thomas, tell me this is all a terrible mistake."

"Of course it's a terrible mistake. Samantha will rue the day she took on Thomas Smithton," he said, putting books into a liquor store box.

Maddie sat down with relief. "So, it's all lies. Why would all those girls say these things?"

Thomas stopped and gave her an accusatory look. "Are you doubting me?"

"No! I just don't understand it. Why would they say you forced them to have sex with you?"

Thomas pursed his lips in perplexed annoyance. "You see, that is the falsehood of it. They stand there with their tight sweaters and short skirts, asking stupid questions after class. They're falling all over me and then accuse me of forcing them to have sex!"

"What?" Maddie's voice was low, stunned. "You did it? All those nineteen year olds? Those *children*?"

"Don't be such an idiot." He turned back to his packing. "Every one of them wanted it. Enjoyed it. I can't help it if girls all have stupid illusions of living happily ever after just because they've been laid."

"So it's all their fault? They seduced you and you couldn't help yourself, is that it?"

Thomas stopped and thought for a moment. "No. I suppose it's partly your fault, too."

Maddie stood up. "My fault? How is your shagging these freshmen my fault?"

"Well, if you'd been more satisfying, I wouldn't have had the energy or inclination, now would I?"

Maddie walked the campus that day feeling like the top of her head had been blown off. A spring rain pelted her face, but she'd barely noticed. Incoherent thoughts tracked through her mind mixed with images of Thomas, her parents, the newspaper headlines.

A litany of defining words ran through her mind: betrayed, manipulated, used, demeaned. Thomas was a big phony and she was a bigger idiot for not seeing through him.

Her stomach and chest hurt as if she'd been physically assaulted. She became one of the walking wounded.

Maddie stared into Grammy's ghostly image once again. "I've learned my lesson, Grammy. I need to be strong and independent, keep my emotions under lock and key. I'll never trust a man's smooth talk again. I should thank Thomas for showing me what men are really like."

Grammy scowled. "That's the biggest load of horse manure I ever heard."

"Oh, what do you know? You're just a figment of my imagination." Maddie pushed herself away from the mirror, and pretended she hadn't seen anything unusual.

Her eyes focused on the early pregnancy test she'd purchased in the grocery store. Still a little early to get a true reading. *Who are you kidding? You don't want to face that possibility yet.*

Being pregnant would blow her carefully built life to smithereens. After leaving Boston in humiliation and despair, moving to Arkansas had been her salvation. She'd spent precious time with Grammy while making her place at Beaver Cove High. While not a great career, she enjoyed working with the teens. She loved the beauty of the Ozarks. Being an unmarried pregnant assistant principal would not be acceptable in this part of the Bible belt. And imagine the wagging tongues in Boston if she returned home unemployed and pregnant.

So, she could get an abortion, right? She imagined lying on a paper-covered vinyl examining table with her feet up in the cold steel stirrups. A shiver ran through her body.

Abortion had always been a social issue until now. Something to discuss in women's awareness groups. Up close and personal, it took on completely new dimensions. Could she scrape away a chance at motherhood?

The whole baby issue was too confusing and so she put it off a little while longer. Like Scarlett O'Hara, she'd think about it tomorrow.

The first week of school went pretty well for Phil. Teaching history to hormone happy teens provided an interesting challenge. Who would have thought it? Phil looked back on the brash, egocentric kid he used to be and knew that the last decade had transformed his inner man. He spent more time considering the people around him, what made them tick. All these kids going through his classroom and across his playing field had stories of their own. Maybe he could make a positive contribution along the way and make up for his screw-ups of the past.

Out on the practice field after school, the fledgling football team hit it hard. Perspiration dripped off adolescent foreheads, drenched uniform armpits. Oh, yeah, Phil loved the smell of turf and sweat. With the first game four days away, they had a ways to go. Phil had decided on three key plays and drilled them over and over.

"Come on, you candyasses! Get in there, Morely! Now, Martinez!"

The quarterback overshot the ball to his receiver.

Phil inwardly groaned, but put a positive spin on it. "All right! That was better. Do it again!"

So intent on his players, Phil didn't notice an observer in the stands until she yelled, "Run, for God's sake! You got rocks in your pants or what?"

Phil turned around and spotted Melissa, his hostile, distant daughter. Their visitations of the last couple weeks remained strained, but at least they had taken place. He'd given up expecting a full weekend. He'd been grateful for a trip to McDonald's and a couple of hours at a movie. But seeing her in the stands might signal a definite improvement in their relationship.

Phil told his assistant, Stu, to run the plays. Stu lacked any athletic ability, but Phil recognized his analytical and leadership abilities as assets for the team.

Phil climbed the bleacher steps two at a time to reach Melissa, who sat in the middle of the empty metal benches. "Hey, kiddo, this is a pleasant surprise. How did you get here? Does your mom know where you are?"

Melissa chewed a wad of gum, pulling a long string out of her mouth once in a while. Her tattered jeans and old, stained T-shirt made him feel guilty. He'd press Pam to buy the kid some decent clothes.

"I rode my bike." Phil noted the bicycle parked in the grass. "Mom doesn't care where I go after school as long as I'm home by five. It isn't that far over here. Thought I'd check out the team. They really stunk last year. Looks like they still stink."

At that moment they watched the receiver fumble the ball. Phil winced.

"It's early in the season yet," Phil said. "So, how's school going? Do you like your teachers?"

"They're all right." Melissa kept chewing and watching the football practice, never making eye contact with Phil. Her long, stringy brown hair hung on her bony shoulders.

Phil jiggled his feet impatiently. "Do you need any school supplies?"

"Nah."

Jeez, talking to his own kid was like conversing with a brick wall. Maybe he should just get back to practice and let her watch. He felt like an idiot trying to make small talk.

Then she looked him straight in the eye. "Mom says you're a drunk. Are you?"

Oh, Christ, here we go. "You know I go to AA meetings. Yeah, I've been a drunk."

"Mom says you only sober up for visitations, but you drink the rest of the time."

Phil bit back a curse and kept his cool. "I haven't had a drink in three years."

"Mom says you're a loser."

Phil rested his hands on his wide spread knees. "Well, I've

had my ups and downs, just like everybody else. I didn't live up to your mother's expectations. But I'm trying to make up for past mistakes. Don't count me out of the game yet."

Melissa stood up. "If you can make this group of hammerheads into a winning team, I guess you wouldn't be such a loser."

She started down the bleacher steps, then stopped and turned around. "Did you know that a cockroach can live six months without its head?"

Phil couldn't suppress a grin. "No, I didn't know that."

"Oh yeah, it's true. I read it on the Internet. See ya." She bounced down to her bicycle.

Phil watched her slim figure mount the bike and push off. The pressure was on. He had to turn these hammerheads into football players.

He had to do it for Melissa.

While Phil conversed with Melissa, Maddie sat in her office making up a list of all the items necessary to be done before tomorrow night's Moonlight Madness Dance. The decoration committee planned a silver orb in the midst of a twinkling galaxy dangling above the gym floor. Randy and his ever-popular stack of CD's and karaoke machine would provide the music. Randy played a zany DJ to perfection.

She began writing a memo to the chaperones to remind them of their responsibilities. She'd finished the paragraph telling them to be vigilant about stopping overt PDA (public display of affection) when she heard a light tap on her door. The small, heart-shaped face of Reba Finn, a sophomore who lived near Maddie's cabin, peeked through the window. She motioned the girl in.

"Hey, Miz Harris," said the shy backwoods girl in a timid voice.

"Good afternoon, Reba. Miss the bus, did you?"

Reba shifted heavy textbooks. "Yes, ma'am. I had to go around and get the books checked out to me 'cause I weren't here yesterday and then I was too late for the bus."

Reba had come to Maddie's attention the previous year as she drove by the girl walking along the mountain road that led to town. Maddie recognized her as a Beaver Cove High student and pulled over. Reba had missed the bus that stopped along the country road leading to her home. Despite a ten-mile walk, the girl was determined to get to school. Maddie gave her a ride that day and several other times during the course of the year. Some mornings Maddie found Reba swinging on her front porch, waiting for the assistant principal to head out the door.

With her quiet manner, big brown eyes, and naturally curly auburn hair, Reba possessed an ethereal quality that intrigued Maddie. Reba had revealed bits and pieces of her life as the year had gone by. The oldest of five siblings, her father was a mechanic of sorts, drove a wrecker to pick up stranded motorists, and liked to compete in car rallies. Maddie always avoided those terribly noisy affairs held at county fair grounds. She couldn't imagine why anyone would want to participate in such a thing. Reba didn't say much about her mother except she "tended the youngins."

"Sit down a minute, sweetheart, while I finish this memo. Then we can be on our way." Maddie returned to her keyboard as Reba slid into a chair.

"Did you have a good summer?" Maddie asked.

"It was fine, I guess. We had a mess of blackberries to put up and the corn was good. My brother, George, got hisself bit by a snake and we thought he might die, but he din't."

Reba placed her burden of books down in the other chair and sat very still in the one she occupied, as if afraid she might damage it. Maddie glanced at the girl in the tattered clothes and recognized the potential. Reba could go either way; her life teetered on the cusp. She might continue in school and break the mold of her background. Or she might drop out of school, become pregnant and only possibly married. Maddie imagined two possible future Reba's: one smiling, educated and confident; the other careworn and tired, holding a baby in her arms, and a small child by the hand.

Maddie didn't want this girl to fall by the wayside. Perhaps, with a little more personal attention, she could point Reba toward a brighter future. Getting her out of her shell might be a good start. "Are you coming to the dance tomorrow night?"

Reba hung her head. "Ah, I cain't do that."

"Why, because you don't have anything to wear?"

Reba nodded her head.

"It's a fifties theme. I'm sure we can find an extra poodle skirt and matching sweater you can wear. You can stay after school and I'll give you a lift home when the dance is over. What do you say?"

Reba's eyes lit up and her little bow mouth widened into a real smile. "I'd really like that."

"Excellent." Maddie hit the print button on her computer. "Gather up your things, I'm ready to go."

The two headed down the hall to the teacher's lounge. Maddie's clicking heels tattooed a steady beat while Reba's holey tennis shoes squished along side. Maddie stopped at the teacher mailboxes intending to slip her memos in the chaperones' slots. When she got to the box marked *Wilcox*, crammed with messages she assumed that the Coach was ignoring or didn't know about his mailbox.

She tapped the memo against her pursed lips. "Hmmm. I think we need to make a detour to the football field. It seems the coach needs a personal delivery."

Phil stood on the sidelines watching his guys make their thirtieth try at the sling shot play. It might be his imagination, but he thought they were improving. Stu drew diagrams on a piece of paper, excitedly sketching out his ideas. Ray Martinez, their quarterback, had made the last five passes to his receiver right on the money.

A flash of yellow caught the corner of Phil's eye and he turned to see the assistant principal making her way through the gate along the sidelines. A girl accompanying her took a seat on the bleachers as she continued her path toward him. He really got a kick out of this chick. Her high heels sank into the soft turf with every step. Her chic little canary colored suit with the matching scarf around her neck looked completely out of place on a football field, but she walked with resolve. He enjoyed the sexy hip action despite the prissy purse to her lips. She appeared a woman with a mission and no amount of mud or wind hindered her way.

Just as she reached him, her heel tripped in a hole and he caught her by the arms as she pitched forward. "Steady, sister. Why women wear those idiotic shoes, I'll never know."

Phil righted Maddie and she quickly regained her composure. She tugged her jacket into place. "Coach Wilcox, I came to remind you that you're a chaperone for the school dance tomorrow night. I've brought you a list of all the duties outlined for the function. Are you aware that your mailbox is full of messages?"

Phil accepted the memo Maddie shoved in his hands, took a glance at it, crumpled the paper, and stuffed it in his pocket. "Yeah, I need to check it out one of these days. So what time does the shindig start?"

"If you'll examine the list currently compressed in your clothing, you'll see you need to be there at 6:30. It's a 50's theme dance. Dress accordingly."

"I'll get out my James Dean costume. You can wear your *Good Morning, Miss Dove* getup." His glance raked over her body. "Or are you wearing it now?"

"What?" Maddie knew she'd just been insulted. Jennifer Jones in *Good Morning, Miss Dove*, was a prim schoolteacher spinster.

"Coach Wilcox, are you *trying* to antagonize me or does it just come naturally to you?"

"I guess you could say it's part of my personal charm. Like being uptight and snobby is part of yours," he said with teasing eyes.

Her baby blues widened behind the glasses. "My first impression of you was that you were an insufferable lout and it hasn't changed one bit."

Phil broke out with laughter. "Ah, lighten up, sweetheart. I'll be at your dance. I'll..." he pulled the paper out of his pocket and started to read from her list, "'guard against PDA, ascertain the presence of alcohol or drugs, and diffuse the onset of violent confrontation.' Sounds like a blast all right. Save a dance for me." He lowered his voice. "You do dance, don't you, cupcake?"

She hated the way he made her feel like a stodgy wallflower. "Of course I dance. I've taken ballroom, swing, polka, even cha-cha and tango lessons."

"Great, we'll show these kids how it's done." He leaned into her conspiratorially. "Listen, I'd love to stand here all afternoon talking to you, but I've got a football team to coach. These guys already probably think you're out here hitting on me, so you'd better go now. I'll see you around." He gave her a wink, turned, and sauntered back to his assistant.

Maddie's mouth dropped open in amazement. The unmitigated gall! The colossal ego. The dumb jock, the jar headed ignoramus... She marched back and picked Reba up with a litany of insults running through her mind.

Phil watched her figure retreating off the field. She had a wiggle to her walk that he had to admire. Yeah, he had to admit it. Nice ass.

Maddie insisted on driving Reba all the way home, something she'd never done before. The girl had always been happy to exit the car at the junction to the main road. But seeing her today with a load of books, Maddie made the turn up the gravel road.

The ride extended much farther than Maddie anticipated, about two miles. It seemed longer because she had to take it slowly, avoiding potholes and washouts. The county obviously didn't consider Finn Lane worthy of any expense for maintenance. Oak trees, sumac, and poison ivy grew thickly along the sides. Maddie sensed a departure from the civilized world. When she rounded a bend and finally glimpsed the Finn residence, she knew she had reached an isolated kingdom.

Mr. Finn and his clan had carved a ramshackle domain in the heart of the woods. The house resembled a modern-day Noah's ark. The original structure had been a long rectangular trailer home sitting on blocks to level it on the hilly terrain. From there, rooms and stories had been added as needed, constructed from whatever materials had been available at the time. Plywood and corrugated metal had come in handy for walls, along with the natural logs from the surrounding hills. Uneven stairs led up to three separate entrances, none of which appeared to be a proper "front door."

Surrounding the building were assorted vehicles that appeared to be missing many vital parts. To the left were two carports shielding sparkling custom-made cars, one painted turquoise blue, the other a gleaming burgundy featuring fancy flame decorations. These were obviously Mr. Finn's competition vehicles. Maddie shook her head at the priorities of people. His daughter wore thrift store cast-offs while his cars looked like a million bucks. Finn's wrecker and a pickup truck sat parked next to a doghouse bearing the sign *Hell Hounds*.

Several assorted dogs started barking up a storm, disturbing the three black cats that sprawled on a stairway. A tremor of terror quivered in Maddie's stomach as the dogs approached her car. Big, black dogs always brought forth a frightened response since she'd been attacked by a neighbor's Labrador when she was five years old. When two large paws and a monstrous head appeared at her window, she had to fight the urge to throw the car into reverse and make a mad dash for paved roads. Her heart thumped a fearful rhythm in her chest.

A door banged opened at the house and a thin, sandy-haired man in need of a haircut came out looking suspicious and hostile.

Reba quickly opened the door and yelled, "It's me, Pa! Miss Harris brung me home."

His whole demeanor changed as he watched Reba getting out of the car. Finn smiled, shoved his hand through his hair, and started down the stairs, yelling at the curs to shut up.

"It's about time you got home. I was 'bout to send the dogs out for you."

Behind him from the open door poured out the Finn children, two boys and a girl. An overweight woman dressed in a tank top and shorts followed, obviously the mother. She balanced a robust baby boy on one hip and held a cigarette in her other hand. She had probably been pretty once, but too many children, carbohydrates, cigarettes, and beer had taken their toll.

When her parents made it to her side, Reba introduced them to Maddie. "Miss Harris, this here is my pa, Wade, and my mom, Ginger."

Wade walked around to the driver's side. "'Preciate you giving Reba a lift. She can be so dad-gum slow, she misses the bus."

"I'm happy to help," Maddie said.

Wade rubbed his hand over the smooth top of the cream Camry. "Nice car." Hollering to his wife, he said, "You'd like one of these babies, wouldn't you, Sugar?"

Ginger smiled, revealing two lost side teeth. "You bet."

Maddie imagined all the Finn children trashing out the inside of her beloved car and inwardly shuddered.

Wade bent down and rested his elbows on the opening where the window was rolled down and said, "You must be the teacher that lives off the main road. Reba always points out your house when we drive by. She seems to have taken a shine to you."

Wade leaned uncomfortably close to Maddie and she pulled back as far as she could. His eyes inspected her and the car interior. She nearly gagged at the smell of stale cigarettes the musty stains on his Budweiser T-shirt. And weren't his pupils unnaturally dilated?

Maddie smiled politely. "I'm the assistant principal, actually. I think Reba is a very special girl. I've asked her to stay tomorrow for the dance and I'll bring her home, if that's all right with you."

Wade stood up. "Yeah, Reba's special, ain't you, baby?

You want to go to that there dance?"

Reba stood clutching her books. A look passed between father and daughter that Maddie caught, but didn't understand. "Yes, I do. I want to go to that dance, Pa."

Ginger put her arm around her daughter. "Course she does. Her first school dance. Let her go, Wade."

Wade winked at Maddie. "They're ganging up on me. Sure she can go! Wouldn't want her to miss her first dance."

Reba heaved a little sigh of relief as she said, "Thanks for the ride, Miss Harris. See ya tomorrow."

Reba and her mother turned toward the house. Ginger yelled at the other three kids. "Get in the house for supper. The hotdogs is probably ready by now." They all waved goodbye as they mounted the stairs.

Maddie pulled her car in gear and tried to decide the best way to turn around when Wade suddenly leaned into her open window again. "They're sure making teachers good lookin' nowadays." He pulled a card out of his pocket and dropped it in her lap. "If you ever need to have your car towed, call me. That's my personal cell phone. I can be there in a flash."

Maddie sensed he meant more than a friendly exchange of business cards and pursed her lips. "I'm a member of the Automobile Club. Thanks, anyway. Good bye, Mr. Finn." She pushed the up button on her electric window opener, forcing Wade to back away.

As she drove off she glanced in her rear view mirror. Wade stared at her as she negotiated the bumpy road. His thin body held a menacing tension. A line from *Othello* flashed in her mind. *Yon Wade has a lean and hungry look.*

Chapter Four

I won't dance

sung by Fred Astaire

Thanks to the decorating committee and the wizardry of Randy's tech crew, the gym's transformation into a glitzy ballroom dazzled the eyes. By six o'clock on Thursday evening, a paper moon hung behind the portable stage. Red and blue stage lights cast a dreamy glow across the lacquered wooden floor and a mirrored ball dangled over the middle of the room spinning flashing reflections of light. Randy had donned a bright blue suit, complete with wide lapels enhanced with satin ribbon and rhinestones for dramatic effect. He stood on the platform adjusting his audio equipment and tuned up the karaoke machine while a few students hung the lights and decorations.

Phyllis Green meticulously fussed at the food table, placing petite sandwiches on trays. She wore a full skirted dress reminiscent of fifties sitcoms. With her straight cut bangs and funny face, she resembled a plump Imogene Coca.

Randy turned on Dean Martin's *That's Amore* just as Maddie and Reba entered the gym. Singing along with Dean, Randy danced down the stage steps, pulled Maddie into his arms, and waltzed her around the empty gym floor. Dressed in a peach colored poodle skirt, matching cashmere sweater, neck scarf, bobby socks, and saddle shoes, Maddie laughed as he twirled her around the room. They glided to a stop beside a grinning Reba.

Randy looked the females up and down. "Wowsers, ladies!"

"Costumes are courtesy of the Beaver Cove drama department. Doesn't Reba look wonderful?" Maddie asked.

Maddie thought the girl adorable in her powder blue flared skirt and matching sweater outfit. Her curly auburn air formed a halo around her sweet face.

"You'd make Laverne and Shirley die of envy. And don't I look fabulous?" Randy struck a pose.

"You're absolutely blinding," Maddie replied. "I've got to go check on the door-keepers. Reba, why don't you assist Mr. Bailey for a few minutes while I make my rounds?"

"Okay."

"Come on, kid," Randy said, "You can be my back-up for *Love Potion Number Nine*."

Phil glanced at his watch as he drove the Skylark to the school. Late. That stiff-necked assistant principal would probably chew his ass about it. It had taken him a while to come up with a fifties look. He assumed a Rebel-Without-A-Cause look leather jacket over gray slacks and a black shirt. He'd have been on time if he hadn't gotten into it on the phone with Pam. Why every conversation had to turn into a battle he didn't know. He'd initiated it to try to keep peace.

"Pam, it's me, Phil."

"Like I wouldn't recognize your voice."

"Listen I just wanted to let you know I mailed the support check today. I included a little extra for some school clothes for Melissa. I expect to see her in something better than the rags she's been wearing."

Pam's voice took on the tone of fingernails scratching a chalkboard. "Don't you dare criticize me, asshole."

"Okay, okay. Sorry. I'd like you to buy some better clothes for her. All right?"

"Well, I can tell you, Phil, an extra ten bucks isn't going to go that far."

"I sent more than ten dollars, for Chrissake!"

"Listen, I gotta go. Don't give me a hard time or I'll swear out a Victim Protection Order against you."

Phil swallowed his infuriated reply. "Wait. Are you going to let Melissa come to the game Saturday?"

"She said something about it." He could hear the calculation in her voice. "We'll see. We'll see how much extra money you sent. Bye."

Phil pounded the steering wheel remembering the conversation as the school gym came into view. In his current mood, chaperoning a dance sounded worse than getting a tooth drilled.

Dance music blasted through the doors as Phil entered the gym. The end of a beehop song played as Randy pranced in his electric suit on the stage talking to the crowd, telling jokes. Maddie stood next to the food table, flanked by Mr. Manchester and Phyllis Green. Phil decided he might as well face the music and present his tardy butt before Miss Prim and Proper. As he reached the table, she lifted her hand to the side of her mouth and began chanting, "Elvis, Elvis, Elvis." The crowd picked up the refrain and soon the whole room rang with "Elvis, Elvis, Elvis."

On stage Randy posed his hands on his hips and rolled his eyes, feigning modesty. "Well, if you insist..." He nodded toward Reba who manned the karaoke machine. She punched a button and the first blasting chords of *Jail House Rock* reverberated in the room. Randy assumed an Elvis stance and began a lively imitation of the King. The kids ate it up, singing along, pretending to play their electric guitars.

Phil watched Maddie get into the spirit of the moment, clapping her hands in time to the music. Her full skirt rocked rhythmically. Tonight she wore her hair down, curled, and pulled away from her face by a couple of barrettes. She wasn't hiding behind any glasses and her eyes shone as she enjoyed the antics of her friend on the stage. The cashmere sweater made her look soft and touchable.

Just as he suspected, the officious Miss Harris was a babe.

Maddie became aware of being watched and glanced to her left to see Mr. Wilcox staring at her with his macho grin. She immediately straightened up, crossed her arms in front of her and delivered her best "the Queen-is-displeased" expression. Of course, the poodle skirt took away from its effectiveness.

Phil laughed and walked to her, ignoring the other two teachers at her side. The music quieted down to Randy's crooning of *Love Me Tender.*

"You're late, Coach Wilcox," she said.

Phil pointed to his watch. "Your memo said 7:30."

"It did not."

"I'm sure it did."

"I don't think so." She frowned with doubt. Had she made a typo?

He grinned. She was just so easy to play.

Phyllis Green moved in on Phil, taking him by an arm and shoving a plate of dainty sandwiches under his nose. "Coach, wouldn't you like a pimento cheese sandwich? I made them myself. Don't you just love these old romantic songs?"

Phineas Manchester resumed his boring diatribe on the political agenda of the National Education Association to Maddie. He had been leaning over her for the last half hour, expounding his opinions through gaped teeth. She scanned the dancers for inappropriate behavior and tried to tune out his penetrating drone. Lord, her life had come to this–policing teenagers while fending off a middle-aged suitor with bad breath.

Just then a shoving match broke out across the room between two young bucks over a doe-eyed girl in a tight dress. Maddie immediately headed for the melee, certain her stern presence would stop the altercation. By the time she got there, a circle had formed. Bystanders egged them on.

Maddie stepped into the fray. "That's enough, you two boys!"

They totally ignored her.

Bobby Beasley, who came from a long line of good ole boys, shoved his black opponent, Rashid Jackson, again, saying, "Go to hell, Jackson!"

"You first, Beasley!" Jackson pushed back.

Seeing the fight escalating, Phil barged his way through the crowd. Maddie shouted inanities. Idiotically, she put herself right between the two hotheaded teens. Phil knew real punching would commence at any moment and Maddie would get either a black eye or a broken jaw for her troubles if she didn't get out of the way. Phil thought her the bravest, dumbest woman he had ever seen.

Bobby pulled his hand back into a fist, ready to plow around the annoying woman in his path and deck the taunting jerk across from him. Phil caught his arm and the back of his jacket, yanking him off his feet.

"Let's take it outside, Romeo," Phil said as he flipped Bobby around and shoved him toward the side door. Then he took three broad steps to Rashid, grabbed his arm, and pulled him toward the exit. When he caught up to Bobby, he put his hands at the back of both boys' collars and dragged them out the door, leaving Maddie standing in the circle of onlookers.

"All right," she said, "the show is over. Get back to your dancing or I'll pull the plug on the speakers and call it a night."

The crowd broke into pairs and dancing resumed. Randy played a soothing ballad to calm raging teenage hormones. When the song ended, he made an announcement.

"Well, kiddies, I have a nice surprise for you tonight. Before the dance started I had my mike tester sing a song and she really blew me away. I think with a little persuasion, I can get her to perform for you. Come on, give a big hand for Reba Finn!"

The crowd applauded politely, as they murmured among themselves. Most of them had never heard of Reba Finn. Reba took shy steps to the front as the spot engulfed her in white light.

Speaking softly into the microphone, her Arkansas twang echoed in the room. "Hey everybody. I hope ya'll like this song. It's one of my mama's favorites."

Maddie stood amazed and frightened that Randy would push Reba into a situation over her head. The girl didn't need public humiliation at this point in her life. But when the opening notes of the song began, Reba closed her eyes and a transformation took place. She became strong and hit the opening bars of *Stand By Your Man* with all the power of Tammy Wynette.

Maddie drifted to the stage, transfixed as Reba wrung every bit of drama out of the lyric. Maddie glanced at the back of the platform and noted Randy's smile of approval. They exchanged unspoken nods of wonder. Maddie knew her friend had struck gold. He loved finding a talented student to mentor. When the song ended, the room burst into spontaneous applause and Reba jumped a little, as if surprised to find herself before the audience. She gave a frightened smile, nodded, and moved out of the spotlight. Randy put an arm around her, talking excitedly as he started the next song playing.

Phineas sidled up to Maddie. "You quelled that fighting incident admirably. I was getting ready to restrain those ruffians myself."

Maddie looked up at him. "Did you have to stop to tie your shoes?"

Phineas blinked at her. "What?"

Maddie sighed. "Never mind."

He pulled her into his gangly arms. "This is the perfect time for that dance you owe me."

"Oh, I don't think..."

But the determined Mr. Manchester had her in his stiff embrace and nothing short of a scene on her part would disengage him. So, Maddie found herself jammed against his coat lapel doing a box step, wishing she were on the Planet Mars.

Phil returned to the dance floor, having put the fear of God into the two miscreants, looking to have a few words with the reckless Miss Harris. He spotted her in the beanpole English teacher's arms. He grinned at her priceless expression of long-suffering endurance.

Phyllis Green's high-pitched voice reached him. "Oh, Coach Wilcox!"

He pretended he didn't hear her. He couldn't stand the

thought of pushing the saccharine Home-Ec teacher around the dance floor. He made a straight line for Maddie and tapped Manchester on the shoulder.

"Hey, buddy, it isn't fair to monopolize the hottest chick at the dance."

Phineas appeared about to argue when the music changed to a rollicking American Bandstand standard geared to twists and spins that were completely out of Manchester's league.

Phineas gave Maddie a little bow. "I'll get you another drink, Madeleine." He walked off in the direction of the food table, shooting Phil a look of complete disdain.

Phil and Maddie stood facing each other surrounded by energetic teenage dancers. He looked dangerous to her in his leather jacket and dark clothes. She looked damned cute to him in her cuddly fifties get up.

He took her hand. "Let's see what you're made of, Miss Harris."

An irresistible challenge, she spun into his arm and then out again and they were off. They danced in and out, up and down, moving and grooving to a fifties beat. Like Frankie and Annette incarnate, she even slid once under his legs and back again. Before long the spotlight picked them up and everyone stopped to watch, clapping their encouragement. Maddie laughed, following Phil's fast-paced lead. His eyes never left her face as he enjoyed watching her toss her head back in merriment. They danced until the upbeat song mercifully ended. The circle of spectators applauded their appreciation as the couple stood panting holding hands, and they took a bow.

The lights changed, drenching the whole room in a blue tint and Randy began the strains of *Blue Moon.*

Phil gently tugged on Maddie's hand and brought her close to him, swaying to the haunting love song. He held her far enough away from his body to look into her face and talk. "You know how to cut a rug, Miss Harris. But you're a little idiot, you know that don't you?"

Maddie's eyes flashed darkly and she tried to push away. "You are the most insulting person I have ever met."

He squeezed her hand and tightened his grip at her waist. "Getting between two raging bulls isn't a bright move. You could have gotten hurt by those guys, sweetheart."

Maddie looked down. "Oh...I suppose so. I just thought they'd stop."

"Honey, never get between two males during mating season."

She tilted her head up, meeting his gaze. "I'll try to remember that. Thanks for coming to the rescue."

"Anytime, cupcake, anytime."

They continued rocking as Randy's mellow voice crooned about a blue moon and longing for someone to care for. Throbbing music. Pulsing heartbeats.

Maddie couldn't take her gaze away from Phil's face. In the shadowy light he appeared so strong, his square jaw and chiseled features supremely male. A serious, compelling expression replaced the smart aleck smirk. His intense gaze held her as firmly in place as his brawny arms. Something was happening here. She could feel it, a spinning of invisible threads twisting around them as the music played on. She imagined a blue cocoon materializing out of the notes pouring from the bandstand.

"What do your friends call you?" he asked.

"Maddie," she said softly.

Maddie. He liked it. It promised the soft underside of the hard surfaced Madeleine. The cashmere under his hand on her lower back had a sensual feel and he moved his fingers ever so slightly over the texture. He couldn't remember the last time he had felt this good. For the moment the usual burden of bitterness, frustration, guilt, and cynicism lifted from his shoulders and life seemed to have possibilities. Looking into the wide eyes of Maddie Harris, he felt like the man he was supposed to be.

They finished the dance locked in each other's gaze knowing something beyond words was transpiring between them. Something that transcended the mere sexual attraction of a slow dance. Reflections from the mirrored ball glinted on their faces with hypnotizing rhythm, shadow and light, sparkle and space. Like being caught in the beam of that ole Devil Moon…

Chapter Five

There once was a girl who had a curl
right in the middle of her forehead,
When she was good she was very, very good
but when she was bad, she was horrid

Mother Goose

As the school dance spun on, Wade Finn sat in his living room, pissed off. The damned DEA had burned his marijuana fields today. It had been such a sweet operation, growing plots of weed here and there in the hills. Now how the hell was he going pay for his race cars and get to the meets? Busting his butt with the wrecker truck would be a pain in the ass.

As he sat on the sofa in his ramshackle living room nursing a beer and popping a couple pills, he looked around at all the crap in the room. Yeah, he had some nice things, the big screen TV, the workout equipment, video games. He liked his fifty-gallon aquarium with the monster fish that ate the goldfish he fed them. Of course the furniture looked like hell with dirty upholstery covering the couch and chairs. With all these damn kids, what could you expect?

At that moment, bickering children grated on Wade's nerves as they sat around the *Formica* kitchen table finishing off macaroni and cheese. George, age twelve, and Vince, age eight, engaged in a shoving match. Faith, the five-year old, colored a picture until Vince stole her crayons. She screeched like a bobcat. Baby Garth banged his high chair with his cup, jabbering and laughing.

Wade stared at the noisy kids, saw Ginger's fat ass washing dishes at the sink with the ever-burning cigarette dangling out of her mouth and just wanted to punch something. He was strapped with all these mouths to feed when he should be out making a name for himself. He should be on the race car circuit right now being the next, by-God, Dale Ernhardt, instead of sitting around in this hellhole waiting for all the kids to go to bed so he could finally get some with his old lady. Life was so frigging unfair.

He stood up and hollered, "Can't you shut these kids up?"

Ginger twirled around, aware of his edgy mood. But she had worries of her own. With the pot money gone, what were they going to do? She'd tried working before, but making minimum wage down in the town didn't add up to squat. And who would take care of the baby?

She hollered back, "They're not botherin' you!"

"The hell they're not!"

He took angry strides to the table, swept his arm across the surface, sending bowls of sticky pasta flying. "Supper's over! Go to bed!"

Faith howled as chunks of macaroni ruined her pretty colored picture. The baby laughed and threw his bowl onto the floor. George and Vince quickly stood up and ran from the room. They'd played this scene before and knew they could get walloped in a hurry.

Ginger grabbed Garth out of the high chair and hugged him in her arms. As she cast angry looks at Wade, she talked to Faith. "Take your colors and git to bed."

Faith cried, "He wrecked my picture!"

Ginger tried to keep her voice even. "I know. You can make another 'un tomorrow."

Faith wiped her eyes with the back of hands as she gathered up her crayons. When she reached the kitchen door she turned around, looked at Wade, and yelled, "You turd!"

Wade took one step in her direction and she high-tailed it up the makeshift stairs in the hall to the room she shared with Reba.

He turned on Ginger. "You should teach them kids some manners!"

"I'm givin' the baby a bath and puttin' him to bed." Ginger disappeared into the hall.

Wade trudged back to the couch, dug for the remote, and grabbed another swig of beer. As he surfed the channels he hoped there was something good to watch, maybe some wrestling, or a rerun of *Married, With Children.*

On Saturday morning the smell of fall filled the air, a scent of change. Maddie stretched on the running track that encircled the Beaver Cove High football field. A blacktop ribbon surrounded the green grass. She often ran on Saturday mornings before going into her office to catch up on paperwork neglected during the week. She simply couldn't abide facing a backlog on Monday morning. Two hours of undisturbed diligence equaled eight hours of work accomplished during a normal school day.

Dressed in her leggings and matching running gear, she longed to pump her legs and feel the blood rush through her veins. At seven o'clock she had the track to herself with no neighborhood joggers, no teenagers—no disturbing football coaches.

Maddie lifted her feet for a slow warm-up lap, thinking about those heady moments at the dance. It hadn't lasted long, standing there under the spell of *Blue Moon.* But remembering it now rekindled the warmth, recaptured the trance.

Scared the bejeebes out of her.

She liked having control and sensed the Coach resisted anyone's control. He was an arrogant jock and Thursday's slow dance was just some sort of high after their fast jitterbug. Yes, that's what it was–like runner's euphoria. Nothing personal existed between herself and the smug coach. Nothing personal at all. She continued running, congratulating herself on putting the whole thing into perspective.

Phil pulled his car into the football stadium parking lot. The pressure of the day gripped his chest. His first football game as a coach. He'd been awake since four, read the paper, and finally gotten dressed. Standing in his messy apartment, he'd known he should make an attempt at cleaning it up. Then he thought, *screw it*. He'd rather go to school, work out, and get ready for the game. He shouldn't be so nervous over a high school football game, for Chrissake, but he was jittery as hell.

Watching from his car, a running figure caught his eye at the far end of the track, undoubtedly a local early bird. Then he recognized the Camry to his right and he focused on the runner again. A smile filled his face and the tension in his chest eased. Something about Miss Harris–Maddie–made him grin. As she rounded the bend running toward him, he noticed her perfectly coordinated running clothes, purple and black togs, purple leggings, and headband. Yeah, she could be an ad for *Runner Magazine*. He decided a few laps might also do him some good.

As she began her third lap, she unclipped the water bottle attached at her waist and threw her head back for a big gulp.

"It's a mighty fine day for a run, Miss Harris. Mind if I join you?"

He pulled up beside her, coming out of nowhere. She choked on the water, embarrassing herself by spewing liquid out of her mouth in a completely unladylike manner. Coughing, she tripped over her own shoes and would have gone sprawling if Phil hadn't caught her in a bear hug.

"Whoa," he said, "are you all right?"

She pushed away from him. "For heaven's sake! What are you sneaking up on me for?"

"Honey, when these size fifteens hit the pavement, I don't sneak up on anybody. I can't help it if you were in your own little dream world."

Maddie blushed. She'd been reliving that darn dance.

She took a deep breath. "Well, at any rate, I didn't hear you. I wasn't expecting anyone out here this early."

He looked her over admiringly. "Great outfit."

She observed his odd ensemble: blue base ball cap, maroon sweat shirt with the arms cut off over a green T-shirt and brown sweat pants.

Looking very serious, she said, "I have to ask–are you

color blind?"

He dropped back his head and laughed. "No, I just don't give a rat's ass about clothes. I pull things out of the clean clothes hamper."

"Don't you have a dresser? A closet?"

"Yeah, but the clothes don't make it that far. Hey, I'm doing good getting them in and out of the washer and dryer."

"Well, yes, I suppose that's something."

His gaze traveled her body with an appraising grin, making her feel extremely self-conscious.

She cleared her throat. "I like to jog here when I can. It's easier to get a rhythm going where it's flat. It's very hilly where I live."

He was staring at her now and asked in a low voice, "And where do you live, Maddie?"

Feeling like a deer caught in the proverbial headlights, she answered weakly, "In the hills..."

He nodded. "Ah."

They stood there staring at each other like a couple of goofy teenagers until Phil snapped to. "So, did you come to run or flirt with me?"

Embarrassed outrage filled her big blue eyes. "I do not flirt and I certainly wouldn't flirt with you if I did." She pushed off.

Keeping up with her, he said, "No, you'd save that come hither glance for Phineas Manchester."

She rolled her eyes. "Oh, please. Just shut up and run."

And so they did. They ran and ran, keeping pace with each other amazingly well. She was long in the leg at five foot seven, something he admired greatly. Maintaining grace and elegance while sweating around a track took some doing, but somehow she managed it. He imagined her wearing a fancy ballroom gown, himself dressed in a tux, spinning a waltz in a garden setting, the light dim and intimate. He shook his head, thinking, man where did that come from? He was probably getting dehydrated.

After seven laps, they were panting like dogs. Maddie's

water bottle was empty and Phil's throat completely parched. He would have stopped at five laps, but pride is a powerful stimulus. Maddie slowed her pace as they reached the bleachers and stopped to hold onto the front railing, taking measured breaths.

"That's…enough…for me," she said.

"Really?" he said inhaling huge gulps of air. He was about to lie and say he was good for three more laps, but instead spit out, "Thank God!"

They laughed and limped up onto the bleachers.

The early morning breeze felt good passing through their damp clothes as they caught their breath on the metal benches. Maddie grabbed a knapsack she had stowed and pulled out a small towel she draped around her neck. Then she brought out two water bottles and threw one to Phil.

"Granola bar?" she asked.

Phil winced. "Never touch the stuff, but thanks for the water. You do come prepared, don't you?"

"I find a bit of careful planning makes life much easier."

Maddie sat very straight, patting herself with the towel, drank water and looked out over the field. A mockingbird dive-bombed a pair of squirrels playing in a large elm tree that grew near the chain link fence. The slant of the sun sparkled everything with a fresh, clean look.

Phil sprawled back, rested his arms on the bench behind, and locked his gaze on Maddie's profile. Her nose turned up at the end, making her look cute and snooty at the same time.

Laying on a thick accent he said, "So, Miz Harris, where do you holler from? You don't sound like ya'll come from these here parts."

He was teasing her again and, darn it, she liked it.

"I'm from Boston originally, but my father was raised here and I spent my summers in Beaver Cove with my Grammy, uh, Grandmother. What about you? Are you a native?"

"Oh yeah. You can take the man out of Arkansas, but you can't take Arkansas out of the man. I've bounced around a lot, but I guess you could say I've come full circle, hoping to beat the Bender Tigers. Only this time, I'm the coach instead of the quarterback."

She turned and looked at him. "Oh, that's right. Your opening game is tonight. Are you nervous?"

Phil shrugged. "Nervous? It's only a high school football game. It's nothing to lose any sleep over." Maddie's honest blue eyes tore down his defenses. "Listen, I won't kid you. Okay, I'm nervous. These kids might pull it together or they might just get clobbered. It could go either way. These boys are depending on me for leadership and I'm not sure I'm getting through to them. I really don't want to screw this up."

Phil's hand rested on the bench and Maddie instinctively covered it with her own. "I have the feeling you're the sort of person who gets the job done. I've read your resume. You're vastly over qualified for this position. Just do what you've been trained to do and expect the best from your boys. They'll give it to you."

Phil lifted an eyebrow. "Thanks for the vote of confidence." He turned his hand over and captured hers. "So you read my resume, huh? Part of the job or personal curiosity?"

Maddie said nothing and tried to pull her hand away, but he held on tighter and began making little circles with his thumb over her knuckles.

"May I have my hand back, please?"

The sides of his lips turned up every so slightly. "I'm not finished with it yet. You know, I'm curious about you, too. I ask myself what a woman with your education and drive is doing in this hick town. I see you in your little business suits and those awful dark-rimmed glasses and I wonder who you think you're fooling. You try to be a real hard-ass, but, honey, I can see right through you."

She pulled her hand away from his relentless minor caress, feeling breathless. And it wasn't from the running. "I congratulate you on your superior x-ray vision, Mr. Wilcox, but I can assure you I am exactly as I appear. I'm organized, disciplined, and neat–all attributes which appear to elude you.

I dress in a manner suited to my position and I expect a certain amount of respect from the students and the staff. However, every time I'm near you I feel as though you're mocking me, laughing at some sort of private joke at my expense. I can tell you, I don't like it."

Phil's brown eyes crinkled as he leaned a little closer in her direction. "You know what it is, don't you? You want everyone to see you as the assistant principal and I look at you as a woman. You're afraid of being a woman, aren't you, Maddie?"

They stared at each other almost nose to nose. He had seriously ticked her off. She needed some sort of snappy reply. *Afraid of being a woman.* She'd tell him. She'd show him.

She cupped her hands around his cheeks and came at his mouth with intensity, her hot lips taking the smirk off his face. She'd show him who was afraid being a woman.

As she pressed her mouth to his, she anticipated his surprise. *Weren't expecting this, were you, macho man?*

Of course…she wasn't expecting spontaneous combustion. She felt it happening. *Pow!* The strings, the cords of control she'd so carefully laced around her inner woman began popping. She could almost hear them–*zing, ping, snap*! Phil's arms wrapped around her and the kiss transformed from an assault to a surrender. She folded into him, going soft and pliant. Total meltdown.

Phil lifted his head, saying hoarsely, "I take it back."

Maddie blinked, struggling to focus, trying to regain strength. "What? Take what back?"

"The crack about your being afraid of being a woman. Honey, you are *all* woman." His brown eyes smiled, almost merry.

Coming back to her senses, Maddie pushed away and stood up, a little unsteady. "I really have a lot of work to do. I need a cup of coffee." Oh, God, did she need coffee.

She nervously packed her little knapsack, keenly aware of Phil's frank stare.

He said, "Thanks for the run. I feel better about facing the day."

She started to walk down the steps. "Good."

"Are you coming to the game?"

She stopped and turned to look at him. She'd planned on renting a video to watch at home. Her eyes softened. "Of course, wouldn't miss it. I'll be rooting for you."

He smiled a teddy bear grin. "Good."

Maddie stood before her closet at six o'clock that evening, still groggy from an afternoon nap. She'd meant to do laundry and run the vacuum, but weariness overcame her and she crashed on her flowered quilt. She chose a T-shirt bearing the beaver mascot, jeans, and coordinating jacket. Examining her myriad of scarves, she procured an appropriate match and tied it on. The trademark began as a lark at the school and now was expected. Students would think her half-naked without it. At Christmas she received boxes of imaginative scarves from favorite students. Slipping into comfortable flats, she headed for the door just as Randy rang the bell.

She opened the door. He wore a raccoon coat and carried a megaphone. "Who are you supposed to be–Rudy Vallee?"

"You've got it! Going to the first football game of the season is so 1920's, makes me want to do the Varsity Drag. I should have told you to dress as Clara Bow."

"Sorry, you'll just have to settle for plain ole Madeleine Harris, uptight assistant principal." She walked out to the car.

Taking the curvy roads, Randy glanced at her from the driver's side. "You've got to promise me–only one *Coke*."

Maddie appeared highly insulted. "Randall, I am not a foolish college coed any longer. I've learned how to control my natural exuberance at sporting events."

He watched the dusky light play on her face. "Oh, yeah? Do you remember last year's Super Bowl Watch Party? And that was in front of the TV!"

Maddie had washed down *M & M's* with a half liter of *Coke* at Randy's party and nearly come to blows with four of his friends who were rooting for the opposite team. For

Maddie, caffeine and sugar took on drug-like properties.

"I assure you that was a complete aberration. Besides, this is a high school game. How exciting can it get?"

Randy didn't say anything, but Jimmy Durante's voice echoed in his head. *You ain't seen nothin' yet.*

At the Finn household, Ginger put the finishing touches on Reba's hair, gazing over the girl's shoulder into a mirror. Reba chewed her lip and examined her sweater and jean outfit fearing that it made her look fat–all eighty-nine pounds of her.

"You think this makes my butt look big?"

Ginger scoffed, "Don't gripe to me about big butts." She clicked the clip in place. "There! That'll do it."

Reba stared at her reflection, seeing the curly hair, wishing she didn't have freckles across her nose. Still, she liked the ribbed sweater her mom had bought at a garage sale.

Since her singing debut on Thursday, she was suddenly someone people noticed. All day Friday kids said "hi" in the halls and she got invited by some popular girls to hangout with them at the game.

Downstairs, Wade finished packing baggies of pot in his jacket pocket. He intended to sell the last of his supply at the game, an easy way to make some fast bucks. He'd been doing it for years. Everyone thought he was such a big fan. Like anyone could get excited about a half-assed high school football team. Usually he went alone, but tonight Reba had begged to go along.

"Reba, I'm leaving here in five minutes. I ain't waiting for you!" He hollered into the hall.

The walls shook as Reba hopped down the stairs. "Comin' Pa!"

George and Vince yelled at each other over a Nintendo game that had them glued in front of the TV, while Faith sat coloring a picture at the kitchen table.

Wade focused on Reba as she entered the kitchen. "Damn, you look good, girl! Our baby daughter is growing up on us, Ginger."

Ginger entered the room holding baby Garth. "She's the same age I was when I met you." Suddenly Ginger frowned and spoke sharply, "Don't you go off with any boys, Reba."

"I told you, I'm meeting some girls, Mom."

Ginger eyed her suspiciously. "You keep an eye on her, Wade."

Wade slipped on his jacket. "It's just a friggin' Beaver High football game. She can't exactly get lost in the crowd."

"Come on, hurry up." Melissa watched her mom primping before the bathroom mirror. Pam sprayed her bleached hair in place and leaned in close, examining a slight smudge of her lipstick. Mom still liked to think she was a young cheerleader, but the lines around her eyes told a different story. The way she poured over fashion magazines and dressed like Brittany Spears made Melissa want to hurl.

Pam glanced at her tomboy daughter standing impatiently in the doorway, dressed in a backwards baseball cap, torn sweatshirt and loose jeans. Melissa looked and acted like her father, more than Pam would ever admit. The girl was a slob, didn't bother with things that didn't interest her, but could get totally absorbed in a Discovery Channel show about lizards, sharks, tarantulas or any assortment of disgusting creatures.

Despite Pam's best efforts, Melissa displayed no feminine talents. She had the fashion sense of a bag lady. She'd hated dance lessons, but had begged to play softball. Pam detested sitting in the hot sun watching little girls miss the big ball with their clumsy bats. Of course, Melissa had a killer pitching arm.

Pam knitted her eyebrows. "Are you going dressed like that?"

Melissa looked at her mother's outfit–tight turquoise Bermuda pants, topped by a snug scooped-neck sweater that accentuated her bouncy breasts, and asked, "Are you going dressed like *that*?"

Pam examined her profile in the mirror and thought she looked hot. She wanted Phil to see what he was missing. She also wanted to bask in his reflected glory. She was his ex-wife, after all. There had been a big spread in the local newspaper heralding the return of a football hero. While Pam always concentrated on Phil's failures, the reporter had highlighted the successes.

And Pam remembered. There had been good times, high hopes. Days of excitement and nights of passion. God, she missed the glory days. Maybe she could ride Phil back to easy street.

Lord knows her last relationship, if you could call it that, had been a dead end. She'd been dumped by a Florida linebacker and would have been living in her car with Melissa if she hadn't had this crappy house in Beaver Cove left to her by her parents. She'd barely had enough money to ship her precious things won from the divorce back to Arkansas.

So the former cheerleader returned home with a kid to feed and nothing to show for her efforts but a meager support check from Phil. Her job at Wal-Mart was a total bummer. But now with Phil getting his act together and pushing so hard to see Melissa, maybe she could parley his guilt into a little gold for her.

When Melissa had secretly read the article about her dad, the puzzle pieces in her mind regarding her parents shifted. The guy described in the paper was so different from the jerk her mom complained about.

The part that really got her was when the reporter asked why he'd come back to Beaver Cove. "I have an eleven-year-old daughter that lives here. I want to spend as much time with her as possible."

Melissa never cried, but her throat had tightened up and she'd blinked really hard. Maybe her dad wasn't the world-class asshole her mom made him out to be.

Coming back to reality, she yelled at her mom, "We're going to miss the kickoff!"

Pam turned off the bathroom light and walked down the hall. "All right all ready. Let's go."

Melissa tapped her foot as she watched her mom slip on a jacket in the neat little living room of the tiny house. Melissa hated having to be so careful around all Pam's fancy stuff that she'd gotten from the divorce. Her mom had a cow over the vases, candles, figurines, and fussy tables. Her dad must have only been left with his toothbrush, sweats, and old bomber car. She was starting to see a lot of things differently than her mother painted them.

Excitement in the locker room gave off a definite aroma. Male sweat and hormones created an atmosphere that lifted spirits high, putting the braggarts and jokesters in rare form. The timbre of teenage voices, the clang of metal lockers banging open was music to Phil's ears. These kids were all hopes and potential.

Phil finished taping up an ankle for a linebacker, gave last minute instructions to Stu and conferred with the referees. Then it was time for The Speech.

Standing ready in their uniforms, clasping helmets, the team stood at attention before their coach. "All right, listen up. You've made a lot of progress in a short period of time. Use your brains, play smart, no hot-dogging. Remember, no one player is more important than the team. Work together as a solid unit, do the things you've been taught and we'll send the Tigers back to Bender with their tails between their legs. Tonight you're going to show them–Beaver Cove High is back!"

The boys shot onto the field like rapid-fire bullets from a gun as the band blared the school fight song. Phil paused for a moment in the dark passage before he followed them, sending up a prayer to that Higher Power they talked about in AA. "Please, God, help these hammerheads play a good game. Amen."

Wade raced the truck toward Beaver Cove High, dimly aware of a half-moon hanging in the sky. He glanced up, glad to see stars and no damn sign of rain to keep his customers away. His eyes widened at the sight of a packed parking lot.

He fishtailed into a space and whistled low. "Holy shit,

your pa is gonna make out tonight. Listen, sister, you go find your friends and don't get in no trouble. I want your butt back to the truck at the start of the fourth quarter, got it?"

"Sure, Pa." Reba hopped from the truck and ran to the entrance.

Up in the bleachers above the fifty-yard line, Maddie and Randy sat munching popcorn and drinking *Coke*. He bought her a *small* one, which she ungraciously accepted. He could be such a mother hen. Really, she knew her limits.

The Beavers won the coin toss, the ball sailed across the field for the kickoff, and the game was on. Maddie watched Phil pace the sidelines, making remarks to his players as he passed them. She wished she could hear his comments. He held his ground on strong, muscular legs. He motioned his arms in the sharp, distinctive secret signals of coaches. She found herself lingering on the man instead of the game and forced her attention to the field.

Seeing the quarterback toss an interception that caused a turnover, she moaned loudly, just like the thin girl sitting next to her. They frowned at each other in commiseration.

"He looks a lot better in practice," the girl said. "He's just nervous."

Maddie's eyebrows lifted. "You've been watching the practices?"

"Yeah, my dad's the coach."

"Really? You must be...Melissa?" Maddie remembered the name from Phil's personnel file.

Melissa looked up in surprise. "Yeah."

Maddie put out her hand. "I'm Miss Harris, the assistant principal. How do you do?"

Shaking the offered hand, Melissa replied, "Want some *M&M's*?"

Maddie peered into the fragrant opening of the king size bag sitting on Melissa's lap. Merry little colors: bright green, red, blue, yellow, winked at her looking so innocent. Just a handful would taste so good, melt in her mouth. Her fingers sank into the bag and she took a fistful.

"Thank you." She would savor each one, taking her time and enjoy that *one* handful.

Gaining possession of the ball once again, the Beaver receiver found a hole in the defense, making a thirty-yard run on the fourth down for the first touchdown. Maddie and Melissa shot to their feet, screaming. Maddie tossed all the candy in her mouth. When the kicker made the extra point, she happily dipped her hand in the bag for just a little more.

A blonde with big hair wiggled her way up the steps carrying two huge drinks. Maddie saw her surveying the crowd, winking at people she knew. She stopped at Maddie's row, worked her way toward the empty seat next to Melissa, and lowered her tightly clad rear end onto the bench.

Handing the drink to Melissa, she said, "I can't believe the nerve they have to charge three dollars for these."

"Get over it, Mom," Melissa replied as she took a big gulp.

Maddie eavesdropped on the conversation. Phil's ex interested her greatly. She told herself it was professional duty to know as much background information about faculty members as possible. The woman's name was Pam and as far as Maddie was concerned she looked like ten pounds of mud packed into a five-pound bag. Pam squealed a hello at some people, stood, and waved at others.

Pam said, "Baby, I see some friends I'm going to go talk to. I'll be back in a few minutes, okay?"

Keeping focused on the game, Melissa replied, "Whatever."

Just then the Tigers made it into the end zone past a clumsy attempt at defense by the Beavers, leading Melissa and Maddie to groan again.

Maddie sucked the dregs of her *Coke*, causing a gurgling sound. "Your dad's team is going to have to do better than that."

Melissa offered a slug of her mega drink. "Tell me about it."

Randy tapped Maddie on the shoulder. "I see the Finn girl

with some friends. I want to talk to her about transferring into my Intro to Drama class. I'll be back."

Maddie nodded, getting more wrapped up in the game. The caffeine and sugar seeped into her bloodstream, rhythmically pumped by her heart toward her brain. Her attention riveted on the playing field and a sense of anxiety began to overtake her.

The game took on tremendous importance, its outcome crucial to the future of Beaver Cove, perhaps the world. As the Beavers began their next drive, she emotionally struggled with them as they fought for the next ten yards.

A Tiger illegally grabbed a Beaver facemask. She turned to Melissa. "Did you see that?"

Melissa shrugged. "Yeah, the refs are dorks."

Maddie stood and yelled, "Penalty! Penalty!" but the game went on.

Sitting down, Maddie grabbed the drink from Melissa, took a huge swig, and fisted another handful of *M & M's*. The new pals gulped, chewed, and cheered until the halftime with the score tied 14-14. Far too antsy to stay seated in the bleachers, not to mention too full of liquid, they made a dash for the ladies room. Returning to the area in front of the first row of benches, they paced the concrete and discussed strategies for the second half.

"I think Dad should switch receivers," Melissa said.

"Somebody should do something about those biased referees. They're letting the Tigers get away with murder," Maddie replied.

As the band left the field and the players returned, the two fans cheered and whistled their team back onto the sides. Phil looked up into the stands, recognized the boisterous boosters, and gave a small salute. Maddie and Melissa waved back enthusiastically.

"Go Beavers!" they said simultaneously.

As the third quarter progressed, Maddie got into full fan-from-hell persona, her concentration becoming intense, obsessed. Tunnel vision focused only on the ball, players and refs made her oblivious to her surroundings or the effect of her cat-calls on innocent bystanders.

"What kind of call was that? What are you, blind! Come on, defense. Don't be a bunch of pantywaists!"

Phil sent Stu over once requesting that she tone down her enthusiastic cheering.

Shocked at the reprimand, Maddie replied, "Of course. I'm simply rooting for the home team."

But like a four-year-old told to shush, Maddie's exuberance could not be contained. She cheered; she moaned; she made loud comments about the intelligence of the referees and the dirty playing of the Tigers.

When the Beavers got penalized five yards for holding, Maddie yelled, "Oh right! Call that one, but let that punk Tiger fullback do all the clipping he wants! Who's paying you off, anyway?"

Melissa piped in. "Yeah, who's paying you off anyway?"

Phil decided enough was enough. He gave Stu a couple instructions and marched over to the railing where the girls stood above him.

"Miss Harris, a word with you please?" he said, hands on hips.

Maddie gripped the railing and bent over. "Yes, Coach you're doing a fine job, but I can't abide the prejudice of these officials."

He stepped closer, crooked his finger, which made her bend over even farther. "Would you do me a big favor?"

"Of course, anything."

"Shut the hell up!"

Maddie blinked her eyes. "Well! You don't have to be insulting." Glancing at the field, she glimpsed a Tiger viciously knee a Beaver, or so she thought. "I saw that!"

Taking a step up onto the first rung of the railing, she continued her tirade. "You blind, cross-eyed, stupid refs!"

As the Tiger quarterback sprinted into the end zone, Maddie let loose of the top railing, raised her hands in the air and exclaimed, "Oh no!"

Phil noticed the stream of kids and parents on the sidewalk behind Maddie snickering at her exuberance. At that moment a passing fan carrying two tubs of popcorn bumped the small of her back, perhaps intentionally.

She wobbled, a look of panic overtaking her face. Her hands grabbed for thin air as she proceeded to tumble head first over the railing.

"Shit," he muttered as he put his arms out to cushion her fall. Her head crashed into his chest, knocking him down as his arms fastened around her and they both rolled onto the ground.

Coming to a stop in a tangle nose to nose he said under his breath, "You are a pain in the ass, Miss Harris."

Hands from various sideline players pulled them up. Phil dusted himself off as Maddie straightened her clothes, making little grunting noises.

"Are you all right?" he asked

"Of course, I'm perfectly fine," she said, taking a step wherein her ankle completely buckled beneath her. "Ow!"

"Great," he muttered, scooping her up before she hit the ground again. Taking long strides toward the locker room, he held her firmly in his arms.

"Where are we going? Put me on the side with the team. I can watch the game from there," she said.

"Not on your life." He headed into the concrete passageway, turned left and kicked open the door to the men's room. Elbowing his way into a stall, he knocked down the lid with his foot and dumped her on the closed toilet seat.

Standing like Goliath in the lavatory opening he said, "You stay there until the game is over. You'd better be here when I get back."

Gripping the cold enamel of the bowl she sputtered, "But..."

He was already gone.

Standing briefly, pain shot up her leg and she immediately sat down again. Suffering had a sobering effect. Surrounded by the beige metal walls of the stall, the fluorescent beams from the light bulbs hurt her eyes. She leaned her cheek against the cool metal, curled her feet up, and hugged her knees.

Good Lord, I've done it again.

She sat quietly on the stool, feeling her heart pound as the cola/sugar high began to wind down. A line from *A Midsummer Night's Dream* drifted across her mind, *Oh, what fools these mortals be.* Inhaling large calming breaths, her blood sugar descended as insulin pumped from her pancreas. Soon her eyes felt heavy and her chin drooped to her chest.

She dozed unknown minutes until a soft feminine laugh awakened her followed by the definite sound of smooching. She was no longer alone in the bathroom.

"Oh, Wade, you always were a good kisser."

"Yeah, babe, and you was always good at everything, as I recall."

Maddie's eyes widened as she froze in place afraid to make a sound, recognizing the girly voice of Pam Wilcox and the twang of Wade Finn.

Could this evening get any worse?

Female shoes clicked on the concrete floor. "Listen, Wade, I can't stay away too long. Just give me the stuff so I can get back to my kid."

"All right, it's just hard to resist a hot body like yours. Here it is."

"How about a little sample?"

"Sure, why not?"

A match struck and soon the sickening sweet smell of pot filled the bathroom.

Pam purred, "*Mmm...*good stuff. Here."

Maddie heard various sounds of the exchange of goods for money.

"Thanks, Wade, see you around."

"Hey, babe, how about one more kiss for old times sake."

"Sure, why not?"

Low moans issued from Pam's throat, as Maddie imagined the pair grinding their bodies against one another. Then the door opened and Pam's shoes clicked away. Maddie hoped Wade would soon follow, but instead there were small clothing noises and then the unmistakable sound of urinating.

She scrunched her face, shifted her position slightly and the toilet lid made a terrible squeaking sound.

"What the hell..." Wade zipped his pants and made the turn toward the stalls, banging the door open where Maddie huddled.

Maddie gasped as Wade squinted his eyes. "I'll be danged, if it ain't Miss High Tits Harris."

Maddie unfurled her legs and sat as dignified as possible on the closed toilet. "Mr. Finn, it sounded to me as if you were dealing in contraband. I shall call the authorities."

Wade crouched before her. "I wouldn't do that if I was you, teacher lady."

He pulled a switchblade out of his back pocket. A menacing click sent shivers down her spine as it opened. He placed the tip under her chin.

Just then a roar came through the walls of the cheering crowd and Maddie knew no one would hear her even if she were stupid enough to scream.

She tilted her head back as he applied more pressure to her skin with the blade and said, "Don't forget, I know right where you live all alone in that little house by the lake. Why, we're practically neighbors. It wouldn't be nice to call the cops on a neighbor, would it, Miss Harris?"

The sharp blade stung the surface of her skin and she imagined the steel thrust quickly into the soft tissue. She blinked back frightened tears. "No," she said weakly.

His weasily eyes speared her as the smell of stale smoke assaulted her nostrils. "Good answer. 'Cause if I even *think* you've blabbed that high and mighty mouth of yours, I'll come a visitin'. Besides, lots of the cops around here are my cousins and they might not take kindly to you causing trouble for one of their kinfolk. So, you don't know a damn thing about Wade Finn. You got that, Miss Harris?"

Maddie swallowed. "I've got it."

Wade stood, put the knife back in his jeans' pocket. "Been nice passing the time with you. Reba's waiting for me. Or she better be. See you around. Oh, and I really do appreciate you helpin' my little girl the way you do. 'Night."

Wade closed the door, leaving her as he'd found her. Maddie began to tremble, her ankle throbbed, and she thought she might throw up. Raucous noises of cheering fans and brassy music blared through the walls. *Another fine mess.*

The lavatory door banged open again and this time she screamed. "*Ahh*!"

Phil's arms came around her, lifting her out of the enclosure. "Okay, sweetheart, let's take a look at that ankle."

Clasping her arms around his neck, she whispered in his ear as he carried her. "Please, Phil, take me out into the fresh air."

Walking through the dispersing crowd, he set her down on a folding chair on the sidelines, lifted her leg, and examined the ankle. She took deep breaths, gulped the cool moonlit breeze, and tried to regain her equilibrium.

"I think you'll live." He wrapped a bandage tightly around the bulging joint.

She looked down at his wide shoulders, the top of his head. A dizzy feeling of *deja vu* momentarily overcame her. Then she found her voice. "Phil, I think I owe you an apology. I probably owe everyone in the stadium an apology, especially the referees. I can get...carried away."

Phil took a seat on the chair next to her. "Yeah, I'm beginning to figure that out. It's something I like about you–within reason." His voice lowered. "You can be a very passionate girl, can't you, Maddie?"

He had her locked in that chocolate stare of his again. "I don't know, maybe."

"Maybe we'll find out one of these days."

Randy bounced down the stairs unto the field. "Maddie, there you are! I've been looking everywhere. Time to get in our chariot and ride. Great game, Coach."

Phil helped Maddie up as she grabbed his arm. "Oh, I

don't even know...who won?"

He smiled broadly. "We did. 28 to 21."

The two men got on each side of her as she hooked her arms around their shoulders. Her feet barely touched the ground as they traveled toward the parking lot.

Randy grinned at Phil. "Victory is sweet."

Phil grinned back. "You said it, brother."

Chapter Six

I generally avoid temptation, unless I can't resist it.

Mae West

On Sunday Maddie dragged around the house all day, her adrenals completely depleted by the caffeine/sugar overdose. A raging headache and throbbing ankle were added punishments for her crimes.

Her mind replayed her behavior at the game. She'd made a complete fool of herself. A mischievous twin popped out of her psyche to embarrass and humiliate her. Maybe she had some sort of personality disorder. And that wasn't the only thing to worry about. Grammy's presence was becoming more prominent all the time.

Even now her deceased relative's wavering figure stood at the end of her bed. "Yessiree, sister, when you make a fool of yourself, you go all the way. Bet they got some good shots for the school newspaper."

"Shut up, Grammy," Maddie said as she pulled the quilt over her head for an afternoon nap. She just wasn't up to dealing with ghosts, hallucinations, impending schizophrenia, or whatever the visits from Grammy were all about.

Phil pulled up to the curb at Pam's house, girding himself up for another jousting match with his ex. Being her verbal punching bag seemed to be the price he paid to visit his daughter. Still, the kid had enthusiastically cheered the game last night. She'd even given him a thumbs up after the final seconds ticked off the clock and the Beaver victory was in the bag. Pam had snagged Melissa's arm and dragged her off before she could run onto the field to say good-bye.

Now he sucked it up as he stood before the faded front door and punched the bell. *No matter what the witch says, smile.*

The door opened. Pam grinned broadly, hair perfectly in place. She'd traded in her slut-deluxe attire for a pastel pink floral top and white slacks. "Hi, Phil. Melissa's almost ready. Come on in."

Come on in? Jeez, had he stepped into an alternate universe? Cautiously, he edged inside, ready for a bucket of water or something to drop on his head.

"Drink?" Pam asked.

"Uh, no thanks." He stood uncomfortably rocking on his feet.

Pam reached up around the back of his neck. He twitched in surprise.

Her fingers flipped a protruding tag into place. "Honestly, honey, you really need someone to dress you. This old Razorback shirt doesn't go with the Sooners sweats." Her voiced turned to a purr. "But, a real man makes any outfit look good."

Okay, now he knew the Pod people had taken over her body. He backed up and yelled down the hall. "Hey, half-pint, shake a leg or we'll miss the opening scene."

Pam ran a long, polished nail down his arm. "What are you going to see?"

Phil's back was pressed against the door. No more room for escape. "The latest James Bond. The opening stunt is always the best part."

She edged closer. "Gee, I haven't seen it yet."

Okay, enough was enough. He placed both hands on her upper arms and held her away. "What's up, Pam? You need more money, or what?"

"I don't know what you mean." Her cat-green eyes blinked innocently.

He released her arms. "Come off it. What's with the nicey-nicey act?"

She dropped the innocent bit and went for contrite. "You're right. I'm just not sure how to approach you. I realize I haven't been at my most gracious with you for quite a while now. You probably think I'm the biggest bitch in the world. But, I've been doing some soul-searching and have come to realize, I may have been unfair to you. For Melissa's sake, maybe we should be nicer to each other."

Phil lifted a skeptical eyebrow. This turn around in attitude could leave a guy wide open for a sucker punch. Still, maybe he should give her the benefit of the doubt. "You're right. For Melissa's sake, we should bury the hatchet and try to get along before she's totally screwed up."

"I'd like that, Phil." Pam smiled brightly.

Melissa waltzed into the living room wearing new jeans, top, and tennis shoes. "Hey, Coach. I'm ready."

She'd taken to calling him "Coach," which was better than "Loser," but he hoped to get back to "Daddy."

He reached out and hooked an arm around her shoulder. "Hey, kid, you look great. New duds?"

She smiled with unguarded enthusiasm. "Yeah, Mom took me shopping this morning with the extra money you sent."

Major shock. Pam actually giving him credit for something.

"And we had her hair trimmed too. Doesn't she look pretty?" Pam glowed with maternal pride, or so it appeared.

"For sure. I'll be beating the guys off with a baseball bat any day now." Phil tugged Melissa's hand and opened the front door. "See ya, Pam. We should be back in about three hours. Don't call the cops on us."

Pam followed them out on the porch and waved as they headed across the lawn. "Have fun. Take all the time you want."

He glanced over his shoulder. Pam smiled sweetly, but he couldn't shake the foreboding she was a modern-day Dr. Jekyll-and-Mrs. Hyde.

On Monday morning Maddie found herself sitting in the

back of Coach Wilcox's third period history class, having been assigned by McCall to do Phil's teacher evaluation.

Phil had dressed, for once, in an almost-matching sports shirt and slacks. He hooked one leg over the corner of his desk, fielding questions and answers from his students. With the chalkboard and flag as a backdrop, he looked every bit at home in the classroom as he did on the football field.

"What were some of the major events of the 1960's and what are some of the consequences we are experiencing today?" he asked the students.

Maddie sat ramrod straight behind her student desk, appearing on the outside as professional as possible. But inside, Phil was getting to her. The sound of his voice, strength of his gestures, and his wonderful broad chest made her want to cuddle. She knew what his arms felt like wrapped around her, even if he was just hauling her like a sack of potatoes from the football field.

His honest rapport with the students impressed her. He didn't shove dry facts down their throats, but engaged them in a thoughtful discussion of turbulent times–Vietnam, civil rights, the assassinations of the Kennedy brothers and Martin Luther King.

"What else happened in the 1960's?" he asked.

Reba Finn spoke up. "Women's Liberation."

Phil nodded. "Very good. And what impact has that had on your life?"

Reba shook her head. "Not a whole helluva lot."

The class laughed, but Maddie thought of the Finn stronghold. No, women's lib had definitely not made it to that distant corner of the earth. Looking at Reba, Maddie determined right then and there that somehow she would shepherd the girl to a better life. The Wade Finns of the world shouldn't be allowed to keep women under their thumbs.

By the time Maddie pulled out of her reverie, Phil had moved onto famous books of the sixties, recommending them for reading– *To Kill A Mockingbird, I Know Why The Caged Bird Sings*, *Catch-22.*

"Miss Harris," Phil asked, "perhaps you can suggest a good book from the women's lib movement."

Without thinking she blurted out, "*Fear of Flying*."

Phil's eyebrows rose.

Back pedaling as fast as she could, Maddie said, "Of course *The Feminine Mystic* by Betty Freidan is probably a much better choice. Yes, definitely."

Oh, Lord, she thought, it's a good thing these kids never actually read. The school board would really be on her backside for recommending books about zipless fucks to fifteen-year-olds. Not that today's teenagers weren't already well acquainted with them.

The bell rang, signaling the end of the class. As the students emptied out of the room, Maddie removed her glasses, zipped up her brief case, and prepared to hobble from the room on her bum ankle. She sensed Phil standing beside her. For a large man, he could move quickly, quietly.

Turning to face him she said, "Well, Mr. Wilcox, you led a spirited discussion with your students. You kept their attention the whole class period. I commend you."

"Back to 'Mr. Wilcox' is it? What do you say you and me blow this joint and escape for lunch. I'll be Phil and you can be Maddie."

He was so close to her she could smell his spicy aftershave and the intoxicating scent of *him*. Lord, he made her downright dizzy.

Desperately trying to retain her professional authority, she said, "You know, Mr. Wilcox, it really isn't proper for faculty to become too familiar with the administration."

He merely dragged one finger on her forearm, making lazy circles, sending shivers down her spine. "Come on, sweetheart, live on the wild side. Let's go to Burger King."

Without conscious thought, she leaned into him and whispered, "Too many students at Burger King. I know a quiet restaurant."

He smiled triumphantly, grabbed her briefcase with one hand and her arm with the other. "We'll take your car. Mine isn't fit for a neatnik like you."

She knew she should have eaten a tuna sandwich at her desk and avoided further entanglement with the formidable football coach. But as she let him lead her down the hall, the title of Tanya Tucker's song ran through her mind. *It's a Little Too Late to Do the Right Thing Now*.

Mama Corleone's Italian Bistro smelled of garlic and rich marinara sauce. Classic checkered cloths covered the tables. Wax-dripped Chianti bottles held flickering candles. Snuggled next to each other in a far corner booth, Maddie and Phil dipped cheese bread in plates of olive oil and balsamic vinegar as they finished heaping plates of spaghetti.

"*Fear of Flying*, huh? Refresh my memory, what's that about?" Phil asked.

"It's a biography of Amelia Earhart," she said with a straight face and picked up her lemon water.

"Uh-huh." He leaned against the rounded vinyl seat back, spreading his arms and stared at her as if studying a puzzle.

Feeling warm under his gaze, the rigid Miss Madeleine attempted staring him down. "Mr. Wilcox–"

"Phil."

"Mister, oh, all right, *Phil*, I wish you wouldn't look at me like a bug under glass."

"I'm just trying to figure you out."

"I've told you before. There's nothing to figure out. I'm a very straightforward, controlled person. No still waters running deep here."

"That's where you're wrong." He leaned his muscular forearms on the table. "Sometimes you really bust loose. Like your little performance at the game the other night. And that kiss in the bleachers. I didn't notice much control going on, sweetheart."

Maddie wilted. Keeping her assistant principal starch could be such a strain. She covered her face with her hands. "There's something about you that brings out the worst in me. It's very embarrassing."

Phil leaned into her, slid her hands down, not letting go. "Maybe I bring out the best in you. I know being with you makes me feel good, real good. Not like the usual screw-up Phil Wilcox at all."

She squeezed his hands back. "You're not any kind of a screw up. I know you've had your ups and downs, but who hasn't? You've given up a lucrative career for a high school coaching job to be near your daughter. Do you realize how rare you are? And from the looks of it, you're shaping up into an excellent teacher and coach."

Releasing her hands, he said, "I'm a drunk who's paying for past sins." His lips thinned to a bitter line.

"Well, at least you're paying. Most people never take responsibility for their mistakes; they only go around blaming others for their problems. The more I'm around you, the more I see admirable qualities."

A grin tugged at Phil's lips. "Damn, Maddie, I think you've got a crush on me."

She flushed, flapped her mouth wordlessly, and then found her voice. "Why do you do that?"

"Do what?"

"Say things to deliberately embarrass me."

"Because I like to see the real you, the soft Maddie beneath the stiff-necked Bostonian pill."

"Well, I wish you'd cut it out."

"No you don't. You want out of that straight-jacket personality you've manufactured." He leaned in closer. "Who did that to you, babe? Turned you into a prickly, punctual, pain in the ass?"

Maddie stared straight ahead. She knew when she'd turned hard and sharp. After the humiliating Thomas Smithton affair, she'd carefully built a brick facade around her heart and this slob football jock was causing giant cracks in it. Fear kept her from letting the walls tumble, exposing her heart to fresh injuries.

Phil took her hand again. "Come on, give. You evidently know my background pretty good. Spill it. You didn't get to be thirty-something without picking up some scars along the way."

"I'm thirty-two and, yes, I did have one rather unfortunate experience."

She gulped a deep breath as Phil simply sat and waited, circling small caresses over her knuckles with his thumb.

"I was engaged a few years ago to a college professor, Thomas Smithton. He was older than I. Very cultured and witty–when he wanted to be. We met my first year teaching freshman composition. He was the head of the English department. I thought he hung the stars and the moon. I suppose that was my biggest attraction for him, my absolute adoration of him. The Woodbridge pedigree also went in my favor, along with the Harris money. My mother adored him. Dad tried to warn me he was a user. But I learned that lesson the hard way. Anyway, we had a lovely romance enjoying the best culture that Boston had to offer. He seemed to be a perfect fit in my polished world, all of which proved to be an illusion."

She told Phil everything. Told him of her naiveté, her subjugation to a misogynist lover and the final public humiliation that drove her to Beaver Cove. She recalled her dark days after the newspaper story broke revealing Thomas' immoral behavior and total lack of remorse. And something in the telling freed her.

The baggage of betrayal and disgust slipped off her back for the first time in over three years. Every time she looked back into the strong brown gaze of Phil's eyes she felt him releasing her from the burden. The monolith Thomas represented in her mind began shrinking to the true proportions his petty personality deserved.

After she finished her recitation, they sat side by side in the round booth for a moment and then Phil said, "Well, that guy is yesterday's news. He was a liar and cheat and you're well rid of him. He doesn't sound like your type at all, a lightweight who goes to the ballet and drinks wine."

"Oh really? And what is my type?"

He pulled her so close to him their thighs touched and his

voice seduced her with whiskey tones. "You go for more beefy guys nowadays. Someone who's been around the block a few times and knows a good thing when he sees it. Someone who won't lie, cheat, or let you forget you've got eyes as pretty blue as an Ozark sky. Someone who will never call you Madeleine, only Maddie, honey, sweetheart or babe."

Maddie said softly, "Don't forget 'cupcake.'"

A grin tugged Phil's lips. "You like that?"

"I shouldn't. It's condescending and politically incorrect."

"Come here, cupcake." He drew her into his arms and kissed her in front of the Mama Corleone's wait staff and God. His touch was soft, tender, and perfect. Giving, not taking. Healing, not hurting. Her mouth opened to capture all his flavor. A spectrum of light burst behind her closed eyes breaking into a rainbow of blue, red, and violet through the dark spaces in her heart. *Yes, this is what I've needed.* A small moan rose from her throat as her hands gripped the material of his shirt.

He lifted his mouth as one hand pressed the back of her head against his chest. His ragged breaths matched hers. The scent of him caused a trembling awakening deep in the core of her body and soul.

Phil muttered, "Jeez, I'm going to have to do ten laps and take a cold shower when I get back to school."

Maddie pushed away. "School! What time is it?"

He looked at his watch and winced. "Time to go and make up a good story about our car breaking down."

Dashing back to school, all was quiet in the halls when they arrived. Phil needed to retrieve something out of his mailbox before heading down to the gym. The two walked wordlessly on the shiny floor toward her office. The bond forged between them at lunch still held taut and strong, making Maddie want to jump into his arms and beg for one more kiss.

Instead she turned to him, plastered a Miss Harris prim expression on her face, and said, "Thank you for lunch, Mr. Wilcox. It was most pleasant."

His eyes turned heavy-lidded and his head gave a small

shake. "No more of this bullshit."

Pushing her two steps backward toward a closed door, she felt the door give way and found herself closed in a small janitor's closet with Beaver Cove High's burly football coach.

Phil's hands reached up to the sides of her head, sinking into her hair. "Don't ever call me 'Mr. Wilcox' again unless we're surrounded by students, do you understand? I won't let you put those prissy barriers up between us again. We've got something going here and I really want it. I really want you and you want me too, don't you? Say it."

Maddie felt the walls crumbling. "I..."

His hands moved to her upper arms. "Say it!"

Her voice came out in a breathy puff. "I want you too, Phil."

His lips crushed hers with the intensity of a man finding water after a desperate trek across a desert. He drank and drank, tapping the deep well of her swirling emotions, opening a river buried in the underground caverns of her heart, a gush of silvery passion shooting to the surface.

She never knew when her leg wrapped around his calf or when he backed her against the cool enamel sink, but reality struck in the form of a mop bopping her on the head.

"Ow!" She rubbed the spot as he caught tumbling janitorial equipment, noisy buckets, and brooms bouncing off the wall.

It was so ridiculous, so juvenile, so delicious, they started laughing.

Phil put his arms loosely around her. "Go away with me somewhere next weekend. Let's take this the whole nine yards."

Held by the intensity of his possessive gaze, Maddie knew she would go wherever he wanted, give him everything he demanded.

Oh, Lord, he was going to score a touchdown right in her end zone.

Chapter Seven

Sex: the thing that takes up the least amount of time and causes the most amount of trouble.

John Barrymore

At two o'clock Thursday morning Ginger tossed in her crumpled bed, enduring a restless sleep alone on the undulating water mattress. Exhausted after a full day in the company of her hooligan children, she'd fallen into musty sheets worried about Wade.

He'd hit the road early Sunday morning for a race in Little Rock, pulling his shiny red racer on a trailer behind the pickup truck. He usually called to brag or complain about the outcome of the day, but there'd been no phone calls. Fearsome visions flashed in her mind of his car rolling and bursting into flames.

Wade's call penetrated her dreams. "Ginger! Ginger, baby!"

She imagined he called from a fiery inferno.

"Ginger, get your ass down here!"

Ginger sat up and brushed the hair from her eyes.

"Christ on a stick!" Wade's voice wafted from the front yard.

Thank God, he'd come back home.

Out on the stubby grass, Wade stacked boxes from the truck bed. A steel gray moon cast a harsh light over the cluttered yard. The door banged behind Ginger as she padded outside dressed in a flimsy robe over her thin nightgown.

"What's goin' on?" she asked, coming down the steps.

The dogs circled, sniffing and growling at the boxes Wade set on the dusty ground.

He kicked one mongrel. "Get the hell out of my way, Lucifer." The big black yelped and slunk off.

"I brung our future right here in these boxes," Wade said. "We're gonna be rich, baby."

Ginger tiptoed in bare feet to the stack of boxes and opened a lid, revealing a case of cough syrup.

Pulling out a bottle she said, "What are ya doin'? Opening up a drug store?"

Wade set down the last box, hooting with laughter. "Oh, yeah! That's it, baby! A drug store, a by-God, drug store. But we're only selling one drug. And it's sweet, baby, it's really sweet."

Wade couldn't stand still. His feet fidgeted and his hand tapped continually against his thigh. "You're gonna cook it and I'm gonna sell it. We're not going to be a small time pot operation anymore, waiting for the damned DEA to screw us."

Wade pulled a baggie out of his pocket and dangled it in front of Ginger's face. Small crystals glinted through the plastic in the porch light.

"What's that?" she asked.

Wade's face drew close to hers, his grin wide, slightly demented. "Crystal meth, baby, speed, spoosh, zoom, whatever you want to call it. We're gonna be rich." He thumped his chest. "I feel great."

He yanked her into his arms; his hard pecker jabbed into her soft belly. "I'm so hot I'm ready to shoot off like a pistol."

Continuing to grind Ginger against him, he kneaded her bottom while whispering his plans into her ear. "I'm going to take over Beaver Cove and the whole county. We can make the stuff right in the kitchen with crap I can get at Wal-Mart. I met this guy at the meet and bought the recipe from him. And, baby, wait until you feel it. It's the best shit I ever had."

Ginger didn't understand everything Wade mumbled on about–red phosphorus, lithium, ammonia nitrate. She only knew he was home, happy and wanted her. Leading him into the house back to their room, she pulled him down onto the waterbed and pretended they were high school sweethearts again. For a little while she could forget about the dirty laundry, the unpaid bills, the things she wanted and would never have. When Wade ran his hungry hands and lips over her body she was pretty Ginger again, Homecoming Queen, Beaver Cove High, Class of 1985.

Thursday evening Phil pulled in front of Pam's house and honked his horn. The front door popped open and Melissa hopped the porch steps quickly, heading for his car with obvious enthusiasm. Her ponytail swung behind her head as she approached him dressed in baggy jeans and a Beaver Cove T-shirt. Walking across the sparse grass, she yanked open the passenger door and bent over to talk to him.

"Turn off the engine, Coach. Mom and I have cooked dinner. She made meatloaf–your favorite."

Phil killed the engine and slowly got out of the car wondering what Pam was up to. A raise in child support? Walking toward the house, he noted the unkempt yard with its pale grass and overgrown bushes. Pam didn't like dirt under her fingernails.

Passing through the front door, the aroma of Pam's meatloaf engulfed him with waves of memories and sensations from a different time and place. A different Phil and Pam.

He stood stock still on the welcome mat gazing at the small living room crammed with possessions of a more luxurious past, a funhouse distorted trip down memory lane. The meatloaf signaled Pam's plan to make love after putting Melissa to bed. At least it used to. The image didn't bring forth any rise in his anatomy at all, just left a dull thud in the pit of his stomach.

Pam's favorite album by Willie Nelson played softly in the background. After all the years of anger and hostility, this sudden show of hospitality scared the hell out of him.

Melissa bopped out of the kitchen and handed him a frosty mug of root beer. "Here. Mom says to use a coaster. Dinner will be ready in a minute."

Pam peeked her head around the corner, her bleached hair

big and puffy. "Hi, Phil. Figured you'd like a home cooked meal for once."

"Uh...thanks."

She waved him toward the living area. "Make yourself comfortable. There's a bowl of beer nuts on the coffee table."

Phil looked warily at her. "Okay…"

The females disappeared into the kitchen, leaving Phil to settle into his old leather recliner. The remote to his once-prized big screen TV sat on the armrest and he mindlessly picked it up and hit the power button. The screen came alive with images grotesquely oversized in the small room. Sound roared from the speakers and he fumbled for the mute button. He gulped his root beer, half expecting an alcohol buzz that thankfully didn't come. Taking a deep breath, he got his bearings thinking, *that was then and this is now*.

Pam obviously held onto the glittering past, now sadly tarnished. On the wall surrounded by a variety of pictures taken of Melissa at different ages, hung the large Glamour Shots portrait taken of Pam during their first year of marriage. Hearing her high-pitched sing-song voice waft in from the kitchen, he remembered the bright-eyed cheerleader with guilt. Somehow his failure as an athlete, father, and man made him responsible for her arrested development. He took another slug of his root beer and sighed deeply.

Melissa came out of the kitchen carrying a steamy casserole dish. "Come and get it, Coach."

Phil turned off the TV and stood. "Sure."

Phil sat down at the round oak dining table, the back of his chair barely missing the nearby wall. Melissa set the meatloaf in the center of table.

Standing straight, she put her hands on jean-clad hips. "Coach, do you know how to make a *Kleenex* dance?"

His mouth quirked. "No, how do you make a *Kleenex* dance?"

"Give it a little boogie."

Phil laughed and decided to make the best of this weird situation. Whatever Pam's game, he'd play along if it meant a better relationship with Melissa.

Pam's green eyes glittered over her beer glass as she finished her meal. "Melissa, your Dad was one hottie. He cruised Main Street with the top down on the Skylark. A real chick magnet. Phil, did you know I locked my keys in my car on purpose when I saw you in the parking lot that first night?"

Actually, he hadn't. *God, was I always such a dumb ass*?

Phil scooped some gravy onto a hunk of bread. "No, I was too busy being the knight saving the damsel in distress."

"So, you tricked him into meeting you?" Melissa asked.

Pam lifted a fork full of peas and smiled smugly. "Pretty much. Of course I fell for the old 'we've run out of gas' bit on our second date."

Phil inwardly groaned, yeah, he had been a big time dumb ass.

Turning to Melissa, Phil sought to change the subject. "So, are you going to try out for the basketball team?"

"What?" Pam squealed. "I thought you were going to go out for cheerleader."

"I've told you I don't want to be a dorky cheerleader." Melissa lowered her face, looking from under knitted brows. "I watched the basketball players this week and I can't handle a ball like that."

"Sure you can," Phil said waving his fork. "You just need practice. You're a natural athlete like your old man. You need to get a basket up in your driveway."

"Like I have time to deal with that," Pam said.

Pushing back his empty plate, Phil said, "I can do it. If you'll let me."

Phil stared a challenge to Pam. *Will you really let me into her life or is this just an act?*

Pam smiled a cat grin. "Gee, Phil, that's real sweet of you. I guess if Melissa has her heart set on basketball, we should encourage her."

"Fine, I'll bring a pole and basket over on Saturday," he said, then remembered his date with Maddie. "No, it'll have to be Sunday afternoon."

The sudden thought of Maddie brought warmth to his gut. Looking at Pam in the harsh yellow light reflected off the old foil wallpaper, he compared her to Maddie. Like comparing a garish rhinestone necklace to a fine diamond pendant. One was cheap, the other classy. But which one did he deserve?

After dinner, Phil helped Melissa with homework while Pam cleaned up the kitchen. Then it was time for him to go back to his apartment.

Pam said, "Melissa, you get ready for bed. I'll walk Dad out to his car."

Melissa gathered up her schoolbooks and papers as Phil crossed to the door. "Thanks, Coach. Hey, do you know how long you would have to fart to equal the power of a nuclear blast?"

Putting his hands in his pockets, he said, "How long?"

"Six years."

"*Mmm.* I know some guys that could be secret weapons." He gave her a wink. "Good night, baby."

Melissa trotted into the hall, calling over her shoulder. "Good night, Daddy."

His hand froze on the doorknob. She hadn't called him Daddy in six years. Something in his chest contracted.

Pam sashayed out of the kitchen. "I've wrapped some meatloaf up for you to make sandwiches."

Phil snapped out of his reverie and opened the door. "Uh, great."

She slid her arm through his, walking with him. "I think it's wonderful that we've called this truce. I mean all the arguing really doesn't get us anywhere, does it? We both want what's best for Melissa, don't we?"

He stiffly trudged forward with Pam plastered to his side. "I know I do. I'm not sure what you want."

She turned to him as they got to the car, gripping his forearm with a desperate hold. "I know what I want, Phil. I want the life we could have had if you hadn't gotten injured. The life we had before things got ugly and mean. When I saw you the other night on the football field, I realized we had something awful good back then."

"There's a lot of water under that bridge. A lot of whiskey, bourbon and beer, too."

Sliding a hand around his waist, she said, "I'm willing to make a fresh start. We've got a kid between us. That counts for something."

Phil looked down at her, smelling the beer on her breath, feeling mildly repulsed. "It counts for a whole lot. So, let's keep our focus on Melissa. She's the best part of both of us."

"Yeah, sure," she said standing on her tiptoes and giving his cheek a kiss. "We'll just be good friends and the best mom and dad Melissa could ever want."

The words sounded right, but the way she clung to him and gazed with her heavy mascara eyes sent warning bells jangling in his head. A sense of suffocation threatened to overtake him. He quickly turned and opened his car door and escaped inside.

"Thanks for dinner," he said, shutting the door.

"I'll make chicken fried steak and mashed potatoes next time," she said as he revved up the engine.

Come into my parlor, said the spider to the fly.

Giving her a little wave, he shot forward, and left her standing in the middle of the street. Whatever new web Pam was spinning, he knew he didn't want to get caught.

Warm, blue light filled with iridescent glitter swirled about them on the twisting magic carpet of Grammy's beach quilt. Maddie felt his arms around her, smelled his heady scent, the hair on his chest tickled her nose. Long and languid, her body undulated in primitive response to masterful caresses that knew every secret spot, every magic place of erotic connection. Where his limbs stopped and hers began, she had no idea. They moved as one creature– smooth and rough, soft and hard filling each other's empty spaces. Her lover's face rose above her, blurry, indistinct. She blinked, trying to see through the hazy light. Slowly, his features took form, the eyes focusing first into familiar bronze, next the strong brows and square chin. Recognizing Phil, she reached up and ran her fingers through his short, thick hair. As she smiled, he dissolved before her eyes, leaving her alone on the quilt staring into the night sky. Above the huge moon shone with blinding intensity and she heard laughter wafting across the moon beams, rolling deep like thunder. Then the noise turned shrill. A shrill annoying buzz like, like...

Maddie pounded the alarm clock, bringing blessed silence into her bedroom and sanity into her mind. Good grief, that dream. She'd gotten Phil mixed up with that insane episode of the summer. The clock glowed 5:10. Her pulse raced and she inhaled several deep breaths in an attempt to calm down. This was the day. She'd promised Phil she'd be at his apartment at 6:30. Was she out of her mind? Could she really go off for a clandestine weekend with the overpowering Coach? Would she trade her Bostonian propriety for hot hillbilly love?

When she sat up, her stomach lurched into her throat. No, she surely wouldn't throw up. She never...oh, God. Dashing into her bathroom, she barely made it to the toilet. Afterwards, she sat Indian style on the tile floor, gulping air.

Coward! Lily-livered, weak-stomach priss. Other women engaged in casual affairs. Why couldn't she just relax and enjoy sex like a recreational sport? Like bowling. *Mmm...* It was sort of like bowling, wasn't it? A hard object shooting into a dark hole, causing a great shattering and noisy explosion. Gee, she'd never go into a bowling alley again without noticing the phallic symbolism.

Grammy's face shimmered in the mirror, hounding from beyond the grave. "You're stalling. Don't sit there like a ninny. Worse case of nerves I ever saw. Get your ass up and get dressed."

One thing she had to say for her hallucination, Grammy always made sense. Maddie lumbered to her feet, turned on the shower, and shook the cobwebs out of her mind. Just one cup of real coffee, loaded with sugar and she'd be fine.

* * *

Driving down the mountain toward town, Maddie felt much better by dawn's early light. A homemade cake rested in its neat carrier on the passenger seat. Breakfast. If she was going to sin, she'd sin all the way.

Dressed in a snappy little peachy turtleneck sweater outfit and adorable new flats, she imagined a wonderful romantic weekend of holding hands while window shopping and enjoying a leisurely lunch in a quiet bistro. Maybe they'd go dancing in the evening. Phil had made reservations, told her he'd take care of everything. They'd spoken every night on the phone just before bedtime. She'd lain in bed and enjoyed his masculine voice stimulating her senses, making her feel like a fully feminine creature. It didn't much matter what he said, she loved the teasing way he said it.

The controlling Miss Harris had left all details of their weekend to Phil's discretion. He didn't want any of her uptight lists. He was right, of course. If she'd had her way, every moment would be scheduled. Still, she was a tad nervous about letting Mr. Casual take care of the arrangements. By the same token, if the day turned into a disaster, it would all be on his head.

Finding his apartment complex, she tread up the stairs carrying the cake and knocked on the door marked 2B. Heavy footsteps shook the platform under her and the door opened. The man of her recent dreams stood before her in rumpled sweats.

Grinning widely, he pulled her across the threshold and into his arms. The plastic cake carrier hampered their embrace. "What's this?"

"Devil's food cake. I had a baking urge. We could have some now or wait until later."

"Man, you are my kind of girl–chocolate cake and milk for breakfast."

Warmth whooshed over her. Someone to share her secret sin. Lord, was she falling in love?

He placed the cake on the kitchen counter. "Hey, you look great, but you've got to change."

"Whatever for?"

"Well, those aren't exactly fishing duds you have on."

"Fishing?"

"Yeah, I bought you a new outfit." Tugging one of her hands, he pulled her toward the sofa, where a set of royal blue sweats, tennis shoes and socks lay folded on a cushion. He lifted them in one swoop and thrust them against her chest.

"Here, babe, you hurry and change. We're burning daylight."

Blinking and dazed, Maddie allowed him to shove her into the bathroom, where she dutifully shed her jaunty jacket and pulled on the Dollar General sweatshirt over her turtleneck. Her slacks and flats were replaced by the sweatpants and tennis shoes. Gazing in the smudged mirror at her reflection, she contracted a case of the giggles. If Thomas could see her now. She snapped her fingers at the mirror.

"Take that, Thomas Smithton. I'm an Arkansas country girl now."

Phil tapped on the door. "Hey, cupcake, do you like mustard or mayonnaise on your bologna sandwich?"

So much for that elegant bistro lunch. "Mustard and dill pickles, please."

"You got it."

Grinning like teenagers, they shared cake and milk at his chipped *Formica* table.

And so began their romantic weekend.

Standing on the bank of Roaring River, an ambitiously named lazy stream that opened occasionally into shallow lagoons, Phil watched Maddie concentrate on baiting her hook. The tip of her tongue peeked between her lips as she gamely folded the squiggly earthworm on the sharp steel barb.

"Ah, ha!" she said, glancing up at him. "You didn't think I would do it, did you?"

Holding his fishing pole, he said, "I had my doubts."

Maddie flicked her wrist and cast the thin line expertly into the shimmering water. "I have news for you, buster. Beau

Harris didn't raise the simpering debutante you think I am. I've been deep-sea fishing off the Atlantic and I once shot a six-point buck. I'm a dangerous woman."

Phil suppressed a chuckle. Dressed in fluffy sweats and spanking white tennis shoes, she looked about as dangerous as a *Sesame Street* character. "I'll remember that."

The twisty drive into the park had been fun and light-hearted. They'd talked of school and the previous evening's game. Beaver Cove High had won the second game of the season by three points. The proper Miss Harris sat cheering sedately in the bleachers, drinking a caffeine-free soda while munching popcorn. Occasionally he'd spot her over his shoulder. It seemed she only had eyes for him, but that might have been his besotted ego. He probably only imagined her face lighting up every time he glanced in her direction. She'd waited on the front row of the bleachers for him to send his boys back to the locker room.

When he sauntered her way, she leaned over the railing and smiled softly down on him. "Good game, Coach. See you in the morning." Then she'd turned and left him staring at her beautiful ass swaying into the shadows. He assumed it was beautiful in its natural state. The day would not end without him finding out.

Phil blinked back into the present when Maddie yelped, "Oh, I've got a bite!"

"Pull up to snag his mouth. Now reel him in, sweetheart, keep it steady."

He watched Maddie settle the pole onto her thigh as she fought the wiggling creature at the end of her line. Little squeaks of excitement escaped from her throat as she inched her way closer to the water's edge to land her catch. Suddenly, a shimmering rainbow trout broke the water's surface, rising into the air, still squirming and fighting. Phil dropped his pole and reached out to capture her prize.

"Oh, isn't he a beauty?" she said as the fish flopped in Phil's hand while he released the hook.

"He's a keeper, if you want him."

"Oh, no, I just want to memorize his colors another moment. Then throw him back."

Maddie's eyes glimmered at the wonder of nature pulsing in his hand. She reached out a finger to trace the multicolored shiny scales.

"He really is marvelous, isn't he?" she said. "You'd better put him back now."

As Phil sent the fish back into its watery home, Maddie sat back on the grass, drew up her knees, and clasped her arms about her shins. "Thank you for bringing me up here. I get so busy I don't even notice the beauty out of my back window. But sitting here, I can take the time to notice the changing colors, smell the forest floor." She pointed across the bank at a towering oak covered in crimson and gold fall foliage. "Look at all the shades of red in that one tree."

His gaze never left her face. Her expression of shining enjoyment captured his attention. She was doing it again, lifting his spirits in a way no other person on earth had ever done. Just being with her made the air fresher, the day brighter, the sounds of the birds sweeter.

The air squeezed out of his lungs as reality hit him. At thirty-eight frigging years old, he'd fallen in love. That's what this had to be. He didn't just get a kick out her or think she was cute. He *loved* this complicated, multifaceted woman who brought a grin to his lips with her fancy vocabulary and hidden vulnerability.

Her smile dissolved as she noticed the intensity of his gaze. "Is something wrong? Have I failed a test? Aren't you going to fish some more?"

Reaching for her, he said, "Come here."

Hands tightly clasped, he pulled her up. He wrapped her firmly in his embrace and stared intently into her eyes. "You're mine now."

"Really? I'm a 'keeper,' so to speak?"

"That's right. I've hooked you, reeled you in, and I fully intend to land you."

He began kissing her forehead, leisurely taking his time

across the lids of her eyes, down her cheek, finding an earlobe to suckle and tease.

Feeling her sharp intake of breath, she said in a shaky voice, "I never knew fishing could be so erotic."

"Oh, yeah, and you haven't even seen my rod," he whispered.

"*Mmm*, no… But I think I'm beginning to feel it."

They sank down onto the spongy grass, bathed in the morning light, jogging suit to jogging suit, kissing and kissing like teenagers discovering the first flush of sexuality. Her fingers caught under the ribbed edge of his shirt, pushed the fleecy material up and over his head as her mouth explored the plane of his barrel chest. Oh, God, she moved in such a sweet, familiar way. It was as if they'd done this before. He wanted it to go on and on.

Not in any hurry, he dipped his hands under the elastic of her sweat pants, and enjoyed feeling the soft cheeks of her bottom. Yeah, the sweats had definitely been a good idea. The cottony barrier of material added a tantalizing level of enjoyment to discovering the wonders of Maddie's body. He wasn't so far gone that he intended to strip her bare in the Arkansas wilderness, exposed to any wandering fisherman who might come around the bend. But he just needed a little more of her mouth, her flowery smell, and her sweet surrender in his arms. Hugging her tighter, he felt himself spring into the cleft above her legs. She moaned and arched against him. Oh, jeez, he longed to taste her flavor everywhere.

Suddenly, a snuffling noise interrupted the mood and moist air wiffled up his back. Releasing Maddie, he rolled back. "What the hell…"

She screamed at the sight of a black, slobbering, Labrador dog nudging Phil's shoulder, pawing at his naked stomach. She jumped and scrambled away as Phil sat up and pushed the friendly critter from his face.

Flinching under the ministrations of enthusiastic doggie kisses, he said, "I gotta tell you, fella, it just ain't the same."

He patted the dog's head and felt a stinging object hit his

hand. "Ow!"

"Go away! Shoo! Go home!" Maddie stood several feet uphill, launching pinecones at the black canine, which only captured his interest in a new game. The dog loped in Maddie's direction, bringing forth a genuine look of terror on her face. Phil saw her eyes widen and he knew she was about to turn tail and dash away.

"Don't run, sweetheart! He'll only chase you down!"

But simple reason was no match for her fright and she twirled in nameless fear, running into the woods, screaming like a banshee. Her noise only added to the dog's excitement at engaging in a grand chase. He barked with abandon and dashed on four gangly limbs after her.

"Shit," Phil muttered, as he caught his footing chasing after them with his bare chest scraping every protruding limb in his path. The trees seemed to reach out and slap him. It amazed him how far her fright could carry her, and he lost sight of her twice. Fortunately, the sound of her screams guided his way. He knew when the dog caught her by the increased frenzy of her hollering. Coming over a hill, he viewed Maddie on her knees. Her hands covered her face as she twisted from side to side fighting off the black monster, trying to jab him with her elbows. Her four-legged attacker licked her head enthusiastically.

"Don't–stop!" Her words came between genuine tears and yelps of fear.

Phil ran, intending to pull the dog off, but instead tripped over a root and fell headlong into the tangled duo. Caught now in a morass of thrashing limbs, the two humans and one canine rolled across the Arkansas forest floor, crunching leaves, twigs, bugs, and every nasty thing in the musty earth. Finally, the trio came to a halt in the gritty soil. The dog sprang up and gave himself a good shake. At that moment a rabbit, disturbed by the tumbling intruders, hopped away at hare-like speed. The lab dashed off in happy pursuit. Maddie and Phil lay on the pungent ground, forgotten by the hound.

Flat on his back, Phil turned his head toward Maddie's

huddled figure. She crouched like a kid playing leapfrog, with her forehead in the dirt. Rolling over, he reached an arm around her waist and pulled her into a sitting position. Putting his hands on her shoulders, he examined her face, now streaked with dirt and tears.

"Hey, are you all right?" he asked in a quiet tone.

She nodded and gave a wavering reply. "I think so. I *hate* big, black dogs!" And she burst into tears again.

He gathered her head onto his shoulder and then pulled them both to their feet. "*Shh.* He's gone now. Rabbit hunting, I think."

Leaning back, she blinked away her tears. "I've been afraid of them ever since I was a little girl. I lose all rational thought and become terrorized like a screaming woman in a Vincent Price horror movie."

"Kind of like me around my ex-wife. Come on, let's get back to the river and see if we can recapture the mood we enjoyed before we were so rudely interrupted."

She sniffed. "Okay." Then her eyes widened as they traveled across his naked chest. "Oh, my God."

"Don't worry about it. Just a few scrapes," he said.

Her fingers gently trailed his exposed skin. "I think it's somewhat more than that." The alarm in her expression caused him to look down. Welts and blisters were already forming and a fiery itch ignited in a burst of irritation. Then he surveyed the path they'd just rolled across. Son of a bitch. Poison ivy. Nothing made him more miserable than goddamn poison ivy.

And so their romantic weekend continued.

Chapter Eight

This could be the start of something big

Steve Allen

Phil wanted to call it quits and head back to his apartment to spend the rest of the weekend in itchy solitude.

Maddie would have none of it. "Absolutely not. We've got a perfectly wonderful cabin and I'm not leaving you in that dingy apartment to scratch and make the whole thing worse. I'll find a store while you take a shower and I'll nurse you back to health in no time."

"I don't know, babe. The last time I had poison ivy I swelled up like a toad and became a mass of running sores. I think that might spoil the superman image I'm trying to maintain here. And I'm likely to get grouchy as hell."

Maddie set her shoulders in resolution. "I'll take my chances."

She commandeered him from the fishing site into the car and dropped him off at their quaint wooden cabin nestled among the pines. Next, she headed into the one-horse town in search of *Benedryl*, baking soda, lotion, and the makings for beef stew.

By the time she returned, his hair glistened with the residue moisture of his shower and he wore a Razorback T-shirt and clean sweat pants. The welts on his arms were still on the rise and interesting shades of red streaked his face. She wondered how long he'd be able to see through eyes that appeared to be swelling shut.

She hustled about the minute kitchen, unpacking groceries chattering inane small talk as he built a fire in the stone hearth.

The cabin was nothing fancy, but cozy nonetheless, consisting of a main room, kitchen, bedroom, and bath. A wooden dining table sat before a large picture window looking out onto an Ozark lake. Plush carpet, a sofa, two over stuffed chairs, and a coffee table adorned the living area. The wooden panel walls featured posters of Arkansas wildlife and the native stone fireplace cast a warm glow into the room.

Phil chose a spot on the couch, sat cross-legged, and issued a disgruntled sigh as he sank into the cushion. Maddie approached him with two pills and a glass of water.

"Here's some *Benedryl* and I've got a cortisone lotion to rub on you," she said.

Taking her offering, he slugged back the pills. "I gotta warn you, these will probably knock me out."

"Then I'll put a pillow under your head and cover you with a blanket. Now peel off that shirt and let me apply this lotion."

Making a low growl, he obliged her, then paused. "Hey, this stuff is contagious. You probably shouldn't touch me."

"Nonsense. I'm impervious to poison ivy." She put out her hands. "See, I rolled in it, too, and have no reaction whatsoever. I wandered these woods everywhere as a girl and never had a problem. Poor Randy wasn't so lucky."

With that, she shook the bottle and splashed the cool liquid on a clean washcloth and began rubbing his chest and shoulders. He jumped when the wet cloth drenched his fiery skin, then closed his eyes and leaned back into the sofa.

Maddie swept lazy circles across his shoulders and pecs. "You have a wonderful chest."

"That's what all the girls say. Especially when it's covered in blisters."

"No, I mean it. You make me think of a great, warm, teddy bear." The thought ran through her mind like a forgotten memory.

Phil squinted at her through puffy lids. "You make me think of one of those expensive porcelain dolls that only come in limited editions." His voice dropped. "Rare and beautiful."

Her hand froze over his sternum. "Why, Coach Wilcox,

that's the nicest thing anyone has ever said to me."

"Yeah, well," his voice dropped to an embarrassed gruff, "it must be the drugs making me punchy."

"You're not as tough and callous as you pretend to be. I've seen the way you look at your daughter."

Phil smiled. "Melissa...she's something. Always has a joke or piece of trivia on her mind. Yesterday, my phone rang a couple of hours before the game. She says, 'What do you call four bullfighters stuck in quick sand?' 'I don't know, what?' 'Quatro sink-o.'"

They laughed at the corny joke as Phil continued. "Then she said, 'Good luck with the game, Daddy.' She's called me 'Daddy' twice this week. First time in six years."

A lump rose in Maddie's throat. "Do you regret the divorce?"

Phil sighed deeply. "I regret my mistakes. I suppose I regret the marriage. Pam and I were too young, too damned stupid to be married. We looked good together, liked to party. A lot of my marriage is lost in a boozy haze. When I'd come home from practice, Pam would have a shaker of drinks ready and sometimes we'd have ridiculous arguments. We spent all the money that came in. I was making big bucks and we thought it would last forever. Bought fancy cars, but never let the Skylark go. Good thing as it turned out."

"And then you got injured."

"Yeah. 'Hitting bottom' they call it. I hit real hard. I went totally crazy one night on painkillers and alcohol. Smashed up a lot of Pam's beautiful things. She called the cops. I spent the weekend in jail. When I got out, she and Melissa were gone."

Maddie placed a hand gently on his shoulder. "Is that when you joined AA?"

"No, I wasn't that smart. I wallowed for a while. Pam filed for divorce and lived with a linebacker from Florida. I've got to admit her leaving made it easier to sober up. I think I drank as much to drown out her voice as deal with the pain. Anyway, I realized what a lousy father I'd been. I've been trying to make up for lost time, but until recently, I was sure I'd totally blown it."

Maddie gently rubbed down Phil's arm. "I've met Melissa, you know. I think she's delightful and she's very interested in you and the team."

He nodded. "Yeah, this move has been a good thing." He put a hand over hers. "In more ways than one."

They stared into each other's eyes, each stripped bare of pretense.

Phil cupped a hand into her hair. "What are you doing here with a broken down football player? You should be married to a doctor or maybe a senator heading up charities and getting your picture in the society page of the paper."

"I have a genetic flaw."

"What's that?"

"The women in my family seem to a have weakness for country boys from Arkansas."

"Sounds serious."

"There isn't any cure."

"Glad to hear it." Phil yawned. "Damn, babe, I'm getting so sleepy."

Maddie arranged a pillow at the end of the sofa and pushed him into a reclining position, then covered him with a blanket. The sound of his steady snoring soon filled the room.

She stood before the sofa studying her sleeping giant. A warm glow and a cold terror engulfed her at the same time. She could fall in love with this man, become totally, utterly vulnerable to ecstasy and pain. But love no longer meant the stuff of fairy tales to her, living happily ever after and all that rot. Love meant handing your heart over to another person to be squashed under his boot.

Phil already held some kind of power over her. She was here, wasn't she? Probably risking her job, certainly her reputation. And yet she wanted to be here. Wanted to run her fingers through his auburn hair. Wanted him to tease her and call her "cupcake." If she went with her feelings, would she regret it? Or was this another episode of going over the edge, giving into hormonal mania? Perhaps a good tumble in the sheets would get him out of her system.

No, she didn't work that way. She didn't separate sex and love. When she gave her body, her heart and soul went with it. Perhaps his tumble in the poison ivy was a warning. Turn back before it's too late. Heart danger zone.

Then he snuffled, wiggled his nose, and looked so damned appealing despite the rash, she wanted to throw herself on top of him.

"Madeleine Harris, get a hold of yourself," she muttered and decided to get to work on that beef stew. The radio played country western softly as she chopped vegetables and put the meat in the pot to cook. She anticipated the sensual pleasure of breathing in the homey scents of browning beef and onions. Tipping her nose over the steaming concoction, she inhaled deeply and immediately felt a wave of nausea punch her stomach.

Gasping, she pressed a hand over her mouth and stumbled back from the stove. Taking deep breaths, she retreated to the dining table and grabbed the back of a chair for support. What in the world?

How could she suddenly feel so sick? Then she remembered back to the early morning heaves in her bathroom. And how about the incredible sleepiness she'd been experiencing? A time bomb had been quietly counting down to detonation.

Tick, tick, tick. Kaboom! Her mind exploded with certain knowledge.

She was pregnant.

The comfortable veil of denial she'd been living under for the past few weeks was blown to smithereens. The signs had been there, much as she'd chosen to ignore them–no period, increased fatigue, strange cravings.

She sat down in the hard chair and stared out the window, gulping air. The view of the fall colors and the shimmering lake dimly registered in her brain. *You're pregnant.* A breezy gust in the yard brought up a tiny twister, skittering leaves, and twigs into a whirlwind across the uncut grass. Flying particles of debris matched the swirling emotions in her mind.

Pregnant–how wonderful! Every girl dreams about having a baby, the secret longing of every feminine heart. Pure joy rose like a bubble in her brain, only to burst against a wall of fear and embarrassment. Pregnant–how terrible! How stupid, how exciting, how overwhelming...how nauseating. She ran to the bathroom.

A few minutes later Maddie hovered at the sink in the small bathroom, rinsed out her mouth, splashed cool water on her face, and gently dabbed it dry with a fluffy white washcloth. Madeleine Harris stared at her reflection in the medicine cabinet mirror, a single harsh light bulb exposing every pore and approaching wrinkle.

Did it show yet? Was there another telltale crease of truth etched in her skin? On top of earlier insecurities and indiscretions did SINGLE PREGNANT WOMAN blink on her forehead like a neon sign? She searched for signs of puffiness, but that probably came later, after she quit barfing several times a day.

All of a sudden her all-too-familiar schizophrenia overcame her.

"Stop! Wait! This can't be happening."

"I'm having a baby! Isn't it great!"

"It's a disaster."

"It's a miracle."

Colliding emotions of panic and exhilaration sent her into a state of hyperventilation. Stumbling into the kitchen, she grabbed a paper bag from her shopping expedition and thrust it over her mouth. In with the good air, out with the bad air. It took several minutes to vanquish the tingling in her extremities.

She threw down the paper bag. *I can't stand being cooped up here one more minute.*

She pulled on Phil's windbreaker and stormed out into the autumn afternoon. Dry leaves crunched with each step as she made tracks toward the water, her mind working as quickly as her feet.

At that point her thinking processes short-circuited and

became more like a kaleidoscope of images. Her mother's face would tighten and pinch when she learned of her daughter's unplanned pregnancy. Her down-home father might accuse her of "swallowing a watermelon like common trailer trash." She imagined herself slinking out of town to avoid knowing eyes, the Camry loaded with her computer, clothes and other personal belongings. She might give birth in the backseat, or out in the woods like the Indians in the movies.

Stopping at the water's edge, she forced herself to calm down. The wind-whipped lake resembled the sloshing of her disjointed thoughts. Looking to the horizon, she focused on a dim orb in the sky. Good God, it was only three o'clock in the afternoon, but there it hung above her–a three-quarter moon, deceptively innocent, an oversized rock floating across the heavens. But, she knew its power all too well.

Memory flashed back–white light against an inky backdrop. Hot, humid air; her skin dripping wet. Seduced by the stunning beauty of the cosmos and the shining summer moon, she'd answered a whispered call on a lonely night, taking for granted an illusion of privacy and seclusion. But by morning, sparkling dreams had turned to harsh reality. What felt like magical ethereal lovemaking had been nothing more than an anonymous sexual encounter. She'd been tricked by some weird, cosmic prank.

Her trickster was disguised now, resting in a sunlit sky, completely innocuous. But she recognized her tormentor just the same.

Maddie yelled as she lifted her arms high. "Damn you! Damn you, you *damned* Devil Moon!"

Chapter Nine

By the time you swear you're his,
Shivering and sighing
And he vows his passion is infinite, undying
Lady, make note of this:
One of you is lying

Dorothy Parker

Returning to the cabin, temporarily spent of emotion, Maddie went back to the mindless task of cooking, carefully munching a saltine cracker to soothe her stomach. The chop and plunk of carrots and potatoes brought a sense of order to the chaotic workings of her mind. She really needed to start thinking in straight lines, form logical patterns.

Phil snorted loudly and turned over on the sofa, drawing Maddie's attention. Oh, good heavens, she couldn't face him at this moment. How could she explain it to him? She didn't understand it herself.

She crossed the small room and stood over him, so glad he still slept. She'd never be able to hide her jumbled emotions from him. He charged through her defenses like the ace quarterback he was. If he woke up now and read her expression, she'd confess to an unplanned pregnancy brought on by a one-night stand. Mortification chilled her soul.

And what did this new development mean to their budding relationship? Probably the end. In truth, the thought of dealing with the complications of an affair and impending motherhood made her dizzy. Of course, she might opt out of parenthood. She could get a quiet abortion and deal with Phil later, if he still showed interest. Or just let it go. Life might just be a lot easier if she stayed solitary and maintained her quiet life. Oh, so many conflicting emotions.

Ready to jump out of her skin, she considered hopping in her car and driving away into the sunset. But leaving Phil itchy and stranded was a horrible thing to do. She looked about the room, grabbed the cell phone out of her purse, and closed herself in the bedroom.

She heaved a sigh of relief when Randy picked up on the second ring. "Randy, it's me. Could you do me a big favor?"

"Sure, darlin', whatever your little heart desires." Randy's sweet voice helped calm her down.

After making arrangements for Randy to pick her up, she found a pen and wrote Phil a note on the back of a brown paper grocery sack. She slipped back into her Miss Harris assistant principal persona.

Dear Mr. Wilcox,

Thank you for the very enjoyable fishing expedition. I've had a personal emergency and must get back home. I have arranged for transportation. Please enjoy a bowl of stew and the rest of the cake. You may leave my car parked with the keys under the mat in the lot at your apartment complex. I have a spare key and will come by tomorrow afternoon to pick it up.

I hope your rash improves quickly.

Very truly yours,
Madeleine Harris

She was long gone by the time Phil awakened in the early morning hours. He sat up and stretched, figured she was asleep in the bedroom. A light over the stove and the last embers of the fire cast a small glow in the room. The food smelled good and he dished himself up a bowl, drowsily taking it over to the table. He fought to keep from scratching his itchy chest. After a couple of spoonfuls, he glanced down at the paper sack lying at his elbow. He noticed some writing and flipped on the overhead light.

Dear Mr. Wilcox…blah, blah, blah…Madeleine Harris

He shook his head in disbelief. Son of a bitch, he was back to "Mr. Wilcox." What the *fuck* had happened while he was asleep?

And so ended their romantic weekend.

On Sunday afternoon, while an itchy Phil erected a basketball goal in Pam's driveway, Randy drove Maddie to get her car in Phil's apartment parking lot. Like a coward, she'd avoided Phil's calls by taking the phone off the hook. After leaving her some memorable messages, he'd called Randy.

Randy pulled in next to the Camry. "I told him to give you some space, that you had some issues to work out. He didn't like it, but I think I bought you some time."

Maddie sat in uncharacteristic silence, merely nodding her head. He hated the ghostly pallor of her skin. He generally avoided playing serious scenes, but at the moment Maddie needed a counselor, not a clown.

Randy touched his hand on her arm. "You know whatever you decide to do, I'll be there 100% for you. Remember how you got me through that awful summer I got dumped by Fabulous-but-Faithless?"

Maddie managed a wan smile. "He wasn't nearly good enough for you."

"Spoken like a true friend." Randy let his flighty front slip. "Listen, dear heart, I haven't forgotten how you forced me out of my pity party during my darkest days. Let's go to the café and talk this out. Father Randy is always available to the lost and forlorn."

She shook her head, a distant look in her eye. "I'm going to take a drive and think things through. Don't worry about me. I'll find you later. Thanks for everything." Maddie leaned over, kissed him on the cheek, and exited the car.

He sighed. His Maddie, pregnant. An unexpected plot switch in the story of their lives. He'd ponder the possible scenarios over a nice cup of cappuccino at his favorite coffee house.

A beautiful fall day surrounded Maddie as she sped down the road. Fluffy clouds skittered in the indigo blue sky, not that she really noticed. Internal wrestling had kept her up through the wee hours, until exhaustion brought a troubled sleep. The battle for objective thinking over incoherent hysteria still raged behind her eyes. As the oaks, pines, and cottonwoods flashed by in her peripheral vision, she forced intellectual consideration of her options.

Abortion. Certainly a practical, expedient avenue to return to the normal course of her life. She'd had friends in Boston who'd done it. They went to a clinic, come home tired and sore, no worse off than a bad day at the dentist. Their physical recovery had been swift and complete. If they'd suffered some kind of remorse, they'd hidden it well. She was a strong, modern woman. Surely, she could look upon an abortion as a necessary medical procedure and easily put it behind her.

Her other options meant changing her entire life, giving up her job and probably her new home, for a very uncertain future. If she allowed the pregnancy to go full term, she could give it up for adoption; see that it went to a good stable home. Or she could join the legions of single moms and devote herself to the nurturing of the child.

She supposed she could find new employment over the course of time, perhaps swallow her pride and stay in her parents' home while she sorted things out. Lord, moving back home at her age was unappealing. Her mother would drive her crazy, and her father would be looking to force some man into a shotgun wedding. Then she would have to spill the truth of the unknown paternity. *For shame, Maddie, for shame.*

All in all, abortion seemed the most practical decision, under the circumstances. While her mind rattled out all the good reasons to simply rid herself of an unwanted pregnancy, her spirit remained unsettled. She needed a sense of peace before embarking on such a course of action.

She'd driven unknown miles up and down the rural hills, not really knowing or caring where she headed. Coming up on her left, she spotted a sign for the Thorn Chapel. Without conscious thought, she turned in the direction of the arrow and followed the short road into the parking lot. It had been years since she'd come with Grammy for an outing to the famous glass chapel nestled in the rocky Arkansas hillside. She parked her car and stared at the path that led up the hill to the chapel.

The angular top of the glass building glinted in the sun. An architectural marvel of glass and beams, the chapel created an enclosed space where the outside ferns, trees, and bushes of the habitat visually surrounded the worshipper. A center aisle separated a dozen rows of padded pews allowing visitors to sit in prayer or meditation and drink in the unique spiritual power of the wooded site.

Maddie left her car and followed a compulsion toward the chapel. Her feet moved forward, drawn by an irresistible force. She tugged the tall wooden door open and entered hallowed ground. A few visitors sat scattered in the pews, quietly whispering prayers. Maddie wandered to an empty area, and sank onto the velvet-padded pew. Strains of hymns wafted in the air from large speakers.

Sitting quietly, she allowed the atmosphere of the chapel to permeate her being. The air seemed charged with a kind of supernatural power, palpable to even the most spiritually insensitive individuals. Angels resided in this place and whispered eternal truths in the ears of the pilgrims who entered the sanctuary. The puny minds of men shrank in proportion to the mighty mind of God; the arrogance of human ego humbled and transformed.

Maddie began to tremble; her intellectual control slipped as turbulent uncertainty swirled in her solar plexus. She had taken a cold, cerebral survey of her situation, but now her emotions surged to the surface, making her mind spin and split. *Oh, God, what should I do?* She wasn't having a love child, formed from an established, caring relationship. Why, she'd almost been raped, a total stranger coming upon her and taking advantage of her compromised state of mind, not to mention state of dress.

"Hold, on sister." Lord, Grammy appeared again, dimly occupying the seat next to her. "You were pretty much the one who jumped his bones, as I recall. And as for rape, much as you would like to deny it, that was the greatest sexual experience of your entire pathetic love life." Grammy took on solid proportions. "And here's another thing. The child in your womb is not an 'it.' That child is a boy or girl you're fixin' to flush out of existence. You better think long and hard before you wipe away my great-grandchild."

Tears streamed down Maddie's face. She'd been holding the image of an actual baby at bay, but now it came into her mind full blown. A baby in her arms. Next, she envisioned a toddler, pudgy and soft, struggling to take a first step. Then an elementary age child transformed into a handsome young man, a real person who was blood of her blood, connected to her soul. She knew she carried a boy. All of a sudden the wells of maternal hormones gushed through her blood stream, causing her breasts to tingle and she longed to hold the swaddled baby in her arms.

She cried herself out in the chapel. Unlike other crying jags of hysterical proportions, this was a controlled stream of tears that cleansed her soul. She received some sort of absolution that afternoon. The reckless behavior of a hot summer night seemed somehow predestined. Shame, embarrassment, and guilt lifted off her shoulders and scripture came to her. *Go, and sin no more.*

The Dream Man appeared in her mind. That's how she thought of him. Dream Man was going to be a father and he didn't know it. She felt a bone deep need to share her news. Maybe she should run a classified: "If you had sex with a stranger by the lake on the night of August 26, please call..." Such crazy thoughts.

Then she thought of Phil and she felt a longing almost as strong as the yearning emotion for the baby. But she knew her budding romance with Phil was over before it really began.

She'd be going away. The baby needed to become her top priority. Expending the energy necessary to build a relationship with a man right now was out of the question. Besides, Phil would probably drop her like a hot rock anyway. Pregnancy sent men running.

Phil had his plate full trying to reclaim his identity in Melissa's life and build a career in Beaver Cove. He didn't need some pregnant woman bothering him with her problems. She'd do them both a big favor and make a clean break.

Giving Phil up would be the penance to be paid for her sinful behavior. As she marched back up the aisle of the chapel toward the towering doors, her feet kept beat to the strains of *The Old Rugged Cross*, and she hummed it on the long ride back home.

Despite a foul mood and a relentless itch, Phil completed the task of installing the basketball hoop in Pam's driveway. Melissa's excitement and smiling chocolate eyes took the edge off his ill humor. Though he never had the speed or height for a basketball player, his natural ball-handling abilities made him a worthy opponent for a one-on-one game with an eleven-year-old.

He bounced her the ball. "Come on, see if you can get past your old man."

Dribble, dribble, feint to the left, feint to the right. He stole the ball away from her and shot a basket.

"No fair," she squealed.

"That's how the game is played, sweetheart."

He passed her the ball. "Try it again."

Round and round they went–running, sweating and laughing. After spending the last twenty-four hours pissed-off at Maddie and sleep-deprived from the torture of poison ivy, Phil found genuine relief in the company of his wiry, tomboy daughter.

They called a time out and panted to catch their breath. Melissa casually bounced the ball. Gone were the sullen looks of suspicion. More and more she reminded him of a love-starved puppy dog.

Her small hand controlled the ball with surprising agility. "Did you know an elephant weighs less than the tongue of a blue whale?"

"You're kidding."

"No. Can you imagine this big, honkin' tongue in your mouth?"

Sometimes his stupid tongue felt that big and honkin'.

Pam wandered out onto the porch carrying a tray of iced tea. The slant of the afternoon sun glinted on the strategically placed sequins that decoratively drew attention to her bust line. Tight spandex Capri pants wiggled as she crossed the concrete in spike heels. Pam had the goods on display.

"Take a break, you two. Come have a seat on the steps," Pam said.

The players wandered across the grass and gratefully grabbed a glass of refreshment.

Phil had to admit, it hit the spot. "Thanks."

"It's just the way you like it. Sugar and lemon," Pam purred.

"Can Daddy stay for dinner?" Melissa asked.

Phil frowned. "Oh, no, I–"

"Of course. I've already got chicken frying and baked beans in the oven. Say you'll stay." Her big, green eyes pleaded.

Though Pam's getup reminded Phil of a three-dollar hooker, her efforts at reconciliation and peace were growing more convincing. Perhaps he should drop his guard and give her the benefit of the doubt. Maybe there was some class developing under the big hair. "Okay, beats a stale baloney sandwich."

Just then a group of teenage boys careened around the corner in a convertible. Pam's curvy body caught their attention. "Hey baby! I want some!" Whistles and catcalls continued as they slowed down and cruised by.

Pam reacted with the aplomb of a barroom tart. "Up yours, assholes!"

Phil gazed down into his iced tea. *Class, oh yeah, real class.*

As the harvest moon rose in the dark sky, Maddie and Randy sat in their booth at the Hillbilly Heaven Café. He'd ordered the Cajun chicken. She nibbled on macaroni and cheese, the mildest thing she could find on the menu.

Randy lost his appetite as he listened to her plans to quit her job, pack up her belongings and head north. Well, just take an axe and beat him on the top of the head. He needed her; she needed him. Other relationships came and went, but Maddie was forever. He rarely let the world see his serious side. Being a naughty tease and flamboyant entertainer served him well, but the thought of losing Maddie wiped the merriment off his countenance.

Toying with her food, Maddie said, "So, I'll tender my resignation tomorrow morning and tell McCall that I've got a family emergency that requires I move back to Boston."

Randy leaned back in the booth. He'd come up with an idea musing over afternoon coffee. His wonderfulness sometimes stunned him. "I guess that's Plan A. But I have a Plan B that is much better."

Maddie's face formed a determined mask. "I've told you, I'm keeping the baby."

Placing his hand over her fidgeting fingers, he said, "I know, and I think it's great. You'll be a fabulous mother. I'm sure you're following your Karmic path. Plan B is simple and brilliant. Marry *moi*."

Maddie froze. "What?"

"Marry me, dear heart. You won't have to quit your job or leave. We'll be the scintillating Bailey family. We're really family to each other anyway. Why not make it official? Let's face it, this will be my only chance at fatherhood and you know I'd be a great Dad. We wouldn't have a marriage in the traditional sense, but really, darling, how much good has sex done either one of us, anyway?"

Maddie blinked in confusion. She'd stiffened her spine in

resolve to go through with her plans. Suck it up and head back to Boston. Randy's idea threw her for a loop.

"I don't know...How would we work it out? Would you move in with me?"

"Oh, not really. I can't leave Mother, you know that. But who would know the difference? We live a stone's throw from each other as it is. I spend half my down time on your couch already. We'll get married and pretty much conduct business as usual. Being a married man will probably raise my esteem in McCall's eyes. He'll have holes pierced in his homophobic armor." He lowered his voice an octave. "I can be the macho man who fathered your child." He threw back his head and cackled. "I love it! Playing your husband will be my greatest role."

Maddie chewed her lip. Maybe it would work. A quick marriage would keep her life intact and squelch embarrassing questions. Except from Phil. Phil would surely give her a hard time. Maddie expressed her concern over the coach's questions to Randy.

Randy waved his hand in dismissal. "Don't worry about him, darling. You know I'm the king of improvisation. I'll handle him. Unless, of course, you're madly in love with the man and you think he'd like to march down the aisle with you. But, by my reckoning, it had better be a quick trip because you must be about six weeks along and that bambino is going to be obvious very soon."

Maddie shook her head. "Whatever might have developed with Phil isn't going to happen. You're right about time running out. I'm much better off pulling myself together and preparing for motherhood. Phil has the ability to reduce me to a blithering idiot and I need to keep my wits about me. He's not good for my equilibrium."

Randy looked at her from under knitted eyebrows. "*Mmm.* I don't know if I like the sound of that. But never mind, I'm not the jealous type. Okay, let's do this right."

Randy slid out of the booth, stood next to the table, and made a graceful descent to one knee. Taking her right hand in his, he then projected his voice in his most rounded, Shakespearian tones, causing all heads to swivel in their direction. "Madeleine Woodbridge Harris, would you do me the inestimable honor of becoming my bride? I promise to love, cherish and all those marvelous things." Then his voice turned intensely serious and he looked at her with innocent puppy eyes. "Really, Maddie, all kidding aside, will you marry me?"

Feeling a fluttering in her stomach, unsure if it meant joy, trepidation, or nausea, Maddie followed the intellectual instructions of her brain. "Yes, Randy, I'd be honored to marry you."

Randy stood, faced the crowd, and became Petrucchio from *The Taming of the Shrew*. "*You shall become my wife; and will you, nill you, I will marry you! Why, there's a wench! Come on and kiss me, Kate!*"

The teachers sat around the long table in the lounge for the usual Monday morning staff meeting. Phil dunked a cake donut in his tepid cup of coffee and tersely offered one-word answers to any questions that came his way.

Most of the room's occupants quickly got the message to bug off, except, of course, Phyllis Green. "Oh, Coach, what a nasty rash! I know poison ivy when I see it. I make a powerful home remedy made from comfrey and jewelweed, guaranteed to take away itching faster than you can say William Jefferson Clinton. I'll run home at lunch and fetch it back for you. You look poorly, if you don't mind my saying so."

Phil felt like telling her where to stick her home remedy, but managed to come up with a polite reply as he escaped to refill his coffee. Where the hell was Miss Punctuality Harris? Maddie and the gay drama teacher had yet to show their faces.

He'd bided his time, taken Randy's advice to back off and let her work through her "issues." Whatever the hell that meant. Patience was an acquired skill for Phil, not a natural inclination, and he wanted to throw her back into the janitor closet and not let her out until he got some straight answers.

She'd obviously run scared, probably with good reason. Maybe just looking at his ugly, spotted mug was enough to send her screaming into the night. Still, the moments before he'd fallen asleep had been sweet. No, something had definitely happened.

McCall called the meeting to order as Maddie and Randy made their entrance. Maddie wore her full, uptight assistant principal regalia, dark-rimmed glasses included. Meanwhile, Randy had given up his usual ribbed sweater and slacks for a getup that looked straight out of the World War II John Wayne movie, *The Flying Tigers,* complete with a bomber jacket and flyer's cap.

Maddie refused to make eye contact with Phil as she took her seat, unzipped her brief case, and opened her traveling office on the table. She appeared fascinated with the order of the pencils and pens in all their neat little slots. Phil watched her with heavy-lidded eyes. She must have sensed his attention even as she studiously remained involved with the contents of her briefcase, because her cheeks took on flaming shades of red.

McCall noted the late arrivals. "Nice of you to join us Miss Harris, Mr. Bailey."

Having shed his shyness and taken on a bold character, Randy looked McCall straight in the eye and said, "Hold on, will you, Chief, while I get the little lady and me a cup of java."

McCall lifted an eyebrow. "By all means. Anybody else need a little extra personal time? Need to file some nails or write a letter?"

Everyone tittered as the meeting got underway. Randy brought back the coffee and then draped a proprietary arm on the back of Maddie's chair.

Phil sat in icy calm as he listened to all the Monday morning crap regarding school fundraisers, junior testing, on-campus smoking problems, and vandalism. He tried to appear gracious as McCall congratulated him on their football win of the weekend. That seemed a million years ago. He ground his teeth as the meeting went on and on. When Phyllis Green talked about reciting the nursery rhyme *Mary Had A Little Lamb* while washing hands to insure destroying all germs, he thought his brain might explode.

By the time McCall finally asked for any more business, Phil wanted to leap across the table and drag Maddie from the room.

That's when Randy stood and said, "Yeah, Chief, I do have an announcement. You know how the old saying goes, 'he chased her until she finally caught him.' Well, I've been chasing this pretty lady for almost twenty years and finally ran her down. Stand up, Sugar." Randy tugged on Maddie's sleeve, bringing her to her feet. Then he put his arm around her as he announced, "Miss Harris has consented to become my wife. Folks, standing before you is the future Mrs. Randall Bailey."

The room burst with excitement, everyone expressing delight and surprise.

"Oh, let me do the cake," Ms. Green squealed.

Mr. Manchester exclaimed, "Well, you could knock me over with the proverbial feather."

Randy held court, improvising as he went along. "We've been fighting it for sometime, but it was just bigger than the both of us…"

Phil remained the only one seated as the rest of the crowd flocked around the betrothed couple and offered best wishes. The moment seemed surreal. He expected Randy and Maddie to stop the show and tell everyone they were enacting a scene from a play, just kidding around. But as the minutes ticked by, reality struck; this was not some early morning skit. He suddenly felt sucker punched. She planned to *marry* the guy. His stomach turned over, threatening to puke up donut and coffee all over an English teacher's lesson plans.

Maddie chatted, nodded, and smiled, but the joy didn't seem to reach her eyes. Damn her beautiful, blue eyes.

He crammed papers into his briefcase, eager to make a hasty retreat muttering, "I don't friggin' believe it."

Stopping just before the door, he made a quick pivot, shooting Maddie a piercing stare from across the room, over the shoulders of her well-wishers. He'd caught her following his departure and now had her trapped in his line of vision. Anger grew in his gut, the taste of betrayal rising in his mouth with the bitterness of bile. Shaking his head slowly, his eyes turned cold as they projected his disgusted thoughts; Sinatra had it about right–*The Lady is a Tramp.*

Chapter Ten

It's not the men in my life; it's the life in my men

Mae West

Maddie carried Phil's accusing gaze in her mind's eye throughout the day. She saw the hurt and anger, felt it stab her chest. At first, guilt flooded her emotions, but as the day wore on she managed to rationalize her actions into a self-righteous, loving act of martyrdom. Putting the baby first must be her top priority, not some heated romance with a football thug. She conjured up every negative trait Phil possessed, selectively ignoring any redeeming features she had discovered.

He was a foul-mouthed, overbearing, condescending, disorganized slob. He had no appreciation of the arts, decorating, or window-shopping. They had absolutely nothing in common when she got right down to it. Except…some sort of chemistry, some sort of deep personal understanding. *No, no, mustn't go there.* Some things were not meant to be. She had to zip up her urges good and tight and send Phil on his way.

Phil took his initial frustrations out on a punching bag. His students came next. His early morning gym class caught hell for gum chewing and normal fooling around. The usual laid back coach with the dry sense of humor morphed into a hard-assed Jack Nicholson-type commander from *A Few Good Men.* He turned a gym class basketball game into a serious rivalry. Two students wound up in the nurse's office.

In his third hour history class, he announced a pop quiz on the assigned chapter. As groans arose from behind the desks, he slapped a ruler so hard on his podium the students jumped at the noise, then froze in silence.

"I've been letting you kids get away with murder: turning in late assignments, talking out of turn, hearing you whine about your problems. Well, no more. I'm not doing you any favors letting you screw off. It's a dangerous world out there and if you're not ready for it, the sharks will eat you alive." He paced the room. "If I give you an assignment, I expect you to come to class prepared, and if you don't, I'll chew your butt so bad, you'll swear I left scars. This is a timed open-book quiz. Open to page thirty-five. You've got exactly fifteen minutes to turn in your papers."

Reba Finn sat at her desk totally unprepared, without text, notebooks, or even a pencil. With the chaos occurring at her house nowadays, just showing up at school was an accomplishment. But, Coach Wilcox knew nothing of the drama going on at the Finn residence, nor at that moment would he care.

Phil towered before Reba's desk, staring down with pitiless disapproval. "Where is your history book, Ms. Finn?"

"I guess I left it at home."

"Did you at least read the assignment last night?"

"I meant to."

Ordinarily, Phil would have just found another book and let the hapless student use it, but he gave into his mean mood. He turned her paper around, and wrote a big "F" at the top.

"If you can't bother to come to my class prepared, sweetheart, then don't bother to come at all." Phil walked back to his desk, a grizzly bear ready for the next stupid salmon swimming upstream.

Reba sat at her desk, as tears began to well in her eyes. All the other students kept their heads down, but cast surreptitious glances her way. Holding on to a shred of dignity, she slowly rose from her seat and walked to the door.

Phil looked up from his papers. "I didn't give you permission to leave."

Reba shot him a watery gaze, chin quivering while forcing herself to keep composure.

Phil winced at the despair in her eyes and felt like a shit. "Go ahead."

Reba made a quick exit as the tears overflowed their confines. She ran into the bathroom and shut herself into a stall.

Maddie found her there, as she made the usual rounds seeking errant students. The sound of familiar female weeping reverberated in the tiled room. Maddie assumed she'd happened upon another jilted girlfriend, a regular occurrence in her line of work.

Tapping on the stall door, Maddie said, "It's Miss Harris. Who is in there?"

Reba flipped the small metal bar back and released the lock, allowing Maddie to push open the door. Reba's swollen eyes and red nose marred her doll face.

Reaching her hand out, Maddie said, "Come on, you can pull yourself together in my office. The bell is about to ring. You don't want to be caught in here when the throng descends."

Reba's jagged recital of Phil's behavior filled Maddie with guilt-tinged fury. Obviously some sort of transference had transpired. She'd heard of his strong-arm tactics in the earlier gym class. Now he'd turned tyrannical in the history class. This is what came from allowing a personal relationship to develop between people who should keep things on a professional level.

She needed to clear the air, set him straight, show him the Woodbridge-Harris starch. After sending a calmed Reba onto her next class, Maddie dispatched a note to Phil.

Dear Coach Wilcox,

Please see me in my office after school to discuss your behavior of this morning.

Madeleine Harris

Phil read the message in the gym as the class monitor waited for his reply. Receiving that note on top of her disappearing act, her failure to return his phone calls, and her ridiculous announcement in the morning meeting, was like waving a red flag before a bull.

He drawled his answer to the courier. "Tell Miss Harris I can hardly *wait* for three o'clock."

As Randy strolled down the school hallway with the bomber jacket draped over his arm, he congratulated himself on portraying the hetero fiancé with true *joie de vie*. Maybe this whole baby thing with Maddie would transform his life. Randy's compartmentalized existence had its satisfactions. He loved teaching, directing, producing the shows; watching young talent unfold.

He tried to keep too busy to notice the huge black hole in his personal life. He could easily blame his dependent mother for keeping any real relationships from developing. He made occasional trips to Little Rock and mingled with the gay community. But he kept acquaintances at arms length. He'd been stabbed in the heart years ago and didn't want to face that kind of pain again. He saw too much switching of partners, in love one minute and bitching the next. Who needed it? Lately, he'd avoided the trips all together because he'd come really close to caring about one person in particular, and it scared the hell out him.

Better to take this opportunity with Maddie to focus on her and the child. She'd need him; the baby would need him; his mother would forever need him. He'd be too busy to notice who he needed.

At 2:55 Randy peeked his head inside the door of Maddie's office. "Hey, love, do you want me to dash you home before I start tonight's rehearsal?"

He'd picked Maddie up for work this morning so they could plan their happy announcement on the way. He'd found her poised over her toilet bowl, upchucking, and managed to pour her into her assistant principal togs and cover the green of her complexion with his cosmetic expertise.

Looking up from her desk, Maddie said, "Not quite yet.

I'm expecting the coach in a few minutes. Why don't you stick around? I could use the moral support."

Randy closed the door behind him, slipped into the bomber jacket, thereby taking on the flyer fiancé character once again. "*If you say three, mister, you'll never hear the man count ten.*"

Maddie smiled. "John Wayne in *The Quiet Man.*"

As she tried to forget her tension headache and allow Randy to divert her mind with amusing anecdotes from his day, Phil slammed the gym door and headed for the main school building. If background music had accompanied his pounding feet, the insistent syncopation from the theme of *Jaws* would surely have been the score of choice. He felt every bit the angry shark circling before the kill.

Ignoring the friendly greetings of secretaries as he passed them on his way to Her Majesty's inner sanctum, he thrust the door open, firmly shut it and stood, feet planted wide like Conan the Barbarian, ready to do battle.

Maddie and Randy riveted their attention on the scowling figure before them.

Phil crossed his arms and raised one eyebrow. "You summoned me?"

Maddie swallowed and gathered all the chutzpah she could muster, searching desperately within herself for the old Bostonian Iron Maiden. "Yes, Mr. Wilcox, I appreciate your punctuality."

"Believe me, sweetheart, I counted the minutes." He pulled the crumpled note out of his pocket. "What is this crap about my behavior this morning?"

Clasping her hands before her on the desk, she said, "It came to my attention that there were two injured players in a highly competitive basketball game this morning in your gym class. I also found Reba Finn crying in the girl's bathroom after you flunked and humiliated her in front of the history class. I can't help but think that my marriage announcement put you in a foul mood, and I will not tolerate a teacher allowing personal emotion to disrupt the order of the school."

Randy watched the vein in Phil's temple pound and considered clamping a hand over Maddie's mouth before the coach lunged across the desk and strangled her.

Phil stepped to Maddie's desk, put his hands down on the cold surface, and leaned in over her. "Well, maybe after you took a powder on Saturday from our cabin, you should have taken my reactions into consideration before walking into the meeting this morning as *The Princess Bride*." Phil shot Randy a look. "And what kind of guy proposes marriage to a chick who's been shacked up with someone else the day before?"

Maddie shot to her feet. "We were not 'shacked up'!"

"Honey, if I hadn't taken that tumble in the poison ivy, we'd have kept the fire burning in that cabin all weekend and never lit the fireplace. You'd have my love bites all over your lily white body."

Maddie's eyes turned ice blue. "You can be the crudest, most vulgar individual I've ever met."

Phil kept his voice to a low growl. "And you're still an irritating, stuck-up, pain in the ass."

Randy was enjoying the show, but he knew his cue when he heard it. Time to play macho lover man. "Well, I guess we'd better come clean, baby." Randy sidled next to Maddie and wrapped a possessive arm around her. "The truth is the little lady was on the rebound. I'd broken off our relationship when she started talking marriage last summer, told her I wasn't the marrying kind. She only went off with you to make me jealous. It worked, too. When she called me on the phone and described your love nest, I knew I had to get her away from you and put my brand on her, pronto."

Pushing back from the desk, Phil took measure of Maddie's stiff composure, locked in Randy's casual embrace. "I'm not buying any of this bull for a minute, but I do know I don't like being played for a sucker. Whatever your game is, I can tell you no guy likes a tease. At least with a five dollar hooker, a man knows where he stands." His voice cut like a knife. "I thought you were something different–a woman with a heart, mind and soul. God help me, I thought you'd be *loyal.*

Christ, I'm an idiot, thinking I'd found gold in you. But you're just like all other women–faithless, lying users. You're just fool's gold. And I was the fool."

Phil turned on his heel and slammed out the door.

Randy released Maddie and heaved a sigh of relief as an actor does when the curtain goes down.

Maddie stood frozen, staring into space trying to put her disjointed thoughts into some logical order, when the door abruptly opened again.

Phil strode across the small room, snagged one arm around Maddie's waist and the other hand gripped the back of her head. "I forgot to kiss the bride."

His lips crushed hers in the urgent need to put *his* brand on her, claim her as his own, throwing logic and common sense to the wind. She'd, by-God, remember him no matter whose arms were around her. His tongue swept her mouth and blazed *his* taste, *his* scent into her memory. He wanted to toss her back on the desk and impale her, thrust himself inside her with a powerful rhythm pounding on and on until they both exploded and he thoroughly possessed the proper Miss Harris. He wanted her lost in passion, fighting, scratching, surrendering, then lying limp and spent beneath him. But he settled for the searing kiss. She'd lost all strength by the time he suddenly released her on buckling knees. A parting glimpse of her gave him a glimmer of satisfaction. Randy had caught her from behind to keep her from completely collapsing on the floor.

Holding the door handle, Phil uttered a final shot. "Let's see if you can do *that* to her, flyboy."

Chapter Eleven

Take my wife--PLEASE...

Rodney Dangerfield

Randy and Maddie drove to Little Rock on Friday afternoon, the last couple to stand before the judge at the courthouse for a quick civil marriage ceremony at 4:45. Two chatty court clerks with deep drawls served as witnesses and offered best wishes. It was a done deal by 5 o'clock. The best friends were now Mr. and Mrs. Randall Bailey.

Standing on the windy old concrete steps before the brick courthouse, they stared at each other, suddenly speechless, each wondering if they'd made a big mistake. Then they laughed. They were still plain ole Maddie and Randy, no matter what a piece of paper called them.

Randy put on a jolly face. "Let's have dinner on the river. I know a picturesque spot where we can watch the sun go down as the barges sail by."

Maddie plastered on a smile. "Sounds wonderful."

As an orange disc sank in the western sky, they sat next to a glass wall in the posh restaurant gazing across the wide expanse of the Arkansas River. Forgetting all about their marriage seemed the most natural course and they discussed Randy's upcoming production of *Dames at Sea* and his decision to cast Reba Finn in the lead role. For some reason, talking about the baby didn't feel right. They didn't know how to approach the subject.

Over entrees of pasta primavera for Maddie and lamb chops for Randy, they worked on ideas for the sets. Randy excitedly sketched on a paper napkin.

The outline of a mock ship took shape as he bent over the table. Neither of them noticed their visitor until a perfectly manicured hand rested on Randy's shoulder. Maddie looked up and inspected a lithe, sandy-haired man in the expensive suit who gazed at Randy with calm familiarity.

"Randall, it's good to see you in town." The man possessed a cultured baritone voice.

Randy's expression of uncomfortable recognition and the stranger's subtle caress where his hand lay told Maddie more than she wanted to know.

Randy pulled back, sloughing off the resting hand. "Hello, Brent."

"It's been a while," Brent said, as he cast a questioning look at Maddie.

Randy made introductions. "Maddie, this is Brent Farnsworth. Brent, this is...my w-wife, Madeleine." Maddie smiled politely as she noticed he'd nearly choked on the "w" word.

Brent blinked at her as if she was a mirage. "Your *wife*? And what does Mother say about that? Or have you kept Madeleine a secret, too?"

Randy stood up, throwing the napkin from his lap down onto the table. "Excuse us, Maddie. Let's go have a chat in the bar, Brent."

Brent shot Randy a steely look. "Yes, let's. It was very nice to have met you, *Mrs. Bailey*."

Maddie watched Randy and Brent walk to the mahogany bar. They carried on an intense, whispered dialog. Randy used a lot of hand gestures in his usual dramatic way. Brent appeared to be the more stoic type. Brent stood straighter and straighter as the conversation continued. He cast Maddie a serious gaze, causing her to quickly look at the river view. She shifted her head back to see Brent turn on his heel and depart the restaurant in rigid anger.

Randy's accustomed mask of impish whimsy was suddenly ripped away, replaced by a soul-revealing, sad countenance. His shoulders drooped as if the weight of the world had been thrust upon them. He stood frozen at the bar staring at Brent's departing back, unaware that Maddie looked on. His face mirrored so much internal pain, she turned away, embarrassed by her unintentional invasion into his private life.

By the time he returned to the table, he'd painted his happy face back on. "How about sharing an order of 'Death by Chocolate' for dessert?" he said as he took his seat.

"Perfect," Maddie agreed.

Their river walk hotel room featured two queen beds, dresser, entertainment center, and full bath. Blue and burgundy tied all elements of the decorating together with efficient monotony. Maddie took the bed closest to the picture window. From the fifth floor the view of the river flowed long and peaceful, even at night. Tall lamps along the winding sidewalk cast a yellow glow as far as the eye could see.

Maddie rested her forehead against the cool glass, standing in her stocking feet, gazing at the water. City lights obscured the stars. No moon appeared in the evening sky, just hazy darkness against the skyline. She longed to get out of her constricting clothes. For the first time, she'd had to find a safety pin to hold her skirt together around her expanding waist.

Randy stepped out of the bathroom, dressed in pajamas adorned with cartoon characters. "It's all yours. How do you like my honeymoon jammies?"

Maddie pulled her equally sexy flannel nightgown out of her bag. "Fetching, very fetching."

She took a long, hot shower that felt heavenly. God, what a stressful week. Surely, she'd been through the worst of it. Now it was simply a matter of putting one foot in front of the other and carrying on like the Woodbridges before her. She hoped that darned, unpredictable Harris blood didn't get her in trouble.

Refreshed by their showers, Randy and Maddie enjoyed a kind of slumber party, watching the romance channel while eating junk food and drinking caffeine-free soda. She fell asleep before eleven o'clock to the sounds of the TV and the blowing air conditioner.

The room was dark and quiet when she awakened two hours later with terrible indigestion. She imagined a sparking firecracker sizzling in her stomach. Groaning as she sat up, she tried not to awaken Randy as she stumbled to the bathroom. She turned on the light and poured herself a glass of water, hoping it would douse her flaming insides. Gulping liquid in the doorway, she glanced back into the room to see if she'd disturbed Randy.

Light pouring out of the bathroom revealed his bed, empty, still perfectly made up. He was gone. The bridegroom had flown the coop. She sat on the edge of the bed and composed a mock press release in her mind.

"The Randall Baileys have returned from their rapturous honeymoon where the pregnant bride endured miserable gas as the groom was off visiting with 'friends.'"

She'd gone through the looking glass into a tilted wonderland.

That's when she noticed it–the full moon now high in the sky. She switched off the glaring bathroom light, crossed to the window in her billowing nightgown, and opened up the curtains as far as they could go, allowing moonlight to bathe the room. The heavenly body remained at once her friend and foe, affecting the tides of her being.

Tonight a mixed mood enveloped her, joyfully sad, as she realized she was no longer alone with the moon. She leaned back on her pillow and placed her hands on the small tight mound forming beneath her bellybutton. A new body, a fresh soul grew every moment of every day, developing in her womb, under her heart. A bubbling thrill coursed through her veins.

But at the same time, she felt so…lonely. She wanted to share the miracle, tell someone about all the minute changes happening to her. But, it wouldn't be Randy. She knew that now. Their friendship only went so far. It didn't go to the deepest intimacies. Tears formed in her eyes as loneliness descended on her like a blanket. She stared up at the moon and sank into the forbidden wish that Phil's warm arms were around her tonight.

Phil puffed an expensive cigar as he sat on the cold concrete steps in front of his apartment staring at the light bulb moon. Smoking wasn't a regular habit, but every once in a while he craved a good cigar. The famous Kipling quote floated across his mind. *"A woman is only a woman, but a good cigar is a smoke."*

His team had barely won tonight's game, thanks to a last minute interception and sprint into the end zone. He should have been happy. The team was three for three; Melissa had joined the squad as water girl and personal advisor to the coach. His life counted for something again. So, why did he feel hollow and empty inside?

Sum it up in three words–Madeleine Woodbridge Harris. Christ, he probably needed to add the *Bailey* by now. The earlier anger of the week had been easier to deal with than these sorry blues. He had to laugh at himself, looking over his shoulder all night long for Maddie's honey blond hair in the crowd. Instead, he found only bleached blond Pam waving wildly at him at every opportunity.

He'd known about Randy and Maddie's hurried trip to Little Rock, having overheard gossip in the teacher's lounge. Still, he'd been foolish enough to hope the rumor was false. Shoot him for being a friggin' idiot. That overwhelming, territory-marking kiss he'd left on Maddie had backfired on him big time. While instilling his taste and scent in her, he'd inhaled *her* essence, implanted *her* flavors in the center of his psyche. Which was why he sat shivering outside in the cold, attempting to put a damper on his ardor. It beat tossing and turning in his empty bed.

A few more puffs on the cigar focused his thinking. What the hell had happened? Why would she run off to marry that twinkle-toes? The facts just wouldn't add up in his mind. She was the kind of woman who would have a big to-do wedding, a lah-dee-dah affair back in Boston with the upper crust. This turn of events resembled an old-fashioned Arkansas shotgun wedding where the bride was barefoot and pregnant.

Barefoot and pregnant...

Son of a bitch...He'd be a goddamned son of a bitch.

Phil stood and ground the cigar out under the heel of his shoe. It was the missing piece of the puzzle. The woman must be pregnant. Had Maddie and Randy actually conceived a child? He couldn't buy that one, but he could see Randy being her way out to respectability. So who was the mysterious stud? Some summer fling? At any rate, he knew one thing for sure–it wasn't Phil Wilcox.

No, Phil was just a damn fool who couldn't get one woman out of his mind. He knew he'd be watching her whether he wanted to or not. How soon before she wore blousy outfits? How soon before Randy performed another teachers' meeting skit to announce the coming of the stork? This time there'd probably do a scene from *Father Knows Best*. Randy might smoke a pipe and call Maddie "kitten."

She'd obviously made her bed, now she could lie in it, without Phil Wilcox.

As he took heavy steps toward his apartment door, he told himself to forget the woman, turn on ESPN, and fall asleep in his recliner. But instead he continued to his dim bedroom and lay back on the bed, hands folded behind his head and stared up at the passing moon through the small window. He'd have sworn a face appeared before the shining orb, a face with wide blue eyes surrounded by soft wheat hair dancing in the breeze.

He flipped on his clock radio. A haunting, melancholy Elvis asked the musical question, *Are You Lonesome Tonight?* Phil's heart beat along in 3/4 time.

Yes, damn it, he was lonesome tonight. He fell asleep with empty arms.

Reba Finn scooted her bottom on the wooden ledge as close to the open window as possible as she gazed at the man on the moon. Even though it was the middle of the night, she couldn't sleep because of all the noise and smells rising from downstairs. Her folks had a houseful of people, all hyped up on the stuff her mom had learned to cook. The stink of the chemicals gave Reba a headache and she hated the way it made everyone act–wild and scary. The pot hadn't been so bad. The smell of it had always been a part of her life, making people quiet and spaced out, not loud and crazy.

Reba gulped a deep breath from the cold air of the open window, which chilled, but brought relief to her throbbing head. She pulled her knees to her chest and wrapped her arms about her shins, feeling air swirl around her naked legs covered by a thin nightgown. Faith stirred in her sleep, snuggling a doll in her small bed. Reba looked back into the room, seeing the slant of the loft roof in the blue evening light. The rough unfinished room with its unpainted rafters and walls served as the girls' sanctuary from the rest of the family. Faith's crayon colored pictures decorated the short walls and Reba had managed to paint a garage sale vanity a cheery yellow to brighten the room.

Sometimes Reba's fertile imagination allowed her to escape reality, and she could be a kidnapped princess waiting for her prince charming to break into the evil castle and carry her away. Other times, she just huddled in her bed and managed to sleep away a bad day. Now, she had a new dream, a dream given to her by Mr. Bailey. Maybe she could sing her way out of this hellhole and take her brothers and sister with her.

Noise from the downstairs got suddenly louder and meaner.

"Don't you tell me about racing! You don't know your ass from a hole in the ground!" Wade's voice came through the floor loud and clear.

Fear tinged Ginger's voice. "Let him go, Wade!"

"Get away from me, you stupid bitch. If it weren't for you and those damn kids, I'd be on the circuit right now. You're just nothing but a weight around my neck–a fat, stinking weight!"

Even through the walls, a slap resounded followed by objects crashing to the wooden floor.

Ginger's sobbing reply pierced Reba's soul. "I hate you!"

A spaced-out male voice joined the melee. "Hey, man, take it easy. I didn't mean nuthin' by it."

"I'm getting the hell out of here," Wade said. "Gonna find me a woman who doesn't look like a damn pig. This shit better be cleaned up by the time I get back."

The screen door slammed. Reba watched Wade's rangy figure climb into his truck. It peeled out onto the gravel road. Ginger's whimpers mingled with muffled comments from other unknown guests.

Reba inhaled a deep breath and lifted her eyes to the sky, attempting to rise above the disturbing trembling in her stomach. The brightness of the moon offered her hope, brought a hypnotizing sense of calm as she stared and stared at the shining celestial body.

"Star light, star bright, first star I see tonight
I wish I may, I wish I might
Have the wish I wish tonight."

And some wishes are granted by that old Devil Moon.

Chapter Twelve

I wonder who's been sleeping in my bed?

The Three Bears

Wade's truck jostled over the potholed road leading to the main highway. "Damn, fucking bitch…"

He pulled out without looking for oncoming traffic, stomped the accelerator and fishtailed onto the black ribbon of asphalt.

His mind raced in a thousand incoherent directions, shooting images of cars, fireballs and women darted through his head like a waking nightmare. He wanted another hit, needed the burst of euphoria from the crystals, pissed that the elusive state of ecstasy got harder to achieve. He also wanted sex, ached to be buried in a woman and blasted to mindless outer space beyond the reach of inner demons.

The flash of trees in his headlights reminded him of ghostly figures, the living dead stalking sorry sons of bitches in the night. He passed a few mailboxes clustered together for the rural postal worker's convenience. Short fences and long driveways that lead to homes clustered around the lake zoomed by. He slowed down; his mind worked to bring up a steady idea. That Miss Harris lived around here, just around the next bend. *Now there's a sweet piece of ass.* Just thinking of her smooth skin and soft hair made his dick hard. He cut his lights and pulled into her gravel road.

Porch lights seemed to greet him, saying *Come on in, Wade*. He got out of the truck and slammed the door, not bothering to be quiet. An image of her naked, long legs and high breasts propelled him toward the house. He jiggled the front door. Locked. Walking around to the well-lit back porch, he searched in the flowerpots and under the doormat where he found the extra key in typical Arkansas fashion. The back door opened noiselessly.

Making his way through the kitchen into the living room, the outside lights offered ample illumination in the still rooms. He stood mesmerized on the plush carpet, inhaling the clean scent of potpourri, soap, and furniture polish. This place didn't stink of ashtrays and baby shit like his house. Even without another hit of the spoosh, he felt better, less jumpy. He moved toward a hallway and guessed which door opened into her bedroom. A strong lavender aroma hit his senses and pulled him into the room. The bed lay bathed in moonlight from the bay window. Fluffy pillows rested on the thick comforter. No beautiful white body lay sleeping in the bed.

"Shit," Wade said as he realized the house was empty.

He flipped on the reading light that sat on the bedside table, suddenly needing to memorize the room where she slept. His hands traveled over the cottony softness of the comforter. A group of pictures resting on her dresser caught his eye, and he moved around the bed to see them better. Each family snapshot shone in a fancy frame, one of an old lady, another featured a good-looking middle-aged couple. In one shot he recognized the high school drama teacher hugging Miss Harris. His fidgety fingers caused a domino effect of falling photos.

Jesus, he loved the smell of the room and wanted to take it with him. He looked around, spotted an old fashioned quilt folded over a fancy wooden frame and pulled it into his boney hands. Visions of her creamy smooth skin danced in his mind as he buried his face in the center of the cotton squares and inhaled deeply. Yeah, it carried the scent of the room, the scent she must carry on that pale body. Damn, what he wouldn't give to hump her brains out.

The quilt lay nestled next to Wade on the front seat as he pulled out of her driveway. He got a glimpse of the neat cabin in his rear view mirror. The purloined key jabbed his thigh through his jean pocket. He'd missed her tonight. But, he'd be back, oh yeah, he'd be back.

On Saturday afternoon Randy dropped Maddie home, and hurried to his house after receiving a whining call from Mother Bailey. Relief rushed through Maddie's body as she entered her cozy cabin after the long ride home. Carsickness had stayed her constant companion as the vehicle swayed around mountain curves.

When she'd awakened in the morning, Randy snored softly in the bed next to her wearing his cartoon jammies as if he'd never left. Both of them pretended that was the case. She might have nudged him for information about the mysterious Brent, but morning sickness hit with a vengeance. Being an expert on nursing sick women, Randy made her stay in bed and brought her crackers and hot tea from the hotel dining room.

Gratefully home, she dragged her overnight bag through the house into her bedroom, went into the bathroom, and shut the door. After ripping off her traveling clothes, she slipped into her robe and felt much better. As she re-entered the bedroom, the shining bedside light grabbed her attention. Funny, she remembered checking the house for any stray lights left on, and the bedroom had definitely been dark when she'd departed. She scanned the room and quickly noticed the tumbled pictures on the dresser. When she realized the quilt frame stood empty, she gasped.

Gripping the post of the bed for support, a wave of fear and anger washed over her. *Someone's been in my bed, said the mama bear.* Now she knew why the three bears had chased Goldilocks out of their house. She felt violated, as if she'd been physically assaulted by the intrusion.

How dare someone come into her house and steal her things! She paced the room, taking mental inventory. Her jewelry box sat on the dresser, unopened. She flipped up the top, expecting it to be empty or obviously rummaged. To her surprise, every necklace, every earring remained perfectly in place. She sat on the bed and realized no common thief had been in her house. Who would come and take only an old quilt and leave behind valuable gemstones? It was downright creepy.

She left the bedroom and headed into the kitchen to make tea and ponder the situation. Remembering the extra key under the mat, she opened the back door and searched, finding nothing. Great, some weirdo had a key to her house.

The rest of the house seemed undisturbed, but now she could almost feel a change in the atmosphere. It was just her imagination, of course, but she smelled a musty difference in the air. Who would do such a thing? A stranger? A student from the school?

Phil?

Oh my God, was Phil some kind of sneak thief? Would he skulk through her house and take a memento? He hadn't seemed the type, but then Ted Bundy had been a perfectly charming young serial killer.

She dipped her teabag as she sat at the kitchen table, getting madder and madder at the thought of Phil taking this kind of petty revenge on her. It would serve him right for her to call the police and have his apartment searched. She wanted to pick up the phone and let him have it, give him the biggest chewing out of his miserable football-playing life. But, of course, he'd just deny it and make her feel like an idiot. He was so good at that.

She swigged a gulp of calming tea. No, she would bide her time. Wait to catch him slip up somehow in a conversation; look for a flicker of guilt in his eyes. She'd see how long he would play innocent.

Lord, this was the second of Grammy's quilts that had been taken in the night. Looking into the doorway, she saw and heard the old gal herself. "By golly, if I'd known strange men were so interested in my quilts, I'd have just wrapped myself in one to go sparkin' on a Saturday night."

Maddie rolled her eyes at the Grammyism. *Just ignore her and she'll go away.* Maddie needed to change clothes and head to a hardware store. Her cabin would have new locks by evening or her name wasn't Madeleine Woodbridge

Harris...Bailey.

At the Monday morning faculty meeting, Phil carried in a greasy portion of biscuits and gravy that brought a distinctly porcine smell into the closed room. Maddie sat in her chair as Phil stood behind her before the meeting started. He purposely began a conversation with Phyllis Green as he opened his Styrofoam food tray.

"Miss Green, do you make biscuits in your Home Ec class? Nothing better than down home fluffy biscuits dripping in ham gravy."

He stuck his steaming, porky concoction under Maddie's nose. "Care for bite, Mrs. Bailey, before I chow down?"

Maddie gasped when the greasy odor assailed her nostrils. "No, thank you."

Miss Green preened at receiving Phil's attention. "Biscuits are very tricky to make just right, Coach. But, I might have the class try them and send a batch over to your football team, if you like."

Phil continued an innocuous conversation with the cooking teacher as he watched Maddie out of the corner of his eye rise and bolt from the room. Randy quietly excused himself and followed her out.

The two returned after the meeting commenced. Maddie definitely looked a little green around the gills but managed a haughty glare toward Phil. He returned a knowing smirk.

Later, Maddie brought up the subject of school thievery, hoping to catch Phil in a moment of guilt. "We've had a lot of back packs stolen lately. I've organized a patrol of student volunteers to stand guard over the packs during lunch hours. *Petty thievery will not be tolerated.*" She looked directly at Phil during her last statement, hoping to paralyze him with accusation from her ice blue eyes. Instead, he wore an expression of bored indifference. She huffed inwardly to herself. Maddie longed for one satisfying "gotcha" moment in Phil's face.

McCall finished the meeting by assigning duties for the

annual Halloween Haunted House. "Mr. Bailey, your drama department will build the sets as usual."

Randy saluted.

"Coach Wilcox, your football team will serve as monsters and various spooks to scare people as they go through the trail. Miss Har–uh–Mrs. Bailey knows the drill. The two of you can work together coordinating the effort. This is a great fundraiser for us every year and I expect everyone to do their part."

Phil and Maddie glared across the table at each other with unconcealed hostility as the other teachers rose, chatted, and got on their way to class. Randy waved a farewell to Maddie, leaving the coach and the assistant principal to duke it out alone.

"So, Mrs. Bailey," Phil asked, "will you be going to the Halloween bash as a pumpkin this year?"

Maddie sharply inhaled, but maintained her composure. "I haven't made up my mind. If you need a costume, I have a *cat burglar* outfit that would suit you."

Phil stood up. "No thanks. I think I'll stick with my Knute Rockne get-up."

She wished he'd just admit his guilt and quit playing games. "Well, yes, I can see how that would definitely be apropos for you."

"Hey, with me, what you see is what you get, unlike some people I know."

Maddie took to her feet. "I don't appreciate your innuendos. If you have something to say, just say it. Nobody likes a sneak."

Phil slowly walked around the table, stalking her with each word. "Okay, lady, I'll lay it out on the table. Has all the baloney that's been going on been because you're–how should I put it–'in the family way'? In other words, are you by any chance–pregnant? Does that explain the rushed hillbilly wedding?" When he finished speaking, he stood only inches from her face.

Oh my God. She wanted to sink into the floor, but instead pulled dignity about her like a protective cloak. "We'd hoped to let a reasonable amount of time pass before making that declaration, but if you're going to go about spewing forth your brilliant deduction, I guess we'll just move up our timetable. You'll have to find other ways of taking out petty revenge. Of course, you already have."

Phil ran his fingers through his hair. "Jesus, what kind of bastard do you think I am?"

Thinking of him rummaging through her house filled her with irritation. "I'll have to admit that I was very surprised by your actions, but we really don't know each other very well, do we?"

"Surprised by my actions?" He appeared momentarily nonplussed. "Okay, the gravy biscuits were a cheap shot. And you're right about us not really knowing each other. I bought that song and dance about your lost love Thomas, but there's proof positive of other players in the field. And, believe me, I don't care if you had an affair with Bill Clinton. I just don't like being lied to. By the way, who is the father? I'm dying of curiosity."

Maddie's face reflected stony resolve. "Randy is my child's father."

Phil crossed his arms. "Uh-huh."

"Randy will make an excellent father."

"Well, that's your story and you're sticking to it. Just do me a favor, sweetheart, don't play me for a sucker anymore."

Maintaining her ramrod posture, she said, "I never meant to deceive you. I've had to make some plans for my life and they simply don't include you. And I'm grateful I've seen some of your true colors before I got too involved with you."

The bell buzzed for the first hour. Phil clenched his jaw. "I've got to go. See you at the Halloween shindig. Don't forget to bring your broom stick."

Maddie blinked as he slammed the door. She looked up at the painted moon on the wall mural. Suddenly, the picture came to life, the lake shimmering under the bright evening sky. The silvery sphere winked and whispered, "*Trick or treat.*"

Chapter Thirteen

Catch me if you can

The Gingerbread Man

Over the next couple of weeks the weather turned blustery, blowing the final tenacious leaves down to form a carpet of crunchy brown parchment over the landscape. Compacted cedar evergreens punctuated the hibernating hills with dashes of color against the steel blue sky. Gray, leafless trees waved twisted branches like witchy fingers casting spells over hapless humans going through the motions of life.

Phil hunkered down into a routine of school, visits with Melissa, and exhausting workouts. Pam kept up an obvious attempt at reconciliation or at the very least, seduction, but he managed to keep a friendly distance. He knew that beneath Pam's girly smile lay the sharp ability to snap like a barracuda. He wondered when Melissa would come to trust him beyond any ability of her mother to discredit him in his daughter's eyes. Maddie remained an open sore in his consciousness, a nagging tooth; the damned pain in the ass she would always be.

Maddie's morning sickness improved as her middle thickened and her breasts enlarged. Getting organized for motherhood, she ordered prenatal books and began eyeing maternity clothes. She tried to carry on, be a good soldier, keep a stiff upper lip, but her emotions betrayed her. Always a captive of her hormones, pregnancy brought even greater mood fluctuations. Tears came easily for both happy and sad events, like Hallmark TV commercials and the five o'clock news. When she contemplated being a mother, she felt both thrilled and terrified. And the darned loneliness wouldn't leave her.

Even being with Randy had lost its fun. She couldn't muster up her old enthusiasm for pitching in with his next show. Her attention turned inward to the new life within; but joy was elusive with nobody to share the miracle growing within her womb.

The Haunted House took over the gym with dark walls constructed to form a spooky maze of creepy thrills. Black lights hung from the ceiling that brought out ghoulish shapes in the darkness. Secret passages opened to allow monsters access to paying customers wanting to be scared out of their wits, or at least genuinely startled. Frightening tableaus of prisoners chained to walls, a vampire rising from a coffin in a foggy room, and Frankenstein coming to life in the mad scientist's laboratory promised to horrify and delight the residents of Beaver Cove. This year's attraction spilled out into the woods behind the gym, following a spooky path into the haunted hills.

Canned screams blasted from loud speakers piercing the growing darkness as Phil, Melissa, Maddie, and the football team gathered in the locker room. Beaver Cove's jocks now resembled monsters, mummies, and chainsaw murderers.

Maddie wrapped Martinez as the Creature from the Black Lagoon, then sprayed him with dark green silly string that trailed around him. Phil dabbed fake blood on a murder victim's head where an axe appeared to be lodged.

"Stu, you never looked better in your life," Phil said.

"Think I could pick up girls like this, Coach?"

"Well, anything would be an improvement," Melissa sassed.

"Watch it, squirt, or I'll hold you under a cold shower," Stu replied.

"You and who else, four-eyes?"

Other football players joined in. "I'll help!" "Me, too." "I'll wash out her smart mouth with soap."

The over-grown monsters surrounded the skinny eleven-year-old, who looked ready to take them all on. As a dozen pair of hands grabbed her, she squealed, laughed, and yelled,

"Daddy, help!"

Macho male voices imitated her girly tone. "Daddy, help! Daddy, help!"

Melissa dangled in the air, kicking her feet in a futile attempt to escape. Maddie feared the fun might get over zealous and was about to issue a cease-and-desist command when Phil's baritone voice barked over the teenage din.

"Drop her! Nobody throws the coach's daughter in the shower except the coach. You screw-offs better get over to the gym and report for duty to Mr. Bailey. Kick-off is in half-an-hour."

The boys gave Melissa some rough big-brother type shoves and made good-natured farewells as they headed out the door for spook assignments, leaving Maddie, Phil, and Melissa alone in the locker room.

Melissa cleaned up the leavings from monster-making as Maddie and Phil stared wordlessly at each other for a moment. Then Maddie cleared her throat and said, "Well, I guess I'd better get into costume. I've got it hanging back here. I'll just change now that the coast is clear."

Phil nodded curtly. "Sure."

Maddie walked behind a row of lockers, her flats echoing against the concrete and metal of the room. The locker door clanged as she found the costume she'd worn last year. The long black gown of Morticia Adams had floated over her thin body and she didn't think her figure had changed so much yet that she couldn't get away with it one more time. As Maddie pulled off her turtleneck sweater and jeans, she heard Melissa talk to Phil in the center of the room.

"Hey, Dad, do you know what the pirate movie I watched last night was rated?"

"No, what?"

"*Aaarrr*!"

Phil chuckled. "That was a good one, kid."

"I've got something for you, Dad."

"Yeah, it's not fake vomit or exploding gum, is it?"

"Nah, it's something I made for you."

Maddie noted shyness in Melissa's voice and then heard a locker open.

"What is it?" Phil asked.

"It's a scrap book I made. I found a box of all kinds of articles about you from the olden days and I've been saving everything in our newspaper about you and the team."

A bench squeaked as Phil and Melissa sat down. "You made this?"

Maddie couldn't help but hear the awe in his voice.

"Yeah…Here you are in high school, right here in Beaver Cove. You wore your hair long then…That's you and Mom."

As the pages turned, Phil and Melissa made joking comments about his changing hairstyles. A couple of times Phil reminisced about a particular game. Maddie sensed the regret in his voice when he reached a story about his back injury. Then they got to the present-day articles.

Melissa's voice sounded low and subdued. "Did you mean what you said in this article? Did you really move back here so you could be with me?"

"Damn right. It wasn't for the great pay. Why did you think I moved here?"

"Mom said it was because it was the only job you could get. That being a small town football coach was the best you could do."

"Listen kid, I had a good job. But it took me all over the country and kept me away from you. And whether you believe it or not, you're the most important person in my life."

"Really?"

"Do you want me to write it in blood? Cripes, women." Phil's gruff reply brought tears to Maddie's eyes.

"So, do you like it?" Melissa asked.

"Well, it's alright. But it's missing something."

Melissa sounded crestfallen. "What?"

"There's not one single picture of my daughter in here. Not one mention of the day she was born, or the first word she said, which was 'Da', by the way. Those are the most important events in the life of Phil Wilcox, not all this football stuff."

"Oh, Daddy!" Maddie couldn't see it, but she felt sure Melissa had just wrapped her thin arms around her father's neck and given him a big kiss on the cheek.

Phil spoke low. "The scrap book is great, kid. Just like you."

"I love you, Daddy."

"I love you too, baby."

Maddie leaned against the cold metal of the gray locker, struggling to keep a sob from exploding from her lungs. Drat her hormones. *Get a grip, get a grip.*

After a few quiet moments, Melissa said, "I better go. I gotta work the popcorn booth." The door creaked as Melissa left.

Tears streamed down Maddie's face as she struggled into the black dress. As she slipped into her black pumps, she realized the dress was definitely tighter than last year and she couldn't zip herself up.

"Oh, darn!" she moaned.

Phil's voice reverberated back to her. "Do you need some help?"

Maddie wiped her eyes with her fingers, attempting to stem the tide of tears that seemed to always be near the surface. She waddled out to find Phil.

"I'm afraid so. I can't reach the zipper." She rounded the corner of the lockers and held up the front of her dress as she neared him.

"Well, turn around," he said, as his eyes swept over her.

His breath brushed her back as he tugged the metal tab upwards. She still felt a little weepy. "You're a very good father. Melissa's so fortunate to have you."

Phil grunted as he worked to close the zipper. "And here I thought you pretty much consider me dog meat."

Maddie hung her head. She really didn't know what to think about Phil. If he had been her intruder and taken Grammy's quilt, he'd shown no signs of recognition at the countless hints and accusations she'd volleyed his way. She was beginning to have her doubts. And in truth, she missed him. Whatever had transpired between them had been sudden and strong and she missed the banter, the teasing...the understanding. Phil seemed to understand her like no one else in the world.

With a final tug, the dress gripped her body in a completely different manner than the previous year. Phil gently held her shoulders and turned her around to face him. Then his eyes riveted to her bust line. Maddie followed his gaze and saw her rounded bosom bulging over the top of the black dress.

Her hands quickly flew up to cover her nakedness. "It didn't fit me like this last year!"

Phil's mouth formed an appreciative grin. "Oh, the difference a year can make."

Maddie turned and took mincing steps to a mirror. "Oh my God, I look like the Halloween Happy Hooker."

He walked up behind her and gazed over her shoulder into the mirror. "I've got a black cape from a Dracula costume back there. You can cover yourself with that." His eyes seemed mesmerized by her image and they locked gazes in the mirror.

His voice dropped to an unconscious low caress. "You have beautiful skin, Maddie."

He didn't touch her, but she shivered as if he'd stroked her bare shoulder. She could almost feel his kisses on her throat, sparking those special secret places so long denied stimulation. While they stood stock still before the mirror, it seemed their reflections fulfilled their longing to wrap in each other's arms. She watched her head fall back as his mouth dipped to explore the curves of her throat, tease the sensitive moles with the tip of his tongue. Breathing became difficult as she imagined the feathery sensation of his fingers exploring the exposed skin of her chest. Her breasts tingled in anticipation of his touch.

The enchanted locker room mirror caught Phil in its spell also. He relished her taste as his mouth traveled the forbidden territory of her beautiful neck, round and round those raised dots of sensitivity. One hand entwined around her waist as the other gripped the back of her head. Her body fit perfectly against him and his fingers swept across the soft, creamy pillowed flesh pushed above the black material. Her texture and scent filled his senses with an overwhelming feeling of *deja vu.*

She actually moaned, which brought them back to reality. Their reflections once again only stared back at them. They moved away from the mirror and broke the spell.

"I'd better get you that cape," Phil said.

Something teetered on the edge of Phil's mind as he found the costume and brought it back to Maddie's waiting figure. She appeared to be struggling to regain her composure as he draped the cape around her shoulders and then moved to the front of her to tie it about her neck. She lifted her chin to give him better access and that's when his eyes stilled on the trio of moles. He'd just experienced some bizarre fantasy involving those enticing birthmarks and now he was slammed with a memory.

A radiating disc in the sky shimmering silver light on ripples of water. A Moon Goddess white as marble, warm as a waterbed. Three dark dots resting on a long, pulsing throat. Two strangers melting into each other arms, stealing moments of passion and peace. A homey quilt grabbed on impulse.

Phil mechanically finished tying the ends of the strings, stunned by the images and thoughts twirling about in his mind. Could Maddie have possibly been the mystery woman that night? Was *she* the Moon Goddess?

She stepped away from him, oblivious to his revelations. "I must go find Randy. He has the black wig that really finishes off the outfit."

She'd almost reached the door when his voice stopped her. "Maddie, are you by any chance missing a quilt?"

She froze and turned back to him slowly. "So, it *was* you."

Shock charged through Phil's body. "You *knew*?"

"Well, I couldn't be sure, of course. But I'm an intelligent woman. It didn't take me long to figure it out. And really, I understand. People can do strange things when they're emotionally upset. Let's put the whole episode behind us and forget it. Actually, it's a relief to know it was you and not some weird stranger. I would like to remain your friend. You can return the quilt any time it's convenient." She glanced at the wall clock. "Oh, dear, it's getting so late. Randy will have my head if I don't do my part. Everything is such a big production with him. Thank you so much, Phil, for clearing the air. See you later."

With that, she hobbled out the door in her tight dress and cape, leaving Phil completely flummoxed.

Wade and Reba drove up as the crowd gathered to enter the spooky attraction. Wade had been up for twenty-four hours and was buzzed from a fresh hit to get him through the night. He figured to make big money tonight. Word had been spread with key people that he had the goods. He designated a cove of trees in the woods to be his "office" where he'd be open for business.

Valuable little baggies sat in a shoebox in the backseat of the extended cab, guarded by Wade's most ferocious dog, Lucifer. And, of course, Wade's trusty shotgun lay close at hand. The truck kicked up dust as it cut into the parking lot.

Wade's hands rapped a rhythm on the steering wheel as he turned hot eyes onto Reba. "You better have your ass back here at ten o'clock."

Dressed in a ragged white wedding dress, Reba made a wispy Bride of Frankenstein. "Okay, Pa, see you later."

As she opened the door, a figure passed the front of the truck dressed in black, illuminated by the still-burning truck lights. Wade recognized the assistant principal.

"Miz Bailey! Wait up," Reba said.

Maddie stopped. "Hi, there! All ready for the monster mash?"

Reba ran to Maddie's side as Wade eased open his door and approached the two females. A gust of wind caught Maddie's cape and flipped it open, exposing her décolleté to Wade's hungry eyes.

"Evenin' Miss Harris," he said as he leaned against the truck.

"Good evening, Mr. Finn. And the name is Mrs. Bailey now," Maddie replied, as she gripped closed the errant cape.

Reba said, "She married my drama teacher, Pa."

Wade chortled. "Well, ain't that romantic?"

Maddie looked down her nose at her rough-edged neighbor. "We really must be moving along. Come on, Reba, you can pick me up if I trip in this silly dress. I'd forgotten how little room there is around the ankles to take a decent step."

Wade spoke to their departing backs in his most ingratiating tone. "You go and have real good time, sister. Good seein' you, Mrs. Bailey."

Oh, yeah, he thought. It was real good seeing you, hot tits. He hadn't forgotten his night exploring her clean, sweet smelling cabin. In fact, he still had the quilt in his truck. The flower smell had greeted him for about a week whenever he entered the cab, until the stink of dog and tobacco overwhelmed it. Now Lucifer huddled on his new doggie bed in the back seat.

God, the thought of getting his hands on those brimming breasts made Wade's fingers itch and his crotch rise. Maybe he could pull a trick on Mrs. Bailey and get himself a sweet treat. If she really had married the drama teacher, she'd welcome a poke from a real man. And Wade Finn was just the man for the job. He grabbed his merchandise and ordered the dog out of the truck. Business first, and then he looked forward to a little Halloween fun with the honey-assed assistant principal.

Phil sat in the locker room utterly confused. Maddie had behaved so matter of fact about the night on the beach; acted as if they'd shared a mild picnic in the park. Damn, the woman seemed to always have his balls in a squeeze. Didn't she remember the trip to the moon?

"Hello-oo? Phil, are you there?" Pam's voice bounced off the concrete walls as she pushed the door open.

Great, just what he needed.

"Hi, honey," Pam said. Wearing a coat, cinched tight at the waist, she carried in a clothes bag. "I picked you up an outfit at the costume shop. It's just great."

"Oh, hell, I'm just going as a football coach."

"No way, Jose. You gotta have a costume. Look, this is so *you.*" She pulled off the paper to reveal a fake-fur costume. "Ta-da! You're a perfect Fred Flintstone."

She stripped off her coat and struck a pose. "And I'm Wilma!" She strutted in a circle and wiggled her fur-covered fanny.

"Not on your life."

Using baby talk, she cozied up to him. "Come on, Philly-Willy, you know Melissa will love seeing her Mommy and Daddy dressed up together."

Oh crap, she really knew how to play the Melissa card.

He grabbed the costume out of her hand. "Fine. I'll just be a minute." He went back to his office to change.

As he switched clothes, he thought again about Maddie and their bizarre conversation. And the night under the bewitching moon. His mind shifted like a kaleidoscope trying to fit all the pieces together. She'd been by the lake, alone, crying her heart out. It would be like Maddie to give over to private bursts of emotion. He'd seen that side of her a time or two.

He'd been fascinated by the vulnerable figure, utterly drawn, completely attracted. And hadn't he been just as attracted to the woman in the light of day–even covered up by her pain-in-the-ass assistant principal persona?

How could she talk of it so lightly? Had she actually been asleep and only vaguely knew what had gone on? Jesus, he wanted some answers.

Phil shrugged into the get-up and swiveled before a mirror. To be honest, he made a damn good Fred Flintstone. His wide chest and short auburn hair fit the character, but the serious glint in his eye gave old Fred a decidedly dangerous edge. He grabbed a baseball bat to act as a caveman club. Of course, his big running shoes looked a bit out of character, but he wasn't going barefoot over the sticker-filled grassy field, even for Melissa. He stepped back into the main locker room where Pam primped before a mirror.

She flapped her hands in the air. "Sweetie, you look fabulous! I knew you would. Come stand in front of the mirror with me."

He sighed and sidled next to her, staring balefully at their reflection. No magic spells appeared. Just Phil and Pam, looking like a couple of pre-historic dumb asses. Maybe they were a perfect couple. Maybe he should let the Moon Goddess go her merry way and stay with somebody in his class.

Pam slipped her arm under his. "We look good together, don't we? You know, Phil, I've always felt bad that Melissa is an only child. Having a brother or sister would give her someone all her life. Families stick together."

"What are you talking about? You haven't spoken to your sister in ten years."

Pam squinshed her nose. "She's a bitch. But, it wouldn't be like that for Melissa and another child of ours. We'd give our children a happy childhood."

Oh man, she was hinting marriage again. When had he gone from bum to bridegroom? Now, she offered another baby to sweeten the deal.

Another baby.

His mind shifted back to Maddie and the kaleidoscope whirred in his brain again. He traveled to that moonstruck August night, and as he counted the weeks, the realization of his potential paternity smashed him over the head.

Another baby.

He slapped his forehead. "I am such a friggin' idiot!"

"What's the matter?" Pam asked.

He gazed at her, heat rising in his veins as he recalled the years of fighting for every moment he spent with his daughter. The thought of another woman stealing a child away from him really burned his butt. If the lady thought she could call the shots when she carried *his* baby, she had another thing coming.

There was something called DNA testing nowadays. And, brother, did he know his way around the custody courts.

"I gotta get over to the gym right away. They expect me in the photo booth. Pictures-with-the-Coach is supposed to be a big money earner this year."

She grabbed his arm. "Melissa's going to spend the night at a girl friend's. Maybe you could come by my house after this deal is over for a special Halloween treat."

Phil peeled off her fingers. "Uh, I'm still making my way through the leftovers you sent a couple days ago."

A jagged crease formed between her eyebrows. "I wasn't talking about food, dumb shit."

"I really gotta go." The modern day caveman needed to seek out a certain honey blonde who might very well be carrying his child.

"I'll come by the booth and we can take a picture together. What do you say, Fred?"

Phil rolled his eyes as he shoved the door open. "Yabba-dabba-do."

By the time Phil arrived at the photo booth, the haunted house was packed. Randy, dressed as Harry Potter with a cape and round glasses, flitted in a dither dealing with all the anxious fans.

"Coach, thank God you're here! The natives are getting restless." He patted his hands together. "You look marvelous! Doesn't he look downright primitive, Maddie?"

Maddie, now completely garbed as Morticia with a black wig, had rounded the corner to the makeshift photography studio. A Beaver Cove scrim and an American Flag surrounded Phil with a fabulously corny Americana backdrop for pictures with hometown fans.

Seeing Phil's hairy legs topped off by the Neanderthal over-the-shoulder fur garment struck Maddie's funny bone and she hooted with laughter. "Oh, Coach, I believe you're a bit bow-legged."

Phil squinted and said through gritted teeth, "Keep it up,

sweetheart."

Randy pushed Phil into place. "Now don't get your prehistoric hackles up. Maddie, you direct the crowd and just keep them moving along. I've got to go check on the Dracula set."

Maddie took over the organization of Phil's photo booth for the next hour, arranging adoring fans around the continually scowling coach. At least he scowled every time he looked at her. He put a polite front on for total strangers, but when his attention focused on her, she could feel animosity pouring out of him. She didn't know what his problem was, but between his grumpiness, the continual canned screams, and the chemical smell from fake fog, Maddie desperately needed a break and fresh air. She grabbed the wandering axe murder victim, Stu, and put him in charge of the photo set.

When she escaped out a side door, brisk evening air filled her lungs. A bright orange harvest moon cast a pumpkin glow in the All Hallow's Eve night sky. Grateful to be several yards away from the crowded Haunted Forest trail, she found herself near the wooded edge of the gym and looked about for somewhere to sit down and rest her weary feet. Thinking she'd surely find a fallen log or large boulder in the near vicinity, she minced her way up the hill into the trees. Holding onto her wig and cape was a trick, but she managed fairly well, despite the wind that rustled through the barren branches and made whipping sounds appropriate for Halloween.

Unfortunately, the crackling forest noises hid the hushed undertones of human voices. Keeping her concentration on the ground, Maddie didn't stop walking until she saw scuffed boots and jeans come into view. She pushed dangling black hair out of her eyes and looked up to see Wade and a couple of kids standing before her. A big, black dog with yellow eyes gazed at her.

Focused on plastic baggies in the kids' hands, Maddie immediately recognized a drug deal. Angry indignation sparked fearless confrontation. "Wade Finn, I don't care if you're related to every police officer between here and

Bentonville, I am not going to allow you to come on this campus and do your dirty dealings."

The kids lit out in a flash. Wade took a moment to focus in on her. Then he smiled a big, predatory wolfish grin and began taking slow steps in her direction.

"Gosh, Miz Bailey, your timing couldn't be better. I was just ready to close up shop and come a callin' for you. I've been hankering for a real sweet piece of Halloween candy like you."

Good grief, what kind of mess had she gotten herself into this time? A rush of fear-and-flight adrenaline hit her blood stream. She turned on her heels and began running as fast as her tight dress would allow.

Wade barked, "Get her, Lucifer."

Maddie glanced over her shoulder to see the huge hound from hell rise out of the shadows and lope in her direction. *Love a duck*, as Grammy would say.

Pure panic propelled her as she bent down and pulled up the imprisoning hem of her dress as high as it would go. Her screams rang in the air, mingled with the periodic taped screams pouring through the loud speakers. The dog seemed sure of the kill and kept a steady pace with her as she zigzagged down the hill and then stumbled onto the blacktop of the parking lot. The entrance of the Haunted Forest loomed before her and she dashed for the safety of civilization.

"Help! It's going to get me!" she yelled.

People lined up to enter the out door maze moved out of her way and smiled as she entered the path. They thought her "frightened chased woman" imitation highly entertaining.

"Oh, look," one lady said. "There's even a trained dog pretending to track her down."

"Isn't that the drama teacher's new wife? This must be part of the show."

As Maddie screamed and clawed her way through the trail, Lucifer growled and bared his teeth as he closed in on her. Following the man-made tunnel of prison-like walls, Maddie began destroying the displays as she sought any obstacle that might impede the murderous canine's pursuit. She pelted him with jack-o-lanterns, bleeding heads and a life-sized cardboard likeness of Freddie Kruger. At one point, Lucifer gripped the back of her dress with his teeth, eliciting a huge yelp from her throat and a round of applause from her growing audience. Her dress ripped, freeing her legs slightly. She grabbed the annoying wig from her head and threw it in the dog's face, temporarily blinding him.

She turned to the crowd and yelled, "What is wrong with you people? Won't any of you help me?'

But seeing the now bewigged dog shaking his head was so amusing that people just laughed and Maddie took off again. Lucifer became more agitated and began a fierce barking that brought terror to her bones. The phony walls of the path offered her no protection from the demon close on her heels. Blindly, she rounded a corner straight into a massive, spider web display.

"*Ahh*!" She tore at the engulfing sticky strings.

That did it. Total panic. The dog barked and backed her into a corner. Phony, spider threads crept across her face and arms. Her breath came in sharp gasps and her head started buzzing.

"Oh God, oh God, oh God," she muttered as the world spun and went dark.

A sharp whistle followed by a crisp command silenced the dog. "Down, boy."

The obedient mongrel sat back on his haunches. His tongue hung out of his mouth as he panted for air after the big chase. He appeared to have a happy dog grin on his face.

Wade reached out and caught Maddie just as she lost consciousness and scooped her into his arms. "Show's over, folks! Ya'll have a safe drive home!"

The crowd cheered. The hero to the rescue. A redneck hero, yet. Always nice to see a good old boy painted in a positive light.

Wade's boots crunched on the rocky pavement as he carried Maddie toward his truck with the cur close at heel. The crowd clapped appreciatively as the trio disappeared into the shadows.

One spectator wasn't taken in by the show. She knew something really bad was happening. Reba turned and ran in the direction of the gym. She had to find help fast, before her Pa took Mrs. Bailey into his truck and disappeared into the hills.

Reba banged open the closest gym door, which unfortunately took her into a crowd moving the opposite direction she needed to go. She pushed and shoved people out of her way all the time yelling, "Mr. Bailey! Mr. Bailey!" She stopped three monsters to ask if they'd seen him. Finally, she rounded a corner and found herself in the well-lit photo booth where the coach and drama teacher were sharing a Kodak moment by order of principal McCall.

Reba broke in on the pose, speaking through frightened tears. "Mr. Bailey! My Pa's done taken your wife in his truck! He's been talking funny about her every time we pass her house. He's just plumb crazy nowadays and I don't know what he might do to her."

Phil and Randy exchanged a wordless communication and then Phil said, "I'll drive," and they both broke into a run.

Phil took the baseball bat for a weapon and yelled at Reba over his shoulder. "Call the police."

As the men jumped into the seats of the trusty 1981 Skylark, the truck fishtailed out of the parking lot. Fred Flintstone and Harry Potter took off in hot pursuit of the kidnapped Morticia Adams.

And the spirits of Halloween laughed in the howling autumn darkness.

Chapter Fourteen

When the hurlyburly's done,
When the battle's lost and won

Second Witch from Macbeth

Maddie came to as she jostled around the backseat of the extended cab. *Where in the world...* Light and shadow flickered across the torn vinyl seat. A heavy panting sound beside her drew her attention. She swiveled her head to see the undeniable outline of a canine sharing the back bench seat with her. She jerked back and scrunched as far away from Lucifer as possible.

He rested on his haunches and stared at her like a gargoyle from the castle in *Beauty and the Beast.* His fetid breath filled the cab with a sickening doggy stench that threatened her stomach's equilibrium. A blanket lay at her feet and she pulled it up to cover her nose and cut down on the offensive odor.

Maddie began to gather her wits and assess her situation as she forced herself to look forward and ignore the black hound. Wade's skinny neck and shaggy hair was silhouetted in the blue light. He drove with one hand casually resting on the steering wheel.

Be logical, be assertive. Don't show him you're scared.

She rested the blanket in her lap and spoke calmly into Wade's ear. "Mr. Finn, I think you've carried this joke just a little too far. There are laws against kidnapping, you know, and there's a whole school of witnesses who saw you abduct me. Now just pull into that McDonald's and let me out before this situation gets any worse."

Surely the key to bringing sanity to the moment lay in

simple reason and logic. Then she glanced into the rearview mirror and met Wade's crazed stare. His eyes nearly twirled in their sockets. He smiled a jack-o-lantern grin.

I've been abducted by the Hillbilly from Hell.

Wade's gaze seemed to glow red with evil. Hopped-up nervous lunacy rattled his voice. "We're going to a special place I know. It's so deep in the hills a pack of coon dogs couldn't find us, let alone a bunch of dumbass cops. You're going to be my private guest for our personal Halloween party. Yessiree, Wade is gettin' some tonight! You ain't never been fucked until you've been fucked by Wade Finn. I've seen the way you look at me. You want it *bad*."

Maddie's eyes widened indignantly. "What! I certainly don't want you in any way, shape or form. You're severely mistaken, Mr. Finn. Now, I am ordering you this very moment to stop this vehicle and let me disembark."

Wade laughed in demented delight. "Shit, I love the way you talk with all them big, fancy words. I can't hardly wait to hear the long words you'll use when I'm screwing your brains out."

Frustrated beyond fear, Maddie began slapping the back of Wade's head. "Stop... and...let me out!"

Wade jerked his head to get away from her assaults as Lucifer sprang into action. His loud barks blasted the inside of the cab as he thrust his hot body upon Maddie and forced her against the side of the truck.

"*Grrrr*," the dog growled in her ear as he held her pinned beneath him.

Maddie emitted a high-pitched plea. "Please get him off of me!"

"Sit, Lucifer," Wade ordered in a guttural tone. "If you try that shit again, I'll let him tear your fuckin' throat out. You got that, teacher lady? Now lean back and enjoy the ride. I think we got us some company, so we're gonna have us a game of chicken." He emitted a country whoop. "Damn, this is my lucky night."

With that, Wade swerved the truck, tossing Maddie

against the hard side again. She moaned and pulled the blanket about her for protection.

Suddenly, Grammy's face appeared in the window. "Don't worry, I'll take care of this pissant."

Oh great, Maddie thought, what a time to *completely* crack up.

Phil slammed on his brakes to keep from hurtling over the side of the mountain road when Wade swerved the truck, trying to run them off the road.

"Son of a bitch!"

He stomped on the accelerator again, determined to keep the truck in his sights. The lights of Beaver Cove disappeared behind them as they headed out of the valley onto the curvy mountain road.

Randy spoke up. "I'm sure I saw her in the back seat and I think there's a dog back there with her."

"Great," Phil said as he took a fast turn. "She's scared to death of dogs."

"How do you know that? She doesn't share her weaknesses with just everybody."

"I've got news for you, pal. I know a lot more about her than you ever imagined. In fact, I think your wife is having my baby."

Randy's eyes popped behind his Harry Potter glasses. "What?"

"That's right, buddy. I'm the guy that walked off with her quilt last summer."

Wade kept an eye on the rearview mirror, figuring a way to lose his pursuers.

"Those jerkoffs think they can keep up with me, but I'm gonna lose 'em, just you wait and see. Nobody can handle a rig like Wade Finn. So, just wrap up cozy-like in your pretty quilt and sit tight. You do recognize it, don't you? Since I grabbed it out of your bedroom, I've imagined the two of us lyin' on it and doin' you good."

His words crashed in Maddie's brain as if he'd bludgeoned her with a club. Had she understood him correctly? She slowly lifted the edge of the blanket against the cab window and tried to get a better look at its detail. Her fingers traced the outlined stitches of a homemade quilt. At that moment a beam of yellow moonlight illuminated the material in her hands, causing it to mysteriously glow, and she unequivocally recognized Grammy's quilt stolen from her bedroom.

"Oh my God, *you* were the intruder in my house? You stood in my bedroom and ran your dirty fingers across my comforter and photographs?"

She imagined a slimy trail left behind like snail residue marking a clean window. He'd probably dropped vermin in his wake. "I'm calling an exterminator the minute I get home."

The truck jerked wildly as Wade yelled, "Hee-ha! Take that, assholes!"

Maddie attempted to sit upright in the swaying cab as Wade's revelation swirled in her mind. "Wait a minute. Phil told me *he* took the quilt. If *you* took the quilt, then how could…"

Maddie's attention was drawn to the full orange moon that appeared to be following them across the autumn sky. She blinked as a grinning jack-o-lantern face materialized on the surface of the sphere. "OH…MY…GOD!"

The summer night came back to her in sharp detail. She'd felt utterly wretched, lonely beyond description. The sentimental movies, the wine, and chocolate had only served to deepen her mood. When the moon called her toward the lake, her body and soul ached for relief and fulfillment. *Come to me*, he'd whispered. Every fiber in her being yearned for contact and comfort. She must have drifted into a fitful, teary sleep on the quilt because she remembered dreaming of Thomas and suddenly being in his arms. Then the image of Thomas shifted into someone else. The smell was different, so much better. His feel so different, so much warmer. And his touch, oh Lord, his touch inflamed and soothed her at the same time. Yes! She'd longed for this passion to end her lonely torture. *Come on, Dream Man, fly me to the moon.* And he did, beyond her wildest imaginings. The unity had been physical, emotional and spiritual, an all-encompassing life-altering event buried in her subconscious until this moment of awakening.

Maddie focused again on the mischievous moon, whose face appeared to be laughing at his own cosmic prank. "Think you're pretty funny, don't you?"

She shook her head in amazement. The attraction in the light of day had been almost as strong as the midnight encounter, but she'd been utterly blind. It had been Phil all along.

Phil was the Dream Man.

Randy whipped off his fake glasses. "Let me get this straight. You took the quilt from the beach last summer and you broke into her house two weeks ago and made off with another one? What are you doing? Starting a collection?"

Phil pressed the accelerator as far as it could go, but the sharp incline of the road stressed the car's engine and the truck pulled farther away from them. "Shit…What the hell are you talking about? I've never broken into her house. I'm not some damned pervert thief."

"I told her it didn't sound in character to me, but she convinced herself you were the culprit." Randy banged his elbow into the car door as they took a wild curve. "Ow! I hope your insurance is paid up."

Phil tapped his fingers on the steering wheel. "Okay, this is actually beginning to make a little sense to me. Some joker breaks into her place, makes off with her quilt and she automatically thinks I've gone off the deep end and did the deed. That explains all the comments about cat burglars, sneak thieves, and kleptomaniacs. It also brings her speech in the locker room tonight into focus. Randy, I've gotta know. *Am* I the father of Maddie's baby?"

Randy sighed. "If you're the Dream Man, then, yeah, you're the guy." He went into a Perry Mason persona. "Where were you on the night of August 26th from approximately two to four am, Coach Wilcox?"

Phil's memory darted back to that incredible night, even as his eyes stayed on the road. "I was in the arms of a Moon Goddess on a sandy lake beach."

Flapping his hands in resignation, Randy said, "Well, heck, there goes my shot at fatherhood. I guess I'll have to settle for 'Uncle Randy.'"

The truck lights disappeared behind a hillside bend in the road. "Damn," Phil muttered. "So someone broke into her house and took a quilt. Did he take anything else?"

"No, only the quilt. That's why she thought it was you and not a real thief. She couldn't think of anyone else who might be interested in just taking a memento."

Phil grunted. "Well, I'd wager the whacko driving the truck is your man. Christ, the way this guy drives, he must be completely nuts. And the way Maddie talks, she'll be making him even nuttier. We can't let them get out of sight."

When they made it around three more winding twists in the road, a long expanse of highway lay before them exposing a clear view into the distance.

The truck had completely disappeared.

Maddie gasped as Wade cut a sudden left and bounced off the main highway unto an unpaved country road. She splayed her arms wide and spread her fingers against the window and the back of her seat.

"Good grief! You're a complete lunatic!"

Adrenaline rushed through Wade's system and the earlier drugs made him higher than a kite. He felt like the king of the world. "We're almost there, baby! It won't be long before those creamy tits are in my hands. Jeez, I'm getting a boner harder than concrete."

Maddie looked out the window and, to her dismay, saw they were heading deep into the hills on the rutted road. The earlier winding race was a day in the park compared to the insane bouncing speed Wade maneuvered over washouts and fallen limbs. She moaned as she banged around the cab, alternately hitting against Lucifer, the back of the front seat, and the hard truck interior wall.

The dog didn't enjoy the ride, either, and began to whimper. In an amazing switch of mood, the fierce guard dog turned into a helpless pup and plopped his big body across her lap. Their combined weights actually stabilized their movement somewhat. Maddie jammed into the corner with the heavy dog keeping her bottom and legs in place. She patted the big black head and found his fur actually comforting.

Oh my, this night is certainly making strange bedfellows. She stared at the back of Wade's head and knobby shoulder blades. *I'd better figure out a way to avoid becoming his bedfellow.*

Phil banged the steering wheel. "Shit!"

Randy gazed into the empty yawning expanse. "They must have gone off the road somewhere."

Phil stomped the brakes and made a quick u-turn. "Yeah, but where? Keep your eyes out for a turn off."

The brush and hillsides raced beside them as they retraced their tracks. Phil fought to keep down the rising feeling of panic. If that son of a bitch hurt Maddie, he would break his neck. Hell, he would break his friggin' neck no matter what. The sides of the road seemed impenetrable. Where had they gone? He sent up a prayer. *Please, God, help me find her.*

Suddenly, the atmosphere changed. The air took on an odd florescent yellowish hue and straight out of the sky, like a beam from an episode of *Star Trek*, a shimmering tunnel of light illuminated a small turn-off to a path into the hills. Without questioning the supernatural direction, Phil aimed the car for the rocky path and accelerated on the unpaved road.

The men endured the bronco-busting ride in grim silence, punctuated now and then by a groan from Randy. Phil hoped the car would hold together and not bust an axle, gas line, or some other equally vital mechanical part. The magical light disappeared, leaving them in forested darkness. Trees hovered over them, scraping the car's hood and sides as it jostled along the path. They drove on and on until it felt like they must be traveling to the end of the world.

Randy finally spoke. "Are you sure we're on the right road?"

Phil clenched his jaw. "It better be. It has to be."

Then, Phil was forced stop the car. He'd run out of straight road and reached a fork, one heading uphill, the other down. God, which one should he take? No magic light appeared this time to lead the way.

"Damn it all! Which way should I go?"

As if hearing his plea, a human figure appeared out of the shadows into the beam of his headlights. It was a woman, an old country woman dressed in a long dress and shawl.

Randy's voice registered shock. "It's Grammy."

"Who?"

"Grammy Harris, Maddie's grandmother."

"I thought she was dead."

"She is."

The men's eyes locked momentarily in chilling wonder, then turned back to the ghostly figure before them. Grammy's bony arm raised and her hand definitely pointed in the uphill direction. Phil cut his wheels to the right and gave the car the gas. He saluted Grammy's wavering form even as she disappeared into the ether.

"I may have a slug of whiskey when this is all over," Phil said.

"I may join you," Randy replied.

The uphill road turned even steeper and twistier, if that could be imagined. The bottom of the car began to hit larger rocks that grew into boulders requiring Phil to exhibit intricate navigational skill. Trees became sparser as they entered rockier terrain. As they wound up the path, the top of the hill came into view. Silhouetted high above them they could see the outline of a parked truck.

"I think that's it," Phil said.

In the moment he took he eyes off the road, the Skylark made a sickening crunch into a jagged outcropping of granite that pierced the under carriage and ripped the gas line to shreds. The car refused to budge another inch.

Phil pushed open his car door and grabbed the baseball bat. He made tracks in his Fred Flintstone costume up the steep incline. He dimly registered the sound of Randy's opening door and movement behind him. Phil's prehistoric instincts took over and he became a hunter seeking prey. His strong calves bulged as he took long strides up toward the pinnacle. As the top came into clearer view, he saw a cluster of huge boulders and rocky ledges. Pewter light played tricks on the eyes. He'd been around the Arkansas hills all his life and he knew the appearance of solid rock could be an illusion. Secret passages and hidden caves undoubtedly lay hidden in the mountain's interior. He'd need another boost of supernatural help to discern which path to take when he got to the top.

Then he heard the unmistakable sound of his true love's voice echo across the hills. "Really, Mr. Finn, I'm not dressed for this kind of excursion!"

Maddie's knees and shins were a mass of bruises from falling along the stony path to Wade's intended love nest, a hunter's cabin nestled at the end of a long tunnel through the mountain. Wade held one of her hands in a strong grip as he held onto his shotgun with his other hand. Lucifer followed along like a true Hound of the Baskervilles. Maddie tripped and skipped and skidded in her little black pumps and torn black dress, resisting every step along the way.

"I implore you to reconsider this course of action." Her voice echoed against the walls of the tunnel. "The authorities are bound to catch up with you and the punishment you receive will be much more severe if I'm seriously injured."

"I promise you, baby, you're going to love it!" He mercilessly dragged her along.

"I just don't see how that is possible when you totally revolt me. I find you disgusting, repugnant, and utterly undesirable." She gasped for air. "In other words, Mr. Finn, I don't like you!"

He suddenly stopped his relentless tugging and she crashed into him. He let go of her hand, whipped around, and grabbed her chin with punishing fingers. "I don't give a fuck if you like me or not. I've been nice to you, but the truth is, all I want is your sweet piece of ass under my bones and I'm getting sick of your smart mouth. Now shut the fuck up and keep walking or I'll tear that dress off you right here and screw you on the cold cave floor."

Phil rounded a sharp stone corner of the passage to see the dark outline of Maddie facing her captor. Relief washed over him to see her in one piece. Anger quickly followed as he glimpsed the mangy Wade Finn gripping Maddie's face. The moonlit opening of the tunnel behind them lay only a few feet away.

Phil took steady, strong strides toward the pair. "Let her go, asshole. The party's over."

Wade's head swung in the direction of the intruder. He pushed Maddie aside and quickly lifted the shotgun toward Phil's approaching figure.

"No!" she yelled and shoved his arm just as he squeezed off a round. The shot went wild and ricocheted off the jagged rock walls.

"Run, sweetheart," Phil shouted.

Maddie tripped backwards until she felt the damp, stone wall against her back. Her open palms scraped the cutting granite edges. Mixed emotions held her in place. Part of her wanted to run for safety and leave her kidnapper far behind. But she couldn't leave Phil at the mercy of a madman. She'd never forgive herself for taking a coward's flight if Wade proved the winner of the coming battle. She watched Phil's body dive for the ground and roll as Wade got off another blast from the shotgun.

She screamed and covered her ears. Phil lay flat on his back. *Oh, God, don't let him be dead.* He rolled and sprang to his feet. She sagged with relief.

Wade crouched, took aim, and squeezed the trigger again,

but his double barrel shotgun proved to be empty. "Fuck!"

Phil lifted the baseball bat still enclosed in his hand and with the precision that comes from years of passing a football to his receiver, he sent the bat shooting through the air like a guided missile to a designated target.

The end of the bat hit Wade hard in the belly and he doubled over in pain and fury. He looked up to see a burly caveman barreling down on him and turned on his booted heels in a hunched run toward the cave opening.

The two figures passed by Maddie onto the open plateau. Lucifer dashed in their wake, ready to join the fray. Maddie bent down and picked up the baseball bat that had rolled to her feet. She wasn't about to stay out of the action now.

By the time she managed to get into the open on her little black shoes, the opponents were engaged in full hand-to-hand combat. Lucifer circled the battling duo, growling and barking and generally adding to the chaos. Phil got off a strong hook to Wade's chin, but took a dirty kick in the knee. Phil lunged on his good leg and knuckled Wade in the gut. Grunts and cuss words cut through the other sounds of punches hitting bone and tissue.

A winded Wade backed away, faced the dog, and ordered, "Get him, boy!"

Terror struck Maddie's heart when the hulking figure of the killer beast rose in the air. His sharp teeth gleamed in the moonlight as his body slammed into Phil.

Maddie screamed and pitched herself into the battle. Raising the bat in her hand, she gave the dog a good strong whack, getting his attention, but good. He immediately turned his yellow eyes on his attacker and assumed a killer stance. But this time, Maddie overcame her lifelong fear. She stood her ground and stared back into the creature's fathomless depths.

"Oh no, you don't," she said. "Sit, Lucifer!"

"*Grrrr*," Lucifer replied.

Wade's breathy voice issued another command. "I said get 'em, boy!"

His order went unheeded as Maddie and Lucifer engaged in a dog to woman battle of wills. They circled each other in a manner reminiscent of Sumo wrestlers beginning a match.

"I'm not afraid of you," she said. "Now sit your black butt down before I give you another taste of this bat. I don't believe in animal cruelty, but I'll make an exception in your case." With total bravado, Maddie walked to her nemesis until her thigh was just inches from his nose. "I said, *sit*, and I mean it."

Now nearly eyeball to eyeball, the human and canine came to an understanding. Lucifer whimpered and flopped over on his back, the doggy version of surrender.

Maddie smiled triumphantly and reached down to pat his stomach. "Good boy."

Phil watched this exchange as he rose to his feet and caught his breath. He shook his head in wonder and disbelief. Then he heard the sound of running footsteps dashing away and realized Wade was making a break for it. A fresh surge of adrenaline hit Phil's blood stream. No way would he let the psycho escape. He took a large breath of fortifying air and dashed after him.

"You're not going anywhere, you bastard." Phil sprinted up the hill.

Maddie looked up to see the men running off again. Lord, she was getting tired and her feet throbbed in the unsuitable shoes. She longed for her comfortable *Nikes*. She lifted her constricting dress and took up the chase again.

Running up the rocky incline, she skidded to a stop to watch the men renew their struggle. Phil grabbed Wade from behind and punched him in the gut. They fought on the edge of a cliff near boulders jutting from the mountain. In the ghostly moonlight, the rocks seemed like stone sentinels observing the fracas. Maddie hovered nearby, watching, praying, wishing she could help, but afraid she'd only get in the way. Lucifer sat at her side.

Oh, please, God, help Phil.

Wade, wild-eyed and mean, kicked and spewed expletives. Her heart caught in her throat as Phil and Wade grappled at the edge of the plateau. They struggled on the jagged ledge beside a sudden drop-off. Back and forth, each seeming to momentarily have the winning edge.

Phil had engaged in his share of barroom brawls, but he'd never fought a hyped-up crazy-ass druggie before. Wade came at him with frenzied madman strength. He kicked and punched with furious speed. Phil grunted as he took a shot to the kidneys.

Wade laughed in dementia. "Come on, Caveman, get another taste of Wade Finn. I'll leave you for vulture meat and then I'm going to screw her lily-white ass blue."

Phil saw red. He charged Wade with football player might. "There won't be any working parts left on you, pal."

Ignoring Wade's wild punches, Phil systemically beat the tar of him. Weeks of working with a punching bag paid off, as he found his rhythm on his opponent. *Pow, pow, pow.*

Wade jerked away from Phil's assault. Oblivious to pain, he picked up a boulder and lifted it high. Stumbling toward Phil, he tried to crash it on the coach's head. Phil dodged the deadly stone and executed a hard blow to Wade's jaw. The power of the blow and the weight of the rock sent Wade stumbling backward over the precipice onto the jagged protrusions below. His scream filled the air.

Then silence. It was finished.

Phil bent over and placed his hands on his thighs, taking huge gulps of air. Maddie trotted to him in a limping run, her new canine follower close by.

"Phil, oh my God, Phil, are you all right?"

He straightened up slowly. "Yeah, I think so."

She threw herself into his arms. "I was so frightened. You could have been killed!"

His hands traveled up and down her body and then cupped the back of her head. "How about you? Are you hurt?"

She'd begun to tremble from post-trauma letdown. "I'm fine, really."

He looked deep into her eyes. "You're sure? How's our baby?"

A shock of electricity ran down her spine, but only a whisper issued from her throat. "You know."

"Oh, yeah, cupcake. See, I'm the guy that took that first quilt and that loser down there is the creep that took the second one."

She laid her forehead on his warm chest. "I know that now. Oh, Phil this has been such a confusing night. Please, can we go home?"

Just then, Wade must have regained consciousness because he started cussing a blue streak and yelling that his leg was busted. Phil walked to the edge of the cliff and told him they would call for help.

Now with the excitement winding down, Maddie's legs turned to jelly and the familiar urge to burst into tears rose to the surface.

Phil returned to Maddie's side. "Let's get out of here." They took about three steps down the hill when Maddie's legs gave out. She stumbled and nearly fell to her knees. In true he-man style, Phil lifted her off her feet and continued moving toward the mountain's secret passage. In the distance they could hear sirens coming closer. Phil had almost reached the cave when Reba came running from its mouth, her white dress appearing ghostly in the dim light.

"Mr. Wilcox! Mrs. Bailey! Praise the Lord that you're all right!"

Phil halted and set Maddie down. "Reba," Maddie said. "How did you find us?"

"I called the police like Coach Wilcox told me. I figured Pa would head for his hunting cabin so I rode with them here. The officers are coming behind me. They've called a medivac helicopter."

Maddie spoke up. "I don't need any medical attention, but I'm afraid your father does."

"I wasn't talking about Pa. They've called one for Mr. Bailey. He's been shot."

Chapter Fifteen

It ain't over 'til it's over.

Yogi Berra

Phil ducked as the helicopter rose above the craggy hilltop, sending a wake of windy turbulence. Leaves and dust choked him as he watched the copter wing out of sight carrying Maddie, his unborn child, and Randy to a trauma center in Little Rock.

Maddie had rushed out of his arms to the side of her wounded husband. Beaver Cove's drama teacher had lain on the cold cave floor losing blood as battle raged in the Halloween night. A wild shot from Wade's gun had hit Randy in the upper chest. The last Phil had seen of Maddie, she'd been running alongside Randy's stretcher, fear reflected in her wide eyes. He couldn't resist giving her one more reassuring hug before helping her into the helicopter.

Now Phil stood answering questions among a swarm of police and rescue workers as a crew worked at retrieving Wade from the rocks below the cliff. Phil gazed around the scene and glimpsed Reba standing at the edge of the plateau observing the progress of the rescuers. Slow tears tracked down her cheeks. She swiped them away with the back of her hand. He walked to her willowy figure and wrapped a comforting arm around her shoulders.

"I'm sorry about your father," he said.

"At least he's alive." She sniffed. "A worker told me they're stabilizing him."

In the heat of anger, Phil had wanted to kill the guy. Now, in a more reasonable mindset, he felt relieved he hadn't caused a man's death, even a jackass like Wade Finn.

Reba shivered as she leaned into him. "Drugs have turned him mean crazy, like a mad dog."

Wade's broken body was carried up on a stretcher. Semi-conscious, he managed to cuss out the medics. As Phil watched Wade being loaded onto an ambulance, he thought, *but for the grace of God, there go I.* If he'd kept on with the booze, added the haze of drugs, he might be just as whacked-out and destructive.

Reba trembled under his protective arm. "I knew something bad was coming and I couldn't do nothin' about it. Now Pa's hurt hisself and maybe killed Mr. Bailey. I should have stopped him somehow."

Phil gently turned her to face him. "Listen, kid, take it from someone who's learned the hard way. Your Dad is responsible for his actions, not you. He's going to have to face the consequences. You did your best to alert us when he drove off with Mrs. Bailey. And you led the police up here. If it weren't for you, Mr. Bailey would probably have bled to death."

"I hope to God those doctors can save him." Reba sagged, exhausted from the night's chaos.

"Let's get you home, kid."

Reba nodded. "Mama's going to have the shivering fits when she hears what happened."

A cop, who turned out to be Ginger's cousin, drove Reba and Phil to the ramshackle Finn stronghold. The cousin cop told Reba to expect a thorough visit from the police in the morning.

Reba nodded in full understanding. "Guess me and Mama better clean house tonight." In other words, all traces of drugs would be destroyed.

Phil had himself dropped off at the high school where he found Maddie's purse and clothing. After changing out of his costume, he got in the Camry and took off for Little Rock.

He reached the hospital around three a.m. and found the

ICU wing. As he pushed open the beige doors, Phil's gaze traveled across the units of glass walled rooms. His search ended when he recognized Maddie wearing a hospital gown over her torn Halloween costume. A stranger stood beside her at Randy's bedside holding the patient's hand. Phil approached the doorway.

As he entered the room, Randy's weak voice reached him. "I finally got to play a great dying scene and nobody was there to see it."

"I take it he's going to make it," Phil said.

Maddie's expression registered obvious relief when she saw him. "Phil, thank God."

She looked so wan, so exhausted he immediately opened his arms in invitation, which she accepted. She leaned into him and sighed.

Phil glanced at Randy's reclining figure and the unfamiliar friend. "I heard there was a party going on in here and I didn't want to miss out on the fun."

Maddie pulled away from him and managed a small smile. "Phil, this is Brent Farnsworth. Phil Wilcox."

Brent nodded. "Ah, the celebrity coach. You've been making headlines even in the Little Rock paper."

Phil grunted. "Yeah? Must have been a slow news day. So, how's he doing?"

"He's lost a lot of blood and has shattered bones and tissue. Fortunately the bullet went high and didn't involve the heart or lungs. He's going to be all right."

Randy spoke again. "Get her out of here, Coach. She looks worse than I do. And that outfit hurts my eyes."

Phil looked down at Maddie, noting her bedraggled face and hair. Besides the hospital gown over Morticia's shredded dress, she wore green paper shoes on her bare feet. "He has a point. Let's blow this joint."

Maddie appeared torn between duty and exhaustion. "But..."

"I'll stay here with him," Brent said.

Maddie nodded. "All right. I'll be back in the morning."

As they walked down the hospital corridor Phil asked, "Who was that guy?"

"Brent? I think he's the love of my husband's life."

"You have a very strange marriage. Do you know what I think you need?"

"A bath?"

"An annulment."

They stopped at a Wal-Mart where Phil purchased toiletries, a nightgown for Maddie, and various other necessities of life. When they arrived at a Best Western motel, Phil considered his options at the check-in desk. He could go for separate rooms, but he didn't want to leave Maddie alone. A king-size bed seemed like a presumption, so he ordered a room with two beds. He also purchased two bags of peanuts and three candy bars out of a vending machine.

Maddie seemed nearly incoherent as he guided her into the room. It smelled of cleaning fluid and fake potpourri. He threw the key on the dresser and noted the faded floral spreads on the beds. At least the joint looked clean. Maddie hovered at the door, seemingly unable to decide what to do next. He led her toward the bathroom door.

"Take a shower, you'll feel better," he said, as he dumped the Wal-Mart bag beside the bathtub.

She nodded numbly and began fumbling with the strings of the hospital gown. He watched it drift to the floor. Seeing the battered dress under it made him angry all over again at what that maniac had put her through.

"Turn around," he ordered.

Obediently, woodenly, she complied. He undid the zipper and then gave her some privacy in the bathroom. He laid back on a fully made bed, hands locked behind his head. What a helluva night. Bedlam and babies.

Maddie emerged from the bathroom with a towel twisted on her head like a turban. Dressed in the soft pink cotton gown he'd purchased, she reminded him of cotton candy.

"Feeling better?" He lifted up on one elbow, chin resting

on a palm.

Nodding her head, she said, "Much, but I can't seem to put two thoughts together."

"You need to hit the sack. I'm going to take a shower. Try to go to sleep."

Maddie moved toward the bed and yanked the towel off her wet hair. She threw it on the table in an uncharacteristic gesture of messiness.

"Need the hair dryer?" he asked.

"Please."

He brought her the dryer and brush and stood a moment studying her back as she sat on the bed going through the motions of drying her hair. He wondered if she had any idea how beautiful she looked to him right now, watching the graceful sweep of her arm repeating the fluid motion over and over through her clean hair. Her shapeless gown only allowed a hint of the form beneath and he felt a surge of protectiveness that he'd only previously experienced for Melissa. Never in his life had one woman aroused such a varied range of emotions in him.

These past few weeks since she'd disappeared during their weekend getaway, he'd been so damn mad at her, he'd spent hours pounding out his frustrations into a punching bag. Tonight when he'd lost sight of the truck he'd known real fear. Fear as palpable and terrible as a stab in the heart. Later, pure joy and relief flooded his being when she'd limped into his arms on top of that Ozark mountain. The woman was his personal emotional roller coaster.

When he stepped out of the steamy bathroom a few minutes later clad in good old sweats, the lights were out, but the curtains were opened wide to reveal the waning moon and stars. The outline of her body raised the covers in the bed closest to the window. A feminine scent now filled the air. She lay too quiet to be asleep. He walked around to the space between their beds and pulled back his comforter.

Needing to touch her, he turned and placed a hand on her shoulder. "Good night. Wake me if you want anything."

Her voice came out in a high-pitched squeak. "Okay." Two small, uncontrolled contractions of her shoulders jerked under his fingers.

"Oh, man. Are you crying?"

"No," she said in a sob.

He sat on her bed. As she rolled into a tight ball with her back to him he said, "Come on, I can spot a crying woman a mile away." He stroked her soft, freshly cleaned hair. "What's wrong?"

Maddie turned over and looked up at him, the tears turning into a real downpour. "I'm just so tired and confused. This has been such a crazy night. First, I was angry at that rotten drug dealer and then I was scared by his beastly dog and then I was angry when I couldn't get out of the truck." She scooted back and sat up against the headboard. "And when Wade said *he'd* taken the quilt that I was so sure *you'd* taken, I couldn't make sense of it." He handed her a tissue. She dabbed her eyes and then twisted and shredded it as she talked. "Oh Lord, that's when I fear I must have gone out of my mind, because I hallucinated I saw Grammy and…the man on the moon turned into a jack-o-lantern!"

She leaned into him and whispered as if imparting a terrible secret. "I haven't told anyone about this before, but I've been seeing Grammy for some time. She just pops out of nowhere and gives me a piece of her mind. I've tried to ignore her, but she won't go away. And the truth is, I don't really want her to leave. I'm hanging on to my delusion. Do you think I'm mentally ill? Should I commit myself somewhere?"

Phil smiled. "Well, then I'll be right there with you. And so will Randy. We both saw your Grammy tonight. She showed us where you'd gone."

Her eyes glistened in the blue light. "Really? You mean Grammy is an actual ghost?" She heaved a big sigh. "Oh, what a relief."

"Yeah, we saw some other strange things tonight, too. So, let's just chalk it up to Halloween and not worry too much about being crazy."

He wiped some tears from her cheeks with his thumb. "What else is bothering you?"

She sighed heavily. "It all came back to me–that night last summer, I mean. I'd kind of buried it and made up a fantasy about the baby being a sort of Immaculate Conception." A choked laugh rose from Phil's chest, but she continued on in agitation. "Oh, Phil do you think of me as some kind of a pathetic sex-starved spinster having anonymous intercourse with a total stranger?"

He cupped her face with his hands. "Do you want to know how I remember that night? It was great, like something out of a dream. I was in the arms of a Moon Goddess and I didn't come back to find her because I didn't think reality could live up to the illusion. But I was wrong. You're better than any illusion I could dream up. You're a brave, beautiful, smart woman." Dropping his hands from her face, he leaned back. "But, maybe I should be apologizing for taking advantage of you in a vulnerable moment. Should I have just turned around and left that night, Maddie?"

"No!" She placed her hand on his chest. "I said I remembered it all and I did. It was wonderful. Magical. Moments out of time and space, better than any fantasy I could ever have imagined."

With a small smile on his lips he said, "So, what's the problem?"

"It's just come as such a shock, to discover you're the baby's father. I can't quite put it together in my mind."

He pulled away from her as his old feelings of inadequacy bubbled to the surface. "You're not sure you like the idea, is that it? It's one thing to have a hot night in the moonlight. But finding out an alcoholic, broken-down football player is the father of your baby comes as a nasty surprise."

She sat up indignantly. "I never said such a thing! I never thought such a thing. You really need to do something about your self esteem."

He shot her a heavy-lidded scowl. "Thank you, Dr. Laura."

"Look, I realize I've offended you in some way, but I assure you it's been entirely unintentional."

Phil stood and paced the small room. "Offended me? You've completely pissed me off! First, you leave me itching like a son of a bitch in that damn cabin without a word of explanation. Then the next thing I know you've upped and married another guy. A gay guy at that! Yeah, that's done a lot for my 'self-esteem,' as you put it." He walked to the window and stared out over the blinking skyline. "The thing is, I thought there was something happening between us. Something special. Something real. But you weren't honest with me. You didn't trust me enough to tell me the truth."

He turned and looked at her, his eyes boring into her soul. She sat against the pillows, chewing her quivering lip. Her eyes pooled with fresh tears.

Her voice was barely audible as she helplessly shook her head and wrung her hands. "I'm…I'm…sorry. What do you want me to say? I'm *sorry*, okay? These past few weeks haven't been easy for me, either. In fact…they've been dreadful!"

She gave in to the dammed tears, turned on her stomach, and sunk into the pillows. Feminine weepy noises filled the room.

Phil watched her shoulders contract and jerk. *Total female waterworks. How can a guy cope with that?*

He ran his fingers through his hair, sighed deeply, and groaned, "Oh, shit."

Five hours later, they were back at Randy's bedside, now in a private room. Maddie had urged Brent to go home, freshen up, and get something to eat. Brent had given Randy a shave and his color looked much better. She'd been terrified by his deathly pale countenance and bluish lips the night before.

She settled into a chair noting the comfort of the sweats Phil had bought her at Wal-Mart. Maybe the man was onto something. She glanced up at Phil, who looked as out-of-place as a cowboy at a coronation.

"Phil, isn't there something you need to do? Gas up the car? Buy a newspaper? I'd love a decaf latte with extra cream."

Phil raised an eyebrow at Randy. "I think she's trying to get rid of me."

Randy's eyes regained a glimmer of their usual twinkle. "It looks that way."

Phil shrugged. "All right, I'll get lost for a while. Anything else you'd like?"

"A breakfast yogurt with blueberries would be lovely."

He rolled his eyes. "Figures. I'll be back."

Maddie turned to Randy after watching Phil's broad back exit the room. "So, how are you, really?"

"Sore, but mostly glad to be alive. I'll tell you, dear heart, lying in a cave as you bleed to death really causes you to examine your life." His expression turned uncharacteristically serious. "It made me realize I've been a coward in certain areas."

Maddie lifted an eyebrow. "Brent, for instance?"

As they'd been airlifted from the mountain, Randy had been urgent about reaching Brent. In his weakened state, he'd repeated Brent's cell number until Maddie memorized it and promised she'd call when they touched ground. He lost consciousness as soon as she satisfied his request.

Randy nodded and took her hand. "I may be taking a stick of dynamite to my life, but it's something I have to do. I've been running away from who I am for a long time. Keeping so busy, always putting on a clown's face. I'm sick of it."

Maddie smiled in commiseration. "Keeping up a façade can be so tiring, can't it?" She suddenly saw an image of herself decked out in an assistant principal power outfit and realized she and Randy had both been playing out public roles while their true inner selves had been choking. No wonder she occasionally flipped out and he disappeared for days at a time.

Maddie knew that Randy coming out of the closet and taking Brent as his partner would seriously jeopardize his teaching position. And she shuddered to think the hell Mother

Bailey would raise.

Squeezing his hand, she said, "Sometimes you just have to take a leap of faith and follow your heart."

"Such a wise woman. I'm wondering if you follow your own advice?"

Maddie stared down at their joined hands. "Some things are easier said than done." Her emotions regarding Phil remained a confusing Mulligan stew.

Randy asked, "Have you got a mirror and comb on you? I feel a disheveled mess."

Maddie searched her purse and found the necessary items. She held up the mirror, as Randy could only move one arm.

"Oh, God," Randy said. "Getting shot really plays hell with your complexion. I'm absolutely ashen."

"You're absolutely alive. Brent obviously thought you looked better or he would never have left your side for even a little while. I was quite impressed with him last night. He took charge while I was a blithering idiot."

"Have I told you what he does for a living?" Randy asked, as he neatly parted his hair and combed it into place.

"No. Let me guess. Financial advisor? Undertaker?"

"Close. He's a lawyer."

"Ah."

He dropped the comb in his lap and leaned back again onto the raised bed. "You know, honey bunch, I'm afraid I'm not really husband material after all and it appears you've found your Dream Man. The Coach seemed exceedingly interested in the true paternity of your bambino. In light of all that, I've asked Brent to arrange for an annulment." He lifted a hand and went into a soap opera character. "Now, now, no tears. You know it's for the best. You'll get over me. In time."

Maddie smiled. "Never."

Putting on his Ronald Coleman voice, he said *"Tis a far, far better thing I do now than I have ever done before."*

"That's too easy. *A Tale of Two Cities*."

"Well, I've been shot. What do you expect? You come up with one."

And so the soon-to-be *former* Mr. and Mrs. Randall Bailey played Name That Line until Mr. Bailey's Significant Other returned.

A clear azure sky domed above them as Phil and Maddie drove back to Beaver Cove. Their conversation had been perfunctory since they'd gotten up. Fatigue still muddled her brain. Phil's bloodshot eyes revealed his exhaustion. They needed to talk–but later. She ate her yogurt and thanked God the morning sickness seemed to be over.

"How are you feeling?" Phil asked, as if he could read her mind.

"Fine."

"Because if you're going to throw up or anything, I wanna know about it. And there's the last rest stop with bathrooms coming up for twenty-five miles. Should I pull over?"

Maddie blinked in amazement. His concern for her comfort surprised her, even delivered in his left-handed fashion. "I'm fine."

"I've been around expectant women before."

"I'm sure you have."

A few miles of road sped under their tires before Phil spoke again. "So, how do you feel about it–the baby, I mean?"

Maddie swallowed. The baby still remained largely her secret. Once the initial excitement had worn off for Randy, he'd gone back to business-as-usual. And even though Phil had guessed, she hadn't gone public with the news. Now, after weeks of wishing for someone to share her private miracle, she didn't know where to begin.

"I'm fine with it."

"Dammit, woman, talk to me!" He flashed her an exasperated glance. "Most women won't shut up and you're sitting there like a by-God clam."

"Don't yell at me unless you want me crying like a leaky faucet again. I seem to have an interminable supply of tears these days." She took a deep breath and looked at the scenery whizzing by. "How do I feel about the baby? Thrilled, okay?

Thrilled, terrified, and overwhelmed. When I think about being a mother, being completely responsible for another human being, I'm scared. But when I go to the mall and see women with their babies, I tingle with excitement to think I'll have my own child in a few months. I guess you could say I have mixed emotions."

He grunted. "I'm beginning to think that's the story of your life."

She crossed her arms. "All right, Mr. Know-It-All. How do you feel about impending fatherhood? You've had less than twenty-four hours to mull it over. Are you just jumping for joy?"

He took his eyes off the road for a moment and nailed Maddie with a full grin. "Actually, yeah. I can't think of anything that could make me happier."

His warm smile shook Maddie to her core. He did it again, tore away another layer of her protective facade. She'd been building an image of stalwart single parenthood in her mind. Randy's token attempt at fatherhood wouldn't have amounted to much. But taking in Phil's easy acceptance of paternal responsibility threw her for a loop.

She leaned toward him as if conducting a cross-examination. "So, you have no problem with twenty years of financial responsibility? No problem making unknown sacrifices on behalf of a child that you unwittingly fathered with a…uh–"

"If you say 'sex-starved spinster' again I'm going to wash your mouth out with soap at the next Stuckey Stop."

"Well, I find it hard to believe it's so easy, so simple for you to accept."

"But I know something you don't know."

"Oh, do tell."

"I've already got one kid. I know how much I missed. How badly I screwed up." A small smile tugged at his lips. "Maddie, my little moon goddess, you've given me a second chance to do it right."

She turned away, watching the scenery buzz by. "Now

you're making me feel like a regular brood mare."

"Jeez, there's no pleasing you today, is there?" He pulled the car over to the side of the road.

She frowned and felt a bit panicky. "What are you doing?"

He shoved the car into park, turned, and grabbed the sides of her arms. "Let's get something straight. I want this baby. I won't be robbed of another child. I've had to fight Pam for Melissa every step of the way. I don't want to fight you, but I will if I have to."

A lump in Maddie's throat made it difficult for her to reply. "I'm not another Pam. I'd never rob my child of a fine father like you. I'm sure we can work out an acceptable custody arrangement."

His jaw tensed. "Is that the best you can see for us, Maddie? An amiable custody arrangement?" His hands eased their grip and began gently caressing the top of her arms. The serious, searching look on his face seared her soul.

She closed her eyes in defense. "I don't know. You scare me, Phil. The feelings you stir up in me are frightening."

"I know what you mean. I've never known anyone before who throws me so off balance. Being with you is kind of like kicking back a shot of Jack Daniels. You make me hot and befuddle my mind. Ah hell, maybe it's just lust."

His lips were on hers before she had time to consider the wisdom of kissing him. And then she didn't think at all because he felt so good. After weeks of feeling lost and alone, his kiss was like coming home. Her arms furled around his neck as he engulfed her into his broad embrace. He ate at her lips as his hands traveled into her hair. Then he made love to her mouth, sweeping in and taking her breath away. Oh, God, he was like a force of nature. An avalanche, a tornado tearing across the landscape of her emotions.

She lowered her hands and slid them on his chest, pushing back. "Wait. I can't breathe. I can't think. I can't handle this right now."

Phil settled back behind the steering wheel with a smug

alpha male expression, satisfied that his me-Tarzan-you-Jane move had overwhelmed her. "Okay. I'd say I'm sorry, but I'm not. We've got unfinished business between us. And it's not just about the kid. Something started that night under the moon and it's not over yet."

Chapter Sixteen

The course of true love never did run smooth.

William Shakespeare

They were almost to Maddie's house when she thought to ask about Phil's car. "Do we need to go pick it up somewhere?"

Phil shrugged. "Nah. I think my car is toast. I'll have to arrange to get it towed into town tomorrow."

"Oh, I'm so sorry."

"It's not your fault."

"Well, I feel somewhat responsible."

"Listen when somebody kidnaps you, whatever else happens, it's not your fault. Get it?"

He was mildly chastising her for taking on too much responsibility, but old habits die hard. She wanted to fix the situation. "I have a vehicle you can use. Grammy's old pickup truck is in the garage. It's very useful once in a while. I've kept it maintained."

A grin tugged at his lips. "I'm sure you have. Okay. That sounds like a good idea. I was going to have one of the team come and get me, but I think driving around in Grammy's truck sounds like a kick. The old gal won a special place in my heart."

They pulled into Maddie's long drive and stopped before her postcard-perfect cabin. Phil came around to her side and opened her door as she gathered her belongings.

He followed her up the porch steps as she said, "Come in and I'll get you the key to the truck."

Phil checked out the cabin with interest. It reflected

Maddie's personality, a mixture of femininity and practicality. Muted colors and tasteful decorations gave the place a feeling of warmth and peace, so different from the cheap glitzy clutter that filled Pam's house. And it smelled so good. Flowers and soap and sunshine. After a full day of smelling sweat and grass-stained uniforms, coming to a home that smelled like this would be real good.

Maddie returned from the kitchen holding the key out for him. "Here it is. Thank you so much for everything."

He took the key from her fingers, pocketed it, and then grabbed both of her hands. "Thanks. So when's your next doctor's appointment?"

"Why?"

"Answer the question, woman."

"I'm supposed to have an ultrasound on Wednesday at four."

"I'll go with you."

"You don't have to do that."

"I want to be there."

"Oh."

"I know it hasn't penetrated that organized brain of yours, but I'm in this for the long haul. You're stuck with me. Like glue. Like super glue." Tugging her close, he gave her a quick kiss. "Get some rest. I'll see you."

He walked out the door whistling, "*Yes Sir, That's My Baby.*"

After Phil left, exhaustion caught up with Maddie and she napped for three hours. The setting sun sent amber rays through the window as she stumbled into her kitchen. Her foggy head needed a definite dose of medicinal chocolate. She'd baked a devil's food cake to celebrate Halloween. At least that was this week's excuse. Fortified with a sliver of cake and a cup of tea, she pondered the coming week. She turned on a CD to fill the lonely house with a sense of company. Funny, when had she started to think of her house as lonely?

Plopping down on her sofa, she picked up a motherhood magazine and began turning pages when a scratching at her back door caught her attention. A tremor of fear pulsed through her body. After the ghosts and goblins of the previous evening, a multitude of bizarre possibilities crossed her mind as to the origin of the noise. The scratching continued, now accompanied by a whimper.

"Get a grip, Madeleine," she said, as she marched to the door.

Pushing the small window curtain away, she flipped on the light and peered through the glass.

A dark head about three feet high waited at the door. The head tipped back, revealing two yellow eyes and a flopping red tongue from a doggy mouth. Lucifer recognized her, barked a friendly canine greeting, and scratched the door again.

She cautiously turned the knob and stuck her head out. "What are you doing here? Go home!"

Lucifer flopped down on his stomach, crossed his paws, and whined up at her.

"Oh, good grief. I'm not a dog person."

He howled.

"This isn't a good time."

He bayed.

"Well for heaven's sake. All right, but this is only a visit. And you'll have to take a bath."

As she opened the door, he rose and entered the threshold as if he owned the place.

"Come on," she said as she trudged toward the bathroom. She plugged the tub and turned on the faucet. Lucifer's big body brushed against hers as he jumped into the rising water. She half-expected him to take off her hand when she gingerly ran a soapy washcloth across his black back and down his muscular haunches. But he stood stoically and occasionally the muscles between his eyes twitched as if he truly enjoyed being stroked.

Within the hour, a clean-smelling Lucifer lay snoozing before her fireplace. He'd even let her brush his teeth.

They spent a companionable evening together as Maddie made dinner and began to relax. Lucifer snarfed up his ham and cheese sandwich, sniffed his way around the house, and slept again at her feet as she watched TV. He went out before bedtime, which she hoped signaled the end of his visit, but persistent door scratching dispelled that thought.

Too tired to argue, she opened the door and said, "Fine." The two retired to her bedroom.

Lying in her bed, she gazed at the dark creature asleep on the floor next to her. She searched for the normal terror to big dogs that had been a part of her psyche for most of her life. Amazingly, her stomach wasn't churning, her hands weren't clammy. She felt calm. The usually uptight, anal Miss Harris took a deep breath. A small part of her had been set free, released from a life-long fear. Maybe this was just the beginning.

The phone rang. She glanced at the clock. 10:30. Who could be calling so late?

"Hello?"

"Hello, cupcake. How are you? Any ghost sightings tonight?" Phil's voice poured over her like warm honey.

"Grammy probably used up her ectoplasm last night. But I've been entertaining a gentleman friend all evening."

His voice acquired an edgy tone. "Yeah, who?"

"You met him last night. Dark hair, piercing yellow eyes, three feet tall and four legged."

Phil chuckled. "I'll be damned. You sure you're safe with him?"

"I appear to be stuck with him." At that moment, Lucifer sighed and peeked at her through droopy lids.

Phil yawned into the phone. "This has been one helluva weekend for you, hasn't it? Kidnapped, rescued, annulled, adopted by a big dog and finding out a mug like me is the father of your baby."

She asked the question that had been running through her mind. "How did you know, Phil? How did you know I was the woman by the lake?"

"The moles. Those three little love dots you keep under wraps most of the time. I must have known it was you at some level, but when I tied the cape around your neck in the locker room, I suddenly had a hunch." His voice lowered. "That's a very erogenous zone on you, isn't it, sweetheart?"

"Oh…" Maddie flushed as her fingers went to her throat. Suddenly the memory of that summer evening came into full focus. She could feel his mouth on her throat as he held her on Grammy's quilt.

"Listen, babe, I'd love to have phone sex, but I don't think you're that kind of girl and I'd like to hold out for the real thing. I just called to check on you and say good night."

He was melting her down. "Good night, Coach. I don't think you're an insufferable lout anymore."

"Well, that's a load off my mind. I don't think you're such a pain in the ass. So, I guess we're making progress."

Phil and Maddie took their relationship one day at a time. During staff meetings, he winked at her when no one was looking. She tried to wrap up into her stern assistant principal persona and not respond to his inappropriate behavior, but she found herself grinning and winking back.

Their trip to the doctor in Bentonville wound more strings of attachment around them as they watched an image of their child floating in Maddie's womb.

She whispered in wonder. "I'm just sure it's a boy."

Phil clinched his jaw and squeezed her hand hard to keep his emotion in check.

A couple days later Maddie helped Phil pick out a new bicycle for Melissa's birthday. Maddie baked a cake (devil's food, of course) and took it to football practice where the team celebrated their water girl's twelfth birthday and presented her with the shiny red ten-speed bike. Maddie fought back those darn tears as she watched Phil's eyes sparkle when he hugged Melissa, then told her to take two laps for telling corny jokes.

Life's busy routine kept them apart. He had football practice and papers to grade. She had reports to do and meetings to attend. And pregnancy-induced fatigue engulfed her with irritating regularity. In the afternoons, she'd swivel her big chair toward the window and take a little nap, hoping she wouldn't fall onto the floor.

When Reba hadn't returned to school a week after Halloween, Maddie drove to the Finn homestead to check out the situation. The change in the place amazed her. Scraggly grass around the ramshackle house had been mowed and most of the junk in the yard hauled off. A gray-haired man with a country, friendly face stood painting the outside clapboard while a wide-hipped woman hung clothes on a line.

The screen door opened as Maddie turned off her engine. Reba waved, scampered down the steps, and came to the car. Autumn wind swirled her hair.

The dogs gathered around Reba's legs, but she told them to go away and they trudged back to a spot under the house. Maddie eased her way out of the car, only mildly apprehensive about the dogs. She'd come a long way.

"Hello, Reba. We've missed you at school. How are you? How is your family?"

The sun shone on Reba's red hair. "We're doing okay. That's my grandpa and grandma–my mom's parents. Pa wouldn't let them come around much. 'Didn't want them messing with our lives,' he said. But I called them right off when I got home and they've been taking care of everything."

"Where's the rest of your family?"

"The boys and Faith are at school. They've missed too much as it is and I can get a lot more done around here without them. Ma is in the house. She's awful wore out. The cops have been around and we've had to deal with them. Pa's still in the county hospital with a lot of busted bones. When he gets better, he'll probably go straight to jail. There won't be any trial. His lawyer is working out a plea bargain."

Maddie inwardly breathed a sigh of relief. She didn't relish re-telling the night of her abduction before a courtroom of people. Fending off questions from curious students was bad enough.

She pulled her jacket a little tighter against the wind. "I hope you'll be coming back to school soon."

"I'll be back next week. You can bet on it. I know I need to get an education. I don't want to be trapped in minimum wage jobs my whole life."

Maddie nodded in approval. "Nobody can ever take a good education away from you."

Reba reached down and picked up one of the cats circling her feet. "And Mr. Bailey called and said he still wants me to play that part in the musical. I've been practicing real hard." Her face shone with excitement.

"You're going to be wonderful." Maddie's eyes misted realizing her best wishes for Reba might come true. She couldn't resist wrapping an arm around Reba and giving her a big hug. "I know you've had a rough time of it, but you have a special gift that's going to carry you far. I can feel it in my bones."

Maddie joined Phil at McDonald's before school one morning. She fretted over decaf coffee and yogurt as he plowed into a greasy special. "I'm afraid McCall is going to fire me when all the details of my private life come out. Pregnant after a one-night stand. A quickie marriage and a faster annulment. I'll soon be a blooming example of unwed motherhood. I'm not setting a very good model for the students of Beaver Cove High School."

"Your personal life isn't anyone's business except yours." He wiped his mouth on a napkin. "As for your model for Beaver Cove students, these kids are lucky to have a class-act like you on their side. I see the way you encourage them to broaden their thinking. Face it, there are a lot of kids going on to college because the vice principal worked nights and weekends hunting down scholarships on their behalf. And you're all over that school promoting the Science Fair, the Foreign Language Club, finding members for the Debate Team. You name it, Miss Harris is sticking her pretty nose in it. McCall would be an idiot to fire you over appearances."

Maddie wasn't so sure. "I'm worried about Randy's job, too. He's being discreet about his relationship with Brent, but he's not keeping it a secret. The school board may give McCall a bad time."

Phil patted her hand. "I'll handle it. Don't worry. I'll play my ace in the hole."

"And what might that be?"

Phil winked. "Arkansas football-mania."

Phil took the bull by the horns. He entered McCall's office that morning and laid it all out on the table.

Sitting behind his paper-laden desk, McCall shook his gray wooly head as he pieced it together. "So let me get this straight. My prim assistant principal is four months gone with your baby, but she didn't know it was yours until recently. And she'd already married the gay drama teacher to keep her job, but he's now dumping her for his boyfriend."

Phil hooked his ankle on his thigh and leaned back in his chair. "Something like that."

McCall yanked open a desk drawer and pulled out a super-sized bottle of *Tums.* "And you want me to just overlook all this and let everybody keep their jobs."

"If you want to keep a winning football team, that's what I suggest."

After chewing a handful of antacids, McCall said, "I run a tight ship here. I run it my way–McCall's way. I've worked hard at earning my autonomy with the school board. Gossip about a promiscuous assistant principal is going to send them flying over here like a flock of pecking geese. It might be easier on Maddie and the school if she just tenders a quiet resignation."

The muscles in Phil's stomach clenched. If Maddie lost her job, it would be his fault. He'd been the one fully awake, stone cold sober that night. Christ, would he never stop screwing up!

Phil rose and leaned over McCall's desk. "Come on, Doug. This is Arkansas, the state that sent Bill Clinton to the governor's mansion and the White House. You can lay on your Southern charm and pull in some favors. Do this for me, and I swear I'll bust my butt to get you a state championship within three years."

McCall's eyes gleamed. A state championship. God, he'd love to wave that trophy in front of some stuck-up, big-headed administrators he knew. McCall sighed and wagged a beefy finger. "You'd better keep winning ball games, son. And you might think about marrying the girl yourself."

"I don't know about that, Doug." Phil jiggled coins in his pocket, betraying his nervousness over the marriage issue. "I was a pretty lousy husband the first time around. Maddie probably deserves better. Somebody with more class and fewer faults."

"You're selling yourself short, boy. Class isn't about good manners and fancy clothes. Class is about integrity, learning from your mistakes, and treating people right." McCall lifted a shaggy eyebrow. "Why, Phil, you're about the classiest guy I know. Yeah, you dress like a bum and your language is right out of the locker room, but you're showing those boys of yours what it means to be a man. That prissy assistant principal of mine could do a lot worse than you."

Phil left McCall's office wondering. Could he make a real life with Maddie? He'd been afraid to think that far ahead. But he knew he wanted more. More than being a part time dad to her child and a part time man in her life. Dammit, he loved the woman. Why shouldn't he have it all? The wife, the child, the home, the happiness? Maybe it was time to make the big play.

Maddie sat at her desk on the Thursday before Thanksgiving talking on the phone with her mother. "Mom, I'd love to see you and Daddy for Thanksgiving. I just thought you always went to Aunt Agatha's."

Amanda Harris' classy Bostonian accent sang through the phone lines. "We do, but she's still recovering from her hip replacement and really, darling, we want to see you."

Maddie heard her father in the background. "Give me the

phone, for God's sake, 'Manda....Maddie?!"

"Yes, Daddy, I'm here."

"What the hell is going on with you?" Thirty years in Boston hadn't done much to tame his Ozark twang.

"What do you mean?"

"I mean your Grammy Harris has been popping up telling me to get my ass to Arkansas. Says you need me."

Oh great, Grammy meddling from the great beyond.

Maddie heard her parents arguing.

Amanda hissed, "Do you want people to think you're crazy talking to ghosts?"

"Hell, Amanda, half of Boston already thinks I'm crazy and the other half thinks you are for staying married to me. But I do want to know what is going on with our little girl. Maddie, your mother and I will be there next Wednesday for Thanksgiving."

"But..."

"See if you can find that cornbread dressing recipe your Grammy used to make. I'm sick to death of these la-de-dah oyster stuffings I've had to eat all these years at the Woodbridge shindigs. Oh, yeah, and find a jug of that good corn liquor from old man Finn."

Probably Wade's father or a rotten uncle. Maddie ran her fingers through her hair. "I think he's passed on." She sighed, resigned. "It'll be good to see you and Mother."

Beau's voice held a raspy tenderness. "I've missed you, baby. We'll see you next week."

Maddie hung up and covered her face with her hands. The thought of wrestling a turkey made her ill. The thought of telling her parents about her tangled life made her want to crawl into a hole. Damn that Grammy for ratting on her.

She heard a knock and Phil let himself in. Much as she tried to resist, that warm feeling came over her as she surveyed his mismatched clothes. How could such a bad dresser look so good to her?

"Hey, cupcake. What do you say we take off and grab some grub and go to the mall? Maybe do some shopping?"

Maddie blinked her tired eyes. "Did I hear you right? You want to go shopping? What for? Fishing tackle?"

"No, smartass, not fishing tackle. Clothes. I'm tired of looking like a bum and you need to quit cramming into those stuffy suits. It just ain't working anymore, sweetheart. We both need a new look. And I figured you'd be some help picking out shirts for me that don't have beer cans or naked ladies on them."

As they took on the mall, a fresh surge of energy gave Maddie her second wind. She'd been itching to see Phil in good clothes. He had such a wonderful physique and her eyes glowed when he stepped out of the dressing room in a sharp tan shirt and well-cut navy blazer over creased slacks.

He turned in front of the mirror, giving her a killer grin. "Not bad, huh?"

She ran her hands down his lapel, getting it just right. "Coach, you'll have those high school girls swooning at your feet."

He captured her hands. "Yeah, what about the assistant principal?"

She looked straight into his milk chocolate eyes. "She even liked you in your sweats." But she really liked him totally naked in the moonlight. Oh, God, such wicked images. She must have transmitted her thoughts because his eyes traveled to her lips and she could almost taste him.

"I'm not going to tell you how handsome you look because it will go to your head and you're cocky enough." Lord, she wanted to drag his mouth down to hers.

His eyes responded with smoldering fire. "Come on, let's go get you decked out and then we can blow this joint."

He pushed through the maternity racks, pulling clothes he thought looked good. She rolled her eyes at many of his selections, but she let him nudge her toward softer clothes than she usually wore. He sat in a chair and teased her when she modeled the clothes for him. And when they had finished their shopping and had their arms loaded with packages, she couldn't resist standing on tiptoes and kissing him smack on the lips.

As they walked out of the maternity section, they were unaware of being watched by a pair of jealous green eyes. Pam had come to the mall to buy a new Thanksgiving tablecloth. She planned on knocking Phil out with a real homey, come-to-Mama Thanksgiving feast. Seeing him with the assistant principal was like getting punched in the stomach. She'd have to drill Melissa about the two. Bet the little smart mouth had been holding out on her. Then she'd figure out a way to get rid of the holier-than-thou school bitch.

Chapter Seventeen

Give a man a free hand and he'll run it all over you.

Mae West

Grammy's old truck jostled Maddie on the long front seat. They hit a pothole and took a good bounce.

Phil stretched a steadying hand on her. "I think this jalopy could use some new shocks. I'll take her in next week."

It seemed as natural as rain for him to take over a responsibility that she normally assumed. Gazing at his profile, she enjoyed the play of passing lights crossing his features. She could feel it, the bubble of happiness in her chest. Being with Phil calmed her, lifted her, fulfilled her. She'd been fighting it, but, suddenly asked herself… *why*? Why fight this emotion that felt so good, so right? Phil had proven time and again he was no Thomas Smithton. They were as different as sand and butter, as rose petals and stink weed. Lord, she was waxing poetic–albeit, badly–but poetry, nonetheless. It must be love.

There…she'd admitted it. That wasn't really so hard, was it? Of course, she wasn't ready to tell Phil. He hadn't mentioned the "L" word, either. She would have remembered that. So far, Melissa remained the only person who had openly earned that declaration from him. Whether he loved Maddie or not was not the issue at the moment. Madeleine Harris had to face the fact; she'd fallen in love with Phil Wilcox.

She waited for the terror, the trepidation, the need to flee. Time ticked by as they passed a Grandy's, Burger King, and Arby's, but no panic attack clutched her gut. Joy filled her instead. A quiet, sure, grateful happiness that made her want to crawl onto Phil's lap and make love to his teasing mouth. She wanted his arms wrapped around her and his burly chest tickling her face.

Suddenly, she felt a thump. A thump right under her belly button.

She gasped.

Phil turned his head. "What's the matter?"

Maddie couldn't contain a smile. "Nothing. Absolutely nothing. I think the baby just kicked."

Phil grinned, warm as a teddy bear.

Throwing caution to the wind, breaking the seatbelt law, she undid her buckle and slid next to him. "Take this next right."

"That leads up the hill to your house. Your car is still at school."

"If anyone asks, we'll say the battery died." Her voice rasped low, full of unspoken meaning. "Take me home, Phil."

He glanced down at her briefly, made the turn, and then lifted his arm and pulled her next to his ribcage. His hand rested on the side of her swelling belly.

They didn't utter a word as the truck ascended the mountain road, away from the city lights, toward her snug lake cabin. Country music filled the cab, throbbing out songs about lovers from Little Rock, Austin, and Baton Rouge. Phil's scent overtook Maddie's senses; her blood pulsed to the crooning tunes of George Strait and Garth Brooks. She closed her eyes and gave into it, allowing the swaying truck, heartbreak music, and solid man to stoke the fires of passion that simmered just below the surface.

Each turn of the road caused them to rub against each other and soon her hand found its way onto that chest she loved. Small circular caresses tickled her fingertips as they passed across the material covering the skin she longed to explore. She felt him take a shuddering breath and couldn't help smiling. She pulled her legs up onto the bench and tucked herself even deeper against him, gaining greater access to his shoulders, chest, and flat stomach. Needing to feel the real texture of him, her fingers crept to the edges of his shirt, pulling it out of the confines of his belt. Soon the life force under his skin filled the nerves of her fingers and palm, all of his heat moving up her arm, spreading to every fiber of her body.

"God, woman, if we don't get to your house soon, I'm going to have to pull over."

"Do you want me to stop?" she asked, making a long trail with a finger down his abdomen.

"No way. I just want you to know, you're going to get yours when I can take my hands off this steering wheel."

"I'm counting on it." She began raining small kisses along the side of his ribcage, bringing forth a loud, male groan.

Finally, the truck came to a screeching halt and she realized they'd made it up her long driveway while she'd been nibbling around his belly button. Two large hands grabbed her upper arms, spun her around, and pulled her up to meet his hungry mouth. His tongue stroked and tasted as his hand cupped her breast, sending molten liquid between her legs.

This time the groan that filled the cab was female, definitely female.

A scratching and barking at the driver's side window suddenly interrupted growing rapture and the promise of ecstasy. Lucifer, on patrol.

Maddie leaned her forehead onto Phil's chest, took a deep breath, and sat up.

She straightened her clothes. "He's a very good watchdog."

"Swell."

"Do you want to come in?"

"Do you want me to come in?"

"If you don't, I think I'll die."

He grinned. "Well, we can't have that."

He opened the car door, forcing Lucifer back. He greeted and patted the black sentinel. Maddie hopped from her side. She dug through her purse for keys while chatting to Lucifer, who seemed to understand every word she said.

Phil took the key out of her hand as they reached the door, unlocked it, but didn't open it. Instead he turned around and faced her. "This is your last chance to bail out. You can still send me away. Once I step inside, I'm taking you straight to your bed. No cups of tea and polite conversation. I'll slip you between the sheets and the talk might get dirty."

Maddie's legs turned to jelly and she said in a breathy voice, "Sounds good to me."

The next thing she knew, Phil scooped her up and carried her across the dark house and into her bedroom. *Oh my, the big lug could be romantic.* He kicked the door closed in Lucifer's face. A canine whimper echoed from the hall. Poor doggy. Once Phil laid her on the soft bed, began unbuttoning her blouse and nuzzling her aching breasts with his hot mouth, she didn't think about the mundane details of life.

Yes, that feels marvelous. The Dream Man has returned.

Clothes shed like falling leaves and soon the sensations of cool sheets and warm skin enveloped Maddie in a world she'd only imagined. Sensations piled on sensation. Tangy male scents mingled with the lavender potpourri. Phil's fingers explored the curves of her back and hips, smoothed the tender inner thighs. *Good heavens, who knew the back of knees could be so erotic?*

His mouth nibbled her ear lobe. "You're the classiest babe I've even known. You even smell like a million bucks."

"I thought you were going to talk dirty."

"Something about you makes me want to clean up my act. I'll just have to let my actions speak louder than words."

His mouth found hers again, spinning coherent thoughts from her mind all together. *Tumble me, tease me, take me.*

She melted and trembled. Carefully built walls around her heart cracked and crumbled. *Oh my God, I love him; I love him so much it hurts.*

As his hand made circular motions over her stomach and inched lower and lower, she opened for him, wanting him, wet for him.

"Please, Phil…"

She needed to touch him as he touched her. The length, strength, and heat of him throbbed under her fingers. Silky fire drove her to passion she'd never before experienced. It wasn't enough to passively receive. She wanted his textures under her fingers, his tastes in her mouth. And that chest, that broad chest–a playground to explore. She kissed his pecs and stroked him wonderfully erect. He moaned her name.

Her womb ached for him, longed for him. Simply had to have him. She flung one leg over his hips and rose up on her knees. Blue beams poured through the windows. They gazed at each other in the shadowy light.

Phil's face flashed with fire as he scanned her naked body hovering over him. "You are a goddess. A beautiful statue come to life."

She felt beautiful as his hand reached up and grazed her breasts. Power surged through her. Purely, fabulously female, she centered over his strong erection and took him in, following nature to that secret electrified spot. *There, right there*. Slowly, she rocked back and forth, up and down, letting her body direct the moves. *Right there, right there*.

He grabbed her hips and pumped. *Faster, deeper, stronger*. He knew exactly what he wanted and how to do it. *Oh Phil...Oh my God.* Shocks waves pulsed out from her center, spiraled and crashed over her. Her spine arched as she threw her head back and gave into the ultimate uniting of body and spirit.

I'll love you until I die.

She collapsed on his chest, curled her leg over his thigh, and snuggled close, completely spent.

His voice rumbled under her ear. "Good night, Moon Goddess."

She barely got the words out before sleep overtook her, "Good night, Dream Man."

Pam was on the rampage. Melissa had never seen her mother so out of it. She'd been hammered with questions about Dad and Mrs. Bailey or Miss Harris or whatever she was being called nowadays. Melissa was really confused. She'd known Miss Harris was around a lot, but the way Pam always talked about "when your Dad and I get back together," she figured it was all working out the way she wanted it. Dad back home. One, big happy family.

Now, when she really thought about, she realized Dad had been putting up with Mom. Just going along so his visitations would go better.

It was Friday night before another game, the last one before Thanksgiving. A big one. Evidently Pam had seen her Dad and Miss Harris together at the mall the previous night and she'd been ballistic ever since. Now Mom was getting dressed to kill.

"Hand me those earrings," Pam said, sitting in front of the dressing table in her bedroom, like a queen. "Listen, when you see Dad tonight, you be sure and ask him over for Thanksgiving again. I've already talked to him about it, but he'll be sure and come if you let him know you're expecting him. I don't want him going over to that bitch's house."

"I don't think Miss Harris is a bitch. She's always been cool to me."

"Oh, she's a bitch all right. A cold, calculating bitch. I didn't tell you what department they were in at the mall last night, did I? The maternity department! She's got herself knocked up and is looking for another daddy candidate now that your precious Mr. Bailey seems to be out of the picture." Pam spritzed on perfume that made Melissa want to gag. "What is the world coming to, that unmarried assistant principals get pregnant and don't get canned? Or maybe nobody knows about it yet. Maybe she figures to snag your dad so fast, she can keep her respectability. Whatever her game is, I'm getting rid of her."

Watching her mother primping at the vanity, Melissa said, "How are you gonna do that? Shoot her?"

Pam smiled smugly. "I'm not looking to end up in the electric chair. No, I've got a secret weapon and I know just how to use it."

Melissa knitted her eyebrows. "Well, I've got to get to the game. I'll see you later."

Outside, Melissa mounted her bright, new bike and headed for the field. She needed to think this all out. Keep an eye on the grown-ups and see if she could make sense out of everything her mother had been talking about.

Maddie sat in her usual spot on the front row of the bleachers, cheering the Beavers on into the third quarter. The smell of popcorn and turned turf tickled her nose. She wondered if she still glowed from the previous evening's amorous adventure in Phil's arms. She felt like a completely new person–a liberated, happy, maternal Maddie. In love with a rough and tumble football jock and proud of it. Soon, she would tell him. She might even propose. Go straight from the "L" word to the "M" word. Would he faint, run away, or give her a bear hug? She surely hoped for the hug.

She jumped to her feet and cheered as the Beavers took it into the end zone. After they made the extra point, Phil turned around and looked for her. She gave him a thumbs up. He waved; a grin filled his face. Melissa stood next to her father and turned also. Her solemn gaze hit Maddie between the eyes. Maddie's warm glow dulled a little as she felt Melissa's hostility shoot across the football field. *Uh-oh.*

Maddie sunk to her seat and hoped she misinterpreted Melissa's expression. The last thing she wanted was to cause a rift between Melissa and Phil just when they were moving past their troubled history.

Even though she hated to miss a minute of the game, her pregnant bladder simply couldn't be ignored. Phil's child was already an active thumper, a fact that didn't surprise her in the least.

Maddie rose and made her way to the ladies room, hoping she wouldn't miss any big plays.

Florescent lights flickered in the deserted cinder block bathroom. She quickly entered a toilet with a functioning lock. As she maneuvered her new maternity clothes under her coat, she heard someone enter the bathroom. Guess she wasn't the only one with a touchy bladder.

Pam stood, arms crossed, leaning against a sink, obviously waiting for Maddie when she emerged from the stall. Big hair, big boobs, and biker boots. Maddie's mother had a phrase for it–*her taste is all in her mouth.*

Maddie hesitated for a moment and then headed for an empty sink. "Hello."

"Hello, bitch."

Water ran over Maddie's hands as she tried to assess the situation.

She dried her hands and turned to face Pam. "Something on your mind, Mrs. Wilcox?"

Pam took a step in Maddie's direction, her face a grotesque, painted mask. "Yeah, plenty's on my mind. I know what you're up to. I'm on to you and you're not going to get away with it."

Maddie assumed her Bostonian cool. "And what exactly are we talking about?"

"I'm talking about the kid you got in the oven and you trying to snag Phil as the father. I saw you last night. Shopping for maternity clothes at the mall. Very cozy. Very lovey-dovey."

Maddie closed her eyes for a moment. Here it was. She'd known the word would get out. She'd been hoping for a better messenger to the world than Phil's ex-wife.

She held her ground. "All right. The cat's out of the bag. I'm pregnant. Phil's the father. What are you going to do about it?"

Pam took a step back and reached into her tiny purse for her cigarettes. "You mean Phil really is the father? You're not just putting your hooks in him?"

"We can do a DNA test after the child's born if you're going to spread a lot of rumors and speculation. I assure you the tests will show Phil is the father. But I don't see what this has to do with you."

"Oh, you don't, huh?" She lit up her cig. "Listen, Phil is

mine. I've been wondering why he's been so slow to take the bait. I didn't realize you'd been putting out for him. You sure don't look like his type. But, I'm telling you now and you better do as I say and find yourself another daddy for the kid."

"Don't be ridiculous. Phil would never give up his rights to his child. You should know that better than anybody."

"Yeah, you're right. Phil's got a real thing for fatherhood. Melissa is his weak spot. I can get him to do just about anything when I threaten to take away his visitation." She raised a speculative penciled eyebrow, exhaling a cloud of smoke. "And I can do a lot worse than that."

Pam took a few steps away as Maddie felt a chill coming on. Someone tried to open the bathroom door, but Pam had locked it.

"Go away!" Pam said. "We're fixing a busted pipe!"

Maddie kept a calm to her voice she did not feel. "What are you really saying?"

Pam sucked nicotine, highlighting fine wrinkles around her lips. "You've got the hots for Phil, don't you? I saw it last night."

"I love Phil," Maddie said, feeling the blood draining from her head.

"Even better." She strutted in the small enclosure, her heels clicking on the concrete. "If you really love him, then you wouldn't want to see him lose his daughter over you. His daughter, the light of his life. The reason he quit drinking and gave up a big bucks job to coach high school football in this hick town."

Maddie couldn't believe the cruelty Pam was implying. "How can you be so selfish? Would you deny Melissa the love of her father?"

Pam's eyes became green slits. "Unless you dump Phil, I'll turn Melissa against him. I've done it before and I can do it again. Phil is my one hope of getting out of this town. He's on his way now. He could move into coaching in college or the pros. And I'm going to be there with him. Me and Melissa. The way it's supposed to be. I'm not letting some tight-assed bitch take him away from us. If you don't cut it off with him, I'll take Melissa away. I'll tell her how he chose you over us. I'll make her hate his guts. It will be easy." Pam turned to the mirror and patted a few bleached hairs into place. "So, what will it be? Are you going to be responsible for Phil losing his daughter, Miss High and Mighty?"

Maddie felt light-headed and had to grab the sink to keep her balance. She looked in the mirror, hoping to see Grammy Harris for moral support. But all she saw in the harsh light was her ashen face and Pam's cat grin in the background.

Maddie spoke to Pam's reflection. "You're a wicked, evil person."

Pam laughed. "Sticks and stones, sticks and stones. I really gotta get back. Phil might miss me cheering on his team. He's always looking for me. And if you go whining to him about this little conversation, I'll have Melissa out of the state so fast he won't have time to take a picture to remember her by. You dump Phil or he will never see Melissa again."

Pam walked over to the door, flipped back the lock, and sashayed out into the night.

Maddie gazed into the mirror. She leaned in and examined closely. Surely a dozen new lines were about to pop to the surface.

Just before dawn on Saturday morning, and Phil felt great. He sprang out of bed and hit the shower. The forecast was for sunshine and sixty-five degrees. The team had won another game. They'd only lost one so far. His daughter looked at him with eyes of adoration and her mother was no longer making his life a living hell. Dealing with Pam was like crossing a tightrope over a pond of hungry alligators. One false step, and *chomp*, your leg was gone. Or in Pam's case, another equally vital body part. Still, he'd been going along to get along and she seemed to be under control.

But the biggest reason for his euphoria was Miss Madeleine Woodbridge Harris, mother of his unborn child, amazing unleashed lover. Who would have guessed?

Uninhibited, responsive, just plain hot. And she was his.

He got dressed, antsy to get going.

Man was meant to start the day throwing his line into a lake, watching the sunrise, not riding a desk somewhere. He decided to try his luck in Maddie's lake again. He'd never actually gotten the chance to fish at Lake Luna that night four months ago. Might be some good fishing there. Ah, hell, who was he kidding? He wanted to see her. It was too early to call. She'd looked dead tired after the game last night. He'd barely said two words to her before she begged off and left without looking back. But if a man just happened to be fishing in the area and then dropped by later to say hello, he might get a cup of coffee and breakfast. Phil tugged his fishing cap on his head and left his dingy apartment behind.

Driving up the winding hill, he let his mind drift and dream. He imagined taking this drive every day and night, watching the change of seasons in the colors of the hills. Going to work, returning home. His home with Maddie and their son. Yeah, why not? Why not dream big? For him, the thought of a happy home was a big dream. Bigger than winning the Superbowl and a helluva lot more satisfying.

Later, as he cast his line again and again in the sparkling water, he glanced up at her cabin, looking for signs of life. Even with the debris of fall all around, it had a tidy appearance. The picture window that looked out onto the lake gleamed in the morning sunshine. With each flick of his wrist, his resolve grew stronger. He was going to make the big play, ask her to marry him. He wanted her, the whole package: the uptight suits, the smart mouth, the sparkling eyes, the creamy skin. He wanted the woman who looked like she believed in him and the man he could be. And he surely wanted the child she'd be holding at her breast.

He glanced at his watch. Nine o'clock. He didn't know she was such a sack artist. Just then, her porch door opened and Lucifer shot out into the yard, barking and galloping in Phil's direction.

Phil scratched the dog's large head and enjoyed watching

him leap into the water. God, he guessed he wanted her dog, too.

"Come on, boy, let's see if we can beg some food."

Phil and Lucifer made a companionable pair heading up the hill to Maddie's door.

Maddie looked like hell and felt worse. Wrapped in her oldest, rattiest, most comfortable robe, she stood against the kitchen counter, hypnotized by the water dripping from the *Mr. Coffee* basket into the carafe.

She'd paced the floor during the night, until she couldn't stand anymore. Then she curled up on the couch and fell into troubled sleep seeing Pam's wicked lips.

You dump Phil or he will never see Melissa again.

Could she somehow keep Phil at arm's length enough to make Pam happy? Thank God she hadn't confessed her feelings to him. That would make it all the harder. Somehow she had to figure out a way to allow him to have Melissa in his life, even at the sacrifice of her dreams. Melissa was a young girl who needed a father more than Maddie needed a husband. Maddie had successfully lived a solitary life before and she could do it again. Besides, she'd have the baby. She'd see Phil when he had his visitations. That could be enough couldn't it?

No! her heart screamed. She wanted Phil in every part of her life. He filled in her gaps, smoothed her sharp edges. She'd turn into a wizened, prune-faced, sex-starved spinster for sure.

"Get a grip, Madeleine," she said for the umpteenth time.

She needed a shower and a huge slice of cake. Maybe she'd alphabetize her spices again. She just needed some time to pull her unraveling ends together and be the stalwart Woodbridge-Harris her mother had raised. Her mother. Oh Lord, her parents would be arriving in four short days.

It was all too much to contemplate. She needed to go to bed. Hovering under her covers seemed like her best move. She'd taken two steps toward the living room when the back door opened.

"Morning, cupcake! Think you can spare a wandering fisherman a cup of coffee?"

Maddie blinked as if seeing a mirage. "Phil? What are you doing here?"

Phil looked taken aback by her less-than-enthusiastic greeting. "Well, I thought maybe we could have breakfast together. I've been fishing in your lake."

"I'm not feeling very well this morning." She clutched her robe.

"Yeah, I can see you're a little under the weather. Here, you sit down and I'll make you some breakfast."

She sighed. "This isn't a good time."

He dragged her to the table and pushed her into a chair. "You just need one of Coach Wilcox's killer omelets."

"I don't think that's going to do it."

But he paid her no mind and began taking apart her kitchen–frying bacon, scrambling eggs, chopping onions, throwing scraps to Lucifer. Cheerfully making a gigantic mess.

He flipped on her radio and tuned it to country, singing along with Billy Ray, acting the most cheerful she had ever seen him. He told her how great the sunrise had been and replayed some of the best moments of the previous night's game.

She wanted to go jump in the lake.

He tucked into his food with gusto, while she pushed the eggs around on her plate, feeling a throbbing headache coming on. When he finished, he set his dishes aside and leaned back into the chair to stare at her. He opened his mouth to say something and then stopped.

He pushed his fingers through his hair. "I've been babbling like my Aunt Fanny and you've been as silent as a Sphinx. Guess I'm a bit nervous. See, I've been thinking, Maddie. We've got a good thing going between us. We get along. We've got a baby coming..."

Maddie sat up straight. She'd been wishing the interminable breakfast would simply end. And now he appeared on the verge of proposing marriage.

She put a hand on his arm. "Don't say it, Phil."

"Now you don't even know what I'm going to say. See, we're good for each other." He covered her hand and looked at her with the innocence of a puppy. "I love you. I've known it for a good little while. You make me happy and I think we'd make a great team. We need each other. We're right together. Oh, hell, Maddie, either shoot me and put me out of my misery or marry me." He released a deep breath. "There, I said it. I think we should get married. What do you say?"

He looked so happy, she wanted to throw up. Her voice came out hoarse. "I can't marry you, Phil. It just wouldn't work."

An expression of shocked pain flashed across his face before it quickly changed to anger. "Oh, I get it. It's one thing to have a roll in the sheets with the football jock, but you wouldn't want to marry him."

"No, no, it's not like that."

"Then what is it? Explain it to me."

Oh God, she wasn't ready for this. She hadn't rehearsed a speech. She crossed her legs and tried to assume an elegant air. "Well, you're from one world and I'm from another and I don't think we're compatible. You're much too messy. I wouldn't want to be picking up your socks and picking out your clothes." Oh yes she would, she really would.

Phil stood up. "Okay, sweetheart, you're too good for me. I get it. An alcoholic, has-been football player isn't your idea of husband material. Well, let me tell you something, babe. You're passing up a good deal."

She knew that. She knew he was the best thing that had ever come along in her whole life. "It wouldn't be a suitable match, that's all. I think you have many fine qualities, but you're just not my type. I hope we can be friends, for the baby's sake."

He grabbed her chin and forced her to look in his face. "This is so much bullshit. You came onto me the other night like it was for keeps. You didn't say it, but I could feel it in your body, see it on your face. You love me, goddamn it! You look me straight in the eye and deny it. Say it. Say 'Phil, I don't love you.' I don't think you can."

Maddie swallowed and dug deep down to a well of strength she didn't know she possessed. She had to make the lie seem true. In a calm and measured voice she said, "Phil...I...don't...love you."

He released her as if he'd been burned, turned on his heel, and rushed for the door. She flinched at the slam and closed her eyes. Taking a breath, she opened them again and surveyed the incredible mess he'd made making one small meal.

Standing before the sink was the see-through figure of Grammy Harris. "Pitiful, simply pitiful. You've set the Harris womenfolk back 'bout a hundred years."

Chapter Eighteen

Hail, hail, the gang's all here

Gilbert & Sullivan

Phil banged open his apartment door and marched to his gun cabinet. His mind swirled with curses at himself for being such a fool and falling in love. Women! God's joke on man. He'd let Maddie sucker punch him again. Made him take his guard down, then wham! She'd hit his glass jaw, thrown a jab to his gut and generally beaten his brains out.

How could he have read her so wrong? He'd been positive that the cold exterior was only a protective front over a warm, vulnerable, caring interior. What about all those blushing smiles and innocent blue-eyed glances? She'd come apart for him the other night, given herself completely. But it had all been an act. She was some kind of temptress witch, ten times more wicked than Pam.

He unlocked the cabinet and pulled out his best two hunting rifles. Then he stomped into his bedroom, found his duffle bag, and began stuffing it with clothes. He needed to get away. Away from all women and their two-faced, manipulative schemes. He'd head to the backwoods country where the campfires burned low and a man could sit in a hunter's blind and make some sense out of life. Hell, maybe he'd just find a cave and become a, by-God, hermit! He'd let his hair grow and become a bushy-faced old geezer.

With the duffle bag flung over one shoulder and his rifles tucked under the other arm, Phil strode out of his apartment and climbed into the truck. He was going deer hunting, and as far away as he could get from that sweet-faced, black-hearted woman.

Maddie managed to get herself into a functioning mode by Sunday afternoon. Her best chance of making it through Thanksgiving was to banish all thoughts of Phil. Thank God, school was closed for the next week; but she still had to contend with her parents' imminent arrival. And, oh my lord, she needed to prepare a Thanksgiving feast. Time to call in the cavalry.

Sitting on her couch, she picked up the phone and hit Randy's number on her speed dial. He picked up on the second ring.

His merry voice lifted her mood. "Hello, dear heart, how in the world are you? We've hardly talked at all since we've acquired significant others."

"I'm in a fix." Maddie lifted her feet onto the coffee table. "My parents are arriving on Wednesday. How would you, Brent, and Mother Bailey like to join us for Thanksgiving? And bring your wonderful Waldorf salad, your fabulous green beans, your to-die-for home made rolls and a pecan pie?"

"So you're on for the turkey, dressing and potatoes? I suppose the Coach is good for a bag of chips."

Serious guilt pains gripped her chest. "I doubt he'll be here."

"Trouble in paradise?"

Maddie knew she'd burst into tears if she told Randy her sad story and she was sick to death of crying. "I'll tell you about it later. How are you and Brent getting along? Is Mother Bailey making your life miserable?"

"No more than usual. Actually, Brent appears to be winning her over. She enjoys having two of us at her beck and call. So far, we've just been together on weekends. One big, happy, gay family. Brent's talking about building a room addition on for her at his house in Little Rock."

Maddie felt a little stab of jealousy at Randy's happiness. And she was ashamed of herself. "That's wonderful."

"You don't sound too cheery. Has that big brute done

something to upset you?" He put on a Brooklyn accent. "*Do you want I should go and punch his lights out?"*

She managed a chuckle. "No, but I'm thinking of turning Lucifer on Pam. Listen, just bring food and plan on being the life of the party on Thursday. I'm sure we're going to need entertainment by then."

"You've got it. I'll bring my tape of *Moulin Rouge* and do my Nicole Kidman imitation."

"Sounds marvelous."

She hung up and threw herself into a fit of housecleaning. As she scrubbed the toilets, changed the sheets, ran the dust cloth, she fought thoughts of Phil. A boulder-sized lump lodged in her throat. Each time she passed the telephone, she had to stop herself from picking it up and blurting out she loved him, wanted him, needed him.

During the next two days, Maddie kept as busy as possible, working until fatigue forced her to collapse for catnaps on the couch. She'd lay with her hands on her rising stomach and feel the strong thumps of the baby. Fascinated by her changing body, she pulled back her shirt and exposed her naked tummy to watch the ripple of her stomach as the child tumbled inside its fluid sack. She longed to share the moments with Phil, but had to settle for a curious Lucifer, who nudged her hand for attention.

"You want to go for a walk, don't you? Fine."

Maddie hauled her body off of the cozy sofa, pulled on a jacket and scarf, and joined her canine buddy for a stroll down to the lake. It was late afternoon on Wednesday. The cold breeze slapped her face as the crunch of crisp leaves accented each footstep. Water sloshed in white-capped peaks, whipped up by the turbulent wind. High in the sky the distant moon perched like a ghost hovering over the landscape.

She saw it up there, but refused to stand and yell at a traveling rock in the sky. She wouldn't blame the moon, her hormones, or caffeine for her predicament. Somehow, she'd passed that. Much as her heart felt bruised, it wasn't crushed. The love she felt for Phil and the baby grounded her, freed her.

Even though Phil might never know how much she cared for him, she wasn't going crazy. Madeleine Woodbridge Harris was no longer wounded and wound-up. No longer a nervous and edgy fussbudget. The fear of letting people into her heart had melted away. Phil had forced her to open up and love again. Probably love for the first time. He'd charged into her life and torn down her defenses.

What had he called her? A prickly, punctual, pain-in-the-ass. Nowadays she felt softer, gentler, wiser. He'd accused her of being afraid of being a woman and he'd been right. Standing by the cold water's edge feeling her heavy breasts and expanding womb, the wonder of being a woman struck her as a great gift from God. Phil had been a gift also, even if she couldn't keep him.

He'd been a gift from that ole Devil Moon.

Maddie heard a car drive up and turned around to see her parents, Amanda and Beau, opening their doors. Lucifer took off to greet the visitors as Maddie brought up the rear.

Beau held his arms wide. "Maddie, honey!" He engulfed her in a bear hug and she tried to keep her bulging belly from bumping into him.

"Hello, Daddy."

Her mother spoke up. "For heaven's sakes, let's get out of this wind and say our hellos in the house." She screamed when Lucifer jumped up on her and quickly pushed him down. "Good grief! Quickly, Beau, get Maddie indoors before she has a fit over this creature."

"Sit, Lucifer," Maddie commanded, prompting him to plant his black butt in the grass.

Beau scratched his head. "I don't believe it. Girl, you've changed."

Maddie linked arms with her daddy. "Oh, I think you're in for a few more surprises."

She helped them with their luggage and led them into the house.

Beau and Amanda were helping themselves to drinks in

the kitchen when Maddie joined them after a bathroom run. Somehow, Amanda's hair remained perfectly coifed, despite the Arkansas wind. And Beau still had that country-boy-made-good look about him–an open, handsome face in expensive clothes. Maggie saw no point in putting off the inevitable.

Standing nervously before her parents, Maddie fiddled with the hem of her peach and turquoise maternity sweater. "I have some big news and there's no good way to ease into it. I didn't want to tell you over the phone. I'm going to have a baby." She swiveled sideways and pulled her sweater tight over her bulge. "Surprise, you're going to be grandparents."

It took a moment for Beau and Amanda to register the "surprise." Maddie wished she'd thought to buy a video camera to capture the play of emotions that went across their faces. Curiosity, recognition, and shock flickered in a priceless display.

Amanda grabbed Beau's arm for support. "Oh…my…God."

"Good gravy, Maddie-girl, you've struck your mother speechless." He glanced down at the soda in his hand. "To hell with this sissy drink. Have you got any whiskey stored around here?"

Maddie opened the cabinet where she'd stashed the high dollar booze she'd laid in for her dad. "Yes, here, Daddy, I thought you might need this."

Amanda found her voice. "All right, Madeleine, there's obviously been a lot going on in your life that you've failed to mention in our weekly phone calls. Beau, pour a dash of that liquid in my glass and let's sit at the table and all have a little chat, shall we?"

Beau shook his head as he pulled out a chair at the dining table. "Damn, no wonder your Grammy has been hounding me. Now who's the fella that I need to get marching before my shotgun to the preacher?"

"Oh, Daddy, it's a complicated situation." Maddie sank into a chair. "Besides, my annulment from Randy isn't entirely finalized yet. You wouldn't want me to be a bigamist, would you?"

Beau slapped the table. "You married *Randy*? Now why in blazes would you do that?"

"It seemed like a good idea at the time." She straightened the dried rose centerpiece. "Listen, maybe I should start at the beginning. You see, one evening last summer…"

After hearing the convoluted details of Maddie's love life, Beau paced the small space of the kitchen. "I think you're making a big mistake not letting this fella know about the threat from his ex-wife."

Maddie sighed. "I don't want to be responsible for Phil losing Melissa when he's just established a decent relationship with her. You don't know Pam. She'd carry out her threat and disappear. I wouldn't put anything past her."

Amanda perched on her chair like a queen. "Well, she sounds like someone who should be conquered, not catered to."

A familiar raspy voice echoed from the corner. "For God's sake, show some backbone!"

Everyone started as they recognized Grammy's voice. Amanda put her hands over her ears. "This is too ridiculous. Now you have me hearing ghosts."

Taking Grammy's appearance in stride, Maddie continued, "You see, Phil has worked so hard to gain Melissa's trust. I don't want to be a wedge between them."

Beau placed a large hand on Maddie's shoulder. "You've got a good heart, daughter. The fact that you're putting this girl and her father before your own desires shows a lot of character."

Grammy grumbled, "I think it shows she's a ninny. Harris women should fight for their menfolk. I'd have scratched the eyes out of any floozy in Beaver County who'd tried to get her hands on your pa."

Beau shook his head. "Well, that's another approach. Whatever you decide to do about this situation, I want you to know your mother and I will support you one hundred percent."

"That's right, dear," Amanda agreed. "Now that I've had a

moment to let your news sink in, I'm very excited about it. Beau, we're going to have a grandchild!"

Beau chuckled. "That's right. How will it feel to have someone call you 'Grandma?'"

Amanda looked suddenly stricken. "Oh, dear. That will never do." Then she smiled. "But, I won't mind being 'Nana.'"

Maddie's heart swelled as she fully appreciated the love she enjoyed from her parents. She gave them each a kiss on the cheek. "You're being a lot more understanding than I expected about all this. Daddy, I was afraid you'd insist on the shotgun wedding."

Beau shrugged. "You know your Daddy pretty well. But, I can see you're a big girl now, capable of making your own decisions. I just hope for the sake of you and my grandchild that you're making the right one."

A winter storm blew in from the West carrying ice and snow. Sleet rained down in slivered particles, clinging to any solid object. Hour after hour it tumbled down, forming long icicles on tree branches and power lines. As the night wore on, those lines sagged under the weight of the ice until they snapped. Pop! The lights went out all over western Arkansas.

Maddie huddled under her blankets, half-asleep. Lucifer had burrowed under the covers, keeping Maddie's backside warm. She'd been in a crazy dream world filled with monster Pams when the phone rang. Her hand fumbled over her nightstand as she found the phone.

"Hello?" Her voice came out in a froggy rasp.

Randy sounded much too cheerful for the early morning. "Rise and shine, my pet. Uncle Randy has figured out how to save the day."

"What are you talking about?" She struggled to sit up.

"The electricity is down, Sleeping Beauty. There's no way to cook that twenty pound bird you bought."

Maddie groaned. "Oh no…"

"So, we'll go to Plan B, which is to join forces with the community dinner planned at the school. They have the emergency generators working. I've been on the phone with Miss Green and Mr. Manchester, who are organizing the whole affair." His tone turned gossipy. "You know, I think they have something going on between them. Anyway, pack up all your food. I'm sending Brent over to pick it up and we're heading into town to help with the cooking. You and your parents can come down this afternoon to share the meal and then help dish it out. It will put everyone in the holiday spirit."

After hanging up, Maddie crashed back into her pillows. Wonderful, simply wonderful. Her mother would probably go into culture shock–going from Thanksgiving in an elegant Boston dining room to an Arkansas high school cafeteria. Not only that, Amanda Woodbridge Harris would be expected to take her place on the serving line! Maddie began laughing. And laughing. The sight of her elegant mother plopping mashed potatoes onto cafeteria trays for the population of Beaver Cove was something she had to see.

Phil managed to slide and fishtail the truck to Pam's house in the early afternoon. He'd had the good sense to get back to his apartment yesterday before the storm hit or he might be freezing his butt in a hunter's shack. It appeared that Bambi and his mother were safe another year from the deadeye aim of Phil Wilcox. A beautiful buck had been in his sights, but he let the animal pass on by. He'd gotten away more to think than to shoot.

He still felt shrouded in a dark veil, but he decided to get on with his life, such as it was. His obsession with Maddie had to end. The emotional highs and lows couldn't continue. Nor was he willing to be her stud muffin–someone to satisfy her sexual urges when the mood struck her. He wouldn't be her whore. Better to treat her with the detachment he'd been able to muster for Pam. If it weren't for the baby, he'd have nothing more to do with snotty Bostonian pill. Phil shoved the truck in park and took a few more sips of coffee.

Melissa peeked out the curtains of the front window and saw her dad pull up. The aftermath of the ice storm was totally awesome. Sparkling ice crystals glinted in the sun on every tree limb. She would love to go running in the woods and check out all the storm damage, instead of being dragged to the community Thanksgiving dinner. That was okay, though, because she needed to talk to her dad. Questions rolled around in her mind that only he could answer.

Melissa turned around and yelled down the hall to Pam. "He's here, Mom! I'm going out to wait with him in the truck where it's warm."

"Okay. I'll be ready in a few minutes." Pam's voice pierced through the house.

Melissa pulled on her coat and scooted out the door, waving at her dad as she crunched over the frosty lawn.

She yanked open the passenger door. "Hey, Daddy, don't get out. Mom's almost ready. You'll freeze your buns off in the house."

Phil smiled, but Melissa noticed that he had that sad look in his eyes again. He gave her a quick hug. "So, how have you been, kid?"

"Okay." She settled against the brown vinyl seat. "Did you know that rats can't vomit?"

"No kidding? I've been wondering about that."

Melissa knew she only had a few minutes until Pam entered the truck and stunk it up with her crappy perfume. "Hey, Dad, you and Mom aren't ever going to get back together again, are you?"

Phil ran his hand over his face. "No, baby, I'd do a lot of things for you, but living with your mom again is not one of them. We didn't make a good team."

Yeah, she'd figured that out already. Her mom could be so whacko. Like the crap she'd said to Miss Harris in the bathroom at the game. Melissa had seen her mom follow the assistant principal. She'd climbed the outside wall like a regular Spiderman to hear what went on inside.

"So, is Miss Harris having a baby and are you the father?"

"Oh, hell," Phil muttered. "Yes. Where did you hear about it? I should have been the one to tell you."

"It's no big deal." Melissa waved her icy fingers before the warm blowing air of the heater. "It's better than Marilee Sampson's dad who ran off with a holy-roller snake charmer. So, I guess you really like Miss Harris, huh? Are you going to marry her?"

"*No*!" The way he barked the word made Melissa jump.

"Have you asked her?"

"That's none of your business."

"So you have asked her and she turned you down, huh?"

Phil shot her a slit-eyed glance. "You're too smart for your own damn good."

Melissa knew better than to tell him what she'd overheard at the ball game. He'd fly into Pam, who would totally freak out. And Melissa would be stuck with a whacked-out mom for the rest of her vacation. No, there had to be a better way.

Spirits ran high in the Beaver Cove High School cafeteria. Everyone agreed that an ice storm was a beautiful natural disaster. Thankfully, generators ran efficiently, food was plentiful, and a party atmosphere filled the room. Long tables decorated with turkey-and-pumpkin holiday paper created a cheerful ambiance. Miss Phyllis Green had whipped up centerpieces from materials gathered in the woods–pinecones, red berries, sweet gum balls, and such. Miss Green and Phineas Manchester manned the dessert table. She wiped a stray crumb from his cheek, as she batted her cow-eyes at him. He appeared to enjoy the attention very much.

The Finn family occupied a good part of one table. George and Vince kept sneaking the peas and sweet potatoes they hated on Faith's plate until she screeched at them. A subdued Ginger sat feeding baby Garth his supper. Ginger still struggled with all the changes in her life. Part of her missed Wade so bad. When she'd seen him in the hospital all busted up, she'd burst into tears. Later, after hassles with the police and hearing about all the crap Wade had done, she'd flown into a regular hissy fit. She smashed his damn fish tank and would have taken a baseball bat to his precious racecar if Reba hadn't stopped her. And thank God for that. Money from the car sale would keep food on the table a while.

Wade had shamed her and the kids. She wouldn't have ventured in public if she'd had any choice in the matter. Damned ice storm bringing down the electricity. She'd had no choice but to bring the youngins in town for supper. Her lowered gaze traveled the room, expecting people to be muttering about that trashy Finn family. Instead, a couple people she knew offered a friendly wave.

A former high school girlfriend sought her out. "Hey, Ginger! Good to see you."

"Hey, Becky." She'd always liked Becky Malone, with her round, open face. Wade used to make cracks about Becky's "lard butt" and always hustled Ginger away at ball games and stuff. Ginger sat up a little straighter as she realized Wade wasn't around to hassle her about talking to old friends. No, Wade wouldn't be around for a very long time. Ginger managed a small smile. "I like that sweatshirt you've got on."

Becky pulled out the home-decorated holiday shirt from her ample bosom. It sported a turkey getting shot by Indians, all outlined in glitter. "Made it myself. You should come over to my house on Tuesday night. There's a bunch of us that's getting together to make Christmas shirts. We sit around drinkin' margaritas pasting sequins on Santa's belly. It's a blast. Promise me you'll come."

Ginger handed Garth a cookie. "That sounds pretty fun. Maybe I'll be there. Just maybe I will."

At that moment the piano struck up a chord and all eyes moved to the corner where Reba and Randy began a duet of patriotic tunes. Pretty soon the whole room joined in singing *God Bless America, My County 'Tis of Thee*, and *America the Beautiful.*

Maddie and her folks finished eating their food and took places behind the serving line. Brent had everyone well organized: Beau carved the turkey, Mother Bailey dished out green beans, Maddie served yams, and Amanda plopped mashed potatoes and gravy. (Maddie had put Brent up to that.)

Maddie and Beau exchanged amused glances as they watched the cultured Bostonian matron attending her task with grim determination.

Maddie was having a good time. She'd decided to rise above her personal heartache over Phil and enjoy her friends and family. No sense in being a simp. Besides, she'd half convinced herself that she'd be able to find some happy middle ground with Phil. Hopefully, they'd be able to resume their teasing friendship. She couldn't bear the thought of losing his bulldozing personality from her life.

The afternoon crowd became so busy; she barely had time to look up from her spoon. Whenever her dish emptied, she dashed back to the kitchen for a full one. She exchanged quick quips with each diner as they passed by. She didn't realize Phil, Melissa, and Pam were next in line until she had dished golden yams on his plate.

Automatically, she smiled and said "Happy Thanksgiving" as she looked up. Her smile drooped. "Phil…"

With an expression set in stone, he said, "Madeleine," as if he were speaking to a passing acquaintance. A passing acquaintance he had never much cared for.

Her spoon dropped, clanging to the floor as the power of his cool reply hit her. He'd called her "Madeleine." He'd vowed to never call her by that stiff, formal nomenclature.

She knew in that moment that their relationship was irreparably damaged. There would be no teasing banter, no casual resumption of a meaningful friendship. She was being cut off at the knees.

She grabbed a clean spoon and forced herself to mechanically fill Melissa and Pam's plates. For one second she nearly flung yams and marshmallows in Pam's smug face.

Her gaze followed Phil's wide back. He drifted away from her, as surely as Tom Hanks lost his ball buddy in *Castaway*. Maddie wanted to yell at Phil as desperately as Tom had cried, "I'm sorry, Wilson!" Phil was bobbing away from her in a sea of Beaver Cove's humanity.

She turned to Brent and said, "I need a break."

Maddie left her post and exited out of the cafeteria toward the girls' bathroom. She sat on a stool several minutes, trying to compose herself. She couldn't, absolutely wouldn't spin out of control again. But she was close, really close. *Breathe, Maddie, breathe.* Then she heard someone come into the room and figured she should get out before somebody came looking for her. She opened the stall door to find Melissa standing wide legged, hands on hips.

Maddie made her way to the sink groaning, "Why am I always getting trapped in bathrooms with Wilcox women?"

She turned and faced Melissa. The girl was obviously working up the nerve to say something.

Melissa's brown eyes reflected Phil's stubborn genes. "Do you love my dad?"

Maddie took a deep breath. Now she was getting the third degree from the daughter. "I don't think this is an appropriate subject for us to be discussing."

Melissa took an aggressive step toward Maddie. "Bull. He's my dad and if you love him, then I need to know."

Maddie sighed. She was just too tired to lie. "Yes, Melissa, I love your father very much."

Nodding her head, Melissa came to some kind of decision. "Then I think you should fight for him."

Had she heard right? "What?"

"I know all about my mom's threats to take me out of state and turn me against Dad. That's just a bunch of crap. I heard everything she said to you the other night. She doesn't have the money to go to the next county, let alone another state. Besides, I could always just call Dad and tell him where we're at. And she can't make me hate him any more. I'm not a little kid. I know what's going on. She needs to get a life, and it's not going to be with Dad."

Maddie leaned against the cool sink. "I know how important you are to your father. I don't want to be a hindrance to your relationship."

Melissa rolled her eyes. "Chill out, Miss Harris. Everybody I know has stepmothers, brothers, or sisters. And despite what Mom says, I don't think you're a bitch at all. So, if you want Dad, I think you should go for it." Then she gave Maddie a shy little grin. "I'd kinda like to be a big sister."

This sudden change of circumstances brought tears to Maddie's eyes. Phil's daughter had just bestowed her blessings. Hope surged through Maddie. She opened her arms and crushed Melissa against her chest. "Oh, sweetie, you've made me very happy."

"Hey! Cool it, I can't breathe." Melissa gently pushed away. "Just don't tell Mom that you heard anything from me. And I'm going to have to pretend I hate you around her for a while or she'll make my life hell."

"I understand. Your dad is right. You are a great kid." Maddie sniffed back welling emotion.

"Thanks. I better be getting back." Melissa edged to the door. "Say, did you know a baby robin eats fourteen feet of earthworms a day?"

Maddie smiled. "That's fascinating."

"Well, see ya."

"See ya." Maddie turned to the mirror as Melissa disappeared into the hall. She dried her eyes, squared her shoulders, and said, "Okay, Grammy, I'm going to go defend the honor of all Harris womenfolk."

Phil and Pam sat across from each other at the end of a table near the dessert area. Melissa occupied the chair next to Pam, while Doug McCall was on Phil's right. Maddie gulped as she approached her target. It was now or never.

Maddie took a position at the end of the table and looked Pam square in the eye. "Pam, I think you're a mean, nasty, sorry excuse for a woman. You're cruel, selfish, have abysmal taste in clothes and extremely poor grammar. You're not nearly good enough for a man like Phil. I hate to say this to anyone, but I think you're a slut."

Phil spewed a gulp of his apple cider over his plate.

Pam's eyes bugged and she choked down a wad of turkey. "*Ooo*, you are *so* going to pay for that."

"And furthermore," Maddie continued, "I don't intend to let you have him."

Phil growled, "What the hell is going on here?"

Pointing at Pam with disgust, Maddie said, "This woman threatened to take Melissa out of state and completely ruin your relationship with her if I didn't bow out of the picture."

Pam stood up in fury. "Liar!"

Just as Pam was about to bitch slap the tar out of Maddie, a whipped-cream topped pumpkin pie mysteriously rose off the dessert table and flew right into Pam's face.

Several people heard Grammy's raspy voice say, "Take that, you hussy."

Pam wiped the goop from her eyes and nose, grabbed a handful of mashed potatoes, and screeched, "I'll teach you!" Her arm arced back and she pitched a ball of glop at Maddie, who ducked. Becky Malone's big bosom received the splat on her one-of-a-kind decorated shirt.

Becky gasped, then marched forward with the power of a Mack truck saying, "Pam Wilcox, I've hated you ever since I caught you kissing my boyfriend in the tenth grade. You *are* a slut!" And with that she reached down into an available plate, brought up cranberry *Jello,* and smashed it in Pam's kisser.

Recognizing a good thing when he saw it, George Finn stood on top of a table and yelled, "FOOD FIGHT!" Wherein, Vince did his brotherly duty and shot a good portion of yams onto George's forehead.

Well, that was it. Pandemonium broke out as all the junior high boys heeded the call, sending Thanksgiving specialties flying willy-nilly. Amanda yelped when peas and pie landed in her perfectly coiffured hairstyle. Brent shielded Mother Bailey with his body and took most of the hits that came their way. Beau joined the fray and flung handfuls of yams in retaliation. Miss Green leaned into Mr. Manchester and moaned when she saw her carefully arranged centerpieces torn apart for ammunition.

Randy was soundly pelted as he took the mike begging, "Okay everybody, please settle down!"

Doug McCall found himself tangled in an embarrassing jumble of big boobs and thighs as he tried to separate Pam and Becky, now engaged in a full-fledged catfight.

"I'll rip out every strand of your ugly, mall hair!" Becky bellowed, twisting Pam's arm.

"You and who else, fat ass?" Pam replied, as she tried to scratch Becky's face.

Doug groaned when gouged by both combatants.

Phil calmly remained in his seat, as all hell broke loose around him. He gazed across the table at Melissa, who appeared to be the only other person in the room not involved in food flinging. She shrugged, grinned, and then quickly ducked under the table to avoid a faceful of mincemeat pie. Maddie had somehow disappeared after starting all the chaos.

He sighed and raised his iron body out of the chair. Leading with his shoulder, he knocked down George and Vince, as if mowing through the defensive line. He motioned to his scattered football players, who took his lead and began tackling wayward food warriors.

He moved through the room and barked orders. "Cut it out…that's enough…no more, buddy."

Soon, cowering mothers rose and took charge of their battling families (although more than a few women had gotten into the spirit of things) and the tide turned.

Phil stood by an exit and surveyed the room. No one appeared mortally wounded, but all needed a bath. Pam came sniffling and limping toward him on the arm of Doug McCall.

Phil put a hand out and stopped her. "Hey, is what Maddie said true? Did you threaten to keep Melissa away from me if Maddie didn't back out of my life?"

Pam wiped her drippy nose with the back of her potato-encrusted hand. "I was trying to save you from her! You and I belong together. You know we do."

Phil grabbed her shoulders, resisting the urge to shake her senseless. "Listen to me and listen to me good. You and I are *never* getting back together. I am not responsible for your life or your happiness. You've got to move on. The past is over and done. We'll always have Melissa tying us together, but beyond that, there is nothing. Zip. Zilch. Can I make myself any clearer?"

Pam's lip twisted. "You're just hot for that school bitch. It's all her fault."

Jeez, talking to this woman was like slamming into a brick wall of illogic, but he felt a need to set her straight. "And another thing. Don't you ever try to use Melissa against me again. She and I have come to a good understanding. I won't allow you to use her as a tool of your hatred. If I have to, I will go back to court for custody and this time I think I'll win. So, let's just manage a working relationship and cut the rest of the crap. You get me?"

Sniveling in defeat, Pam muttered, "You can be a real asshole."

Phil shook his head and stepped back. Pathetic. "Take her home, will you, Doug?"

McCall tugged her out of the room. "Sure. Come on, Pam. I'll bet you'll feel a lot better when you get all that pie and mascara off your face."

Phil looked for Maddie among the recovering crowd. A honey blond head rose slowly from under a table and he watched her emerge from her hiding place unscathed by food missiles. Smart girl. He'd have been really pissed if she'd put their baby at risk in a stupid food fight. Their gazes met across the room and he read the uncertainty in her face as she walked toward him.

He stood, arms crossed, face expressionless as she stopped before him. "What have you got to say for yourself, Miss Harris?"

She took a deep breath. "I know I made you angry and hurt your feelings, but I didn't want to ruin your relationship with Melissa."

He considered her impassively. "So?"

She bit her lip. "You're not going to make this easy on me, are you?"

"Nope."

"Do you want me to beg? Grovel?"

"Groveling is good."

As much as she loved him, begging and groveling was too humbling and downright irritating. "You can be the most arrogant, bull-headed…"

"That doesn't sound like groveling."

Her eyes flashed. "Well, I won't grovel, but I will tell you this. I think you're a wonderful person. You have integrity, a caring heart, and you take responsibility for your actions. I admire you very much."

"That sounds like a job recommendation. How do you *feel* about me, Maddie?"

This was it. True confession time. She reached out and held his hands, giving in to the need to touch him. "I love you, Phil. I love your wonderful, broad chest and your big, strong arms. Just looking at you, makes me warm all over. I love the way you tease me and tear through my defenses. I feel like you're my missing half. You make me a complete woman. If you don't marry me, I'm afraid I'll turn into a spindly, mean, old maid."

His eyes softened. "Funny. You make me feel like the man I'm supposed to be." He gripped her hands tighter. "When you told me you didn't love me, it felt like a punch in the gut."

"I'm sorry."

"It made me realize just how much I love you. I didn't know how much I wanted you, until I thought I couldn't have you." He tugged her closer to him. "This will be for keeps, babe. I want you by my side. I want that smart mouth of yours on mine when I feel like kissing a woman. If you sign on for this job, it's for life, sweetheart."

Maddie's blue eyes misted. "Sounds good to me."

His arms wound around her as he said, "Come here, cupcake." Then he kissed her in front of God and most of the population of Beaver Cove.

Epilogue

It's like Déjà vu all over again

Yogi Berra

Phil flung the quilt on the sand. Then he placed the wine and glasses on the cottony surface. He lay back on the blanket and waited for his wife to join him under the full moon. God, that moon, filling the sky over the shimmering lake. He could see the dark craters against the white light that radiated into unending space, so similar to that night a year ago, when he first encountered the Moon Goddess. So much had happened in that year. The bitter, beaten, drunken ex-football player had transformed into an upbeat husband, coach, and teacher.

Damn, you're a lucky man, thought Phil Wilcox.

"Did you remember the glasses?" Maddie's voice sailed across the yard from the kitchen door.

"Got 'em. I'm waiting, woman!"

He turned over on his stomach and saw the lithe figure of his wife, now recovered from childbirth, heading his way across the dark yard.

She stopped at the edge of the blanket and placed a monitor down. "Your son is finally asleep. We'll be able to hear him if he wakes up. Of course, Lucifer would come and get us anyway."

He watched her walk to the water's edge. She lifted her hair and craned her neck. "It's so humid. I could really use a swim."

"Go for it, Moon Goddess."

She turned around slowly to face him in the silvery dark light and smiled a knowing, seductive smile. Her hands found the buttons of her blouse as she danced a strip tease shedding her shirt, shorts, and under clothes. Salome taking off the seven veils. He felt himself rising to the occasion and enjoyed moments of mental foreplay, knowing how she would feel, anticipating her delicious milky scent.

She seemed to glide over to him. She knelt down and engulfed him with a mind-blowing sensuous kiss, bearing no resemblance to the Prim-and-Proper Miss Harris whatsoever.

"Catch me if you can, Dream Man." She tore away from him, laughed, and ran into the water, her gorgeous bare bottom glinting in the moonlight as she dove in.

Phil stood and left his clothes in a pile on the sand.

The pair splashed and played in the Ozark lake like a couple of country kids until their moves became decidedly more grown up. Phil lifted Maddie off her feet and carried his Moon Goddess to her soft makeshift bed.

Laying her down he said, "You have such a great ass."

"Oh, Coach Wilcox, you just melt a girl with your sweet talk."

"Shut up, cupcake." His mouth swept hers as she pulled him down and tangled her white legs between his brawny thighs.

And the air filled with iridescent glitter as they entwined themselves on the magic carpet of Grammy's quilt, twisting, swirling, loving under the satisfied gaze of that ole Devil Moon.

Also Available from

Echelon Press

Ain't Love Grand?

By

Dana Taylor

Chapter One

The screen door banged behind me as I stepped out onto my porch that June humid morning. Holding a cup of lemon grass tea, I inhaled the rising daybreak scents of honeysuckle and humus in rural Oklahoma. Orion, my big old yellow cat, wound his chubby body around my legs demanding his daily greeting. He flipped over on his back, exposing his fluffy striped belly to be scratched. Named for a hunting god, Orion lived up to his name, often laying slain rodents or birds at my feet.

"Good morning, Mr. O," I said, burrowing my fingers into his silky fur. "Much as I'd love to spend the day playing with you, I've got to get down to the garden before the sun withers all the herbs to brown twigs."

After a quick stretch, I finished off the tea, slipped into ratty tennis shoes, and plunked a tattered gardening hat on my head. Now that I was approaching the big three-o birthday, I fought the first signs of crows feet. A very stylish OU (University of Oklahoma) T-shirt and matching shorts completed my ensemble.

Feeling an urgency to get to my plants, I grabbed a basket, hopped down the steps of my old Victorian home, and headed across the front yard. Huge elms offered welcome shade as I strode toward my neighbor's adjacent property where I maintained my medicinal herb garden. Coming over the rise, I heard an engine roar that completely drowned out the morning calls of the blue jays and mockingbirds. A pair of cardinals lit out as scampering squirrels shook the top of the cottonwood trees.

I looked down the hill, past the creek. Where yesterday there had been a lush, green meadow, the land was now stripped clear, exposing the bright red clay below. A monster machine pushed the life away and laid waste to my precious herb garden.

I took off full tilt toward the metal contraption. It had already destroyed about half the plot. Noise and dust choked my senses as I ran into the path of the machine.

"Stop! Stop! What are you doing? Stop!" The guy working the controls could neither see nor hear me as I was almost swept into his debris.

Suddenly, I flew head over heels, tumbling through the dirt, weeds, and mangled herbs, the air knocked out of me as I hit the hard ground. Rolling out of harm's way, my body tangled with another person–a very large *male* person.

As we came to a stop, I was lying in the man's arms, coughing as I cleared my befuddled brain.

"Are you all right?" he asked. His face was a bit blurry, what with my eyes watering from the red dust.

"I think so," I sputtered and sat up.

He looked at me with concern and irritation. "Are you out of your mind? You could have been killed getting in the way like that. What were you doing? Who are you?"

The evil machine jerked to a stop. The man sitting in the dirt beside me was covered in dust and I deduced he must have tackled me to escape the Jaws of Death or whatever the machine was called.

"Played a little football in high school, did you?" I asked.

Concern left his face altogether with my cheeky reply. He stood up, dusted himself off, and offered me a hand.

"You didn't answer my question. Who are you?" he repeated.

I steadied my wobbly legs and studied him. I'd seen a few pictures of him in the newspaper, but they hadn't done him justice. He possessed a certain innate power that made me back away. In the photo headlines he'd always worn a suit, usually with the Oklahoma wind flapping his tie as he exited a county courthouse. Blurry photos hadn't revealed the firm granite chin or the flinty steel blue eyes. The mighty Jason Brooks, defender of high profile criminals, loomed before me in the flesh. Actually, he wore jeans and a western shirt, but his hair was too well cut to be anything but a weekend cowboy.

"I'm your neighbor, Mr. Brooks, Perse, uh, Persephone Jones. I live on the other side of the creek."

I walked toward what was left of my garden.

The operator of the mechanical beast hopped out of his seat and asked, "Mr. Brooks, do you want me to finish?"

I turned quickly. "No! Please, I had no idea you'd be developing out here. I've been watching the house go up closer to the highway. I was going to talk to you about the garden."

Bending down, I began harvesting, stuffing leaves and seeds in the makeshift cradle of my shirt. My eyes swept the scarred landscape for my basket.

I glanced at the two perplexed men. "I know this isn't my land, but no one has ever minded my garden. There are some things here that take years to mature. I've got herbs growing that you can't find anywhere else on this continent. People have sent me the seeds and...."

Brooks had heard enough of my rambling. "So, you know that you are trespassing? Is that right?"

"Well, I guess, technically, yes. But I've been cultivating this garden for years. It's very important that–"

"Look, Ms. Jones," Brooks abruptly cut in, "this is now my land and will soon be a landing strip for my plane. I'll give you exactly ten minutes to finish pulling up your weeds and then Andrews here is going to get his job done. I've got an appointment. You'll have to plant your garden on your own property." He thrust his cowboy hat on and walked with a slight limp toward the Expedition parked in the field.

His attitude ticked me off. "Gee, it was swell meeting you, Mr. Brooks. I'll be sure to bring you over a plate of chocolate chip cookies when you move in."

He stopped and slowly pivoted, pinning me with his best hard-ass lawyer stare. I turned my nose up in the air and marched back to my mauled garden.

I put the obliging Mr. Andrews to work and took more than the allotted ten minutes to harvest my remaining herbs. I returned home laden with all the plants my basket, arms, and shirt could hold.

Inside my greenhouse, I set about saving the survivors, grumbling to myself. Why was a high society lawyer moving into Peeler, anyway? He didn't fit in with the common folks. Would he swap stories with the old geezers at the local greasy spoon? I think not. Arrogant, steely-eyed, handsome son of a...

I dumped soil into pots, pressed precious roots into place, and hoped for the best. Once the plants were tended, I headed into the house for a much needed shower. My naked body revealed scrapes and bruises from my morning adventures. Did Mr. Brooks have a few sore spots, too?

By nine o'clock I was rumbling down the country road in my beloved, rusty 1982 Ford pick-up, Lizzie. Two hundred thousand miles and still going strong. A whiff of freshly cut hay drifted into the open widow. Fields gave way to a small grocery and one pump gas station. Soon historic brick buildings came into view. Seeing downtown Peeler's trendy revival of antique shops, odd museums, community theatres, and restaurants always filled me with quiet pride. So much more character than the nearby urban sprawl of Oklahoma City.

Coming back to my hometown to run the family health food store had been a good move. Familiar faces and loving arms had been a balm through the phases of grief. Reflecting on sad twists of fate gave me a moment of wistful longing, but I shook it off. I had moved on, filled my days with purpose. Life was pleasant, even if it lacked passion.

I parked Lizzie in front, where everyone could prominently see the sign on her tail gate–"Mt. Olympus Natural Healing Center, Persephone Jones, Herbalist." Being named for the Goddess of the Seasons had destined me to follow nature's way.

A bell tinkled as I breezed in the door. "Morning, Mavis!" I said and strolled toward the back to put my things down. The scents and sights of the shop engulfed my senses and instilled quiet contentment. Here in this dot of the universe I served the community with my talents and knowledge. Essential oils diffused the air with pungent healing power. Strains of dulcimer music calmed the nerves. Rows of supplements and literature filled half the floor space while a juice bar and comfortable couches invited visitors to stay a while. A blue door welcomed weary customers to relax in the massage room.

"Mornin', darlin'." Mavis waved at me over a rack of literature. Her beautiful, black skin glowed. She moved into the aisle, placing her hands on ample three-children hips. Somewhere along the way, I'd become another one her chicks.

She gave me the once-over. "You look like a tourist advertisement today. *Mmm*, what I'd give for that long pretty hair."

Funny, I always thought being able to fashion gorgeous corn rows or beaded braids would be great fun. My untamed auburn hair defied clippies and assorted hair jewelry. But it went along with the gauzy granny dresses I wore to appeal to the tourist trade. But truth be known, I dressed for comfort, not style.

Mavis took a closer inspection. "Why, girl, what happened to your face? Did Orion get too playful?"

"I rolled around in the dirt this morning with my new neighbor, Jason Brooks."

Her eyes widened. She nodded and smiled. "Oh, yeah, this is going to be good. I'll pour the raspberry tea and then you are gonna tell Mavis *all* about it."

She found my escapade with Mr. Brooks down right hilarious and soon filled the shop with the sound of her raucous laughter. By the time I finished my tale, I'd gotten past anger to the sense of the ridiculous and laughed along.

"If I had any hopes of appearing smart and sophisticated for my hot-shot new neighbor, I completely blew it. He thinks I'm a flake. Of course, I think he's an uptight, stuffed shirt, even if he was disguised in cowboy clothes."

Mavis' eyes gleamed. "I'll bet he looked mighty fine in those clothes."

I sighed. Sighed for things out of reach and beyond my ken–like high society lawyers. "That he did, Mavis. That he did."

Devil Moon Cake

(Devilishly Delicious)

Recipe from Deborah Oakes

1 chocolate sheet cake baked with 3 oz of cream cheese
1/2 jar fudge topping
1/2 jar caramel or butterscotch topping
1/2 can sweetened condensed milk
6 large candy bars of your choice
1 tub whipped topping, softened

Bake a Devil's food or German Chocolate sheet cake adding 3 oz. softened cream cheese to batter. Do not remove cake from the pan.

When it has cooled, make many holes in the top with the handle of a long wooden spoon. Take turns pouring the fudge, caramel and condensed milk over the top and let each soak in before pouring the next. When all the pouring is done, break up 3 of the candy bars and sprinkle over the top of the cake. Then cover with whipped topping. Take the rest of the candy bars, break them up and sprinkle over the top.

This cake is sinfully delicious!

Meet the author:

Born in California, Dana Taylor attended the University of Redlands and graduated with a Bachelor's degree in theatre, with a minor in writing. She met her husband while on an internship at the Oklahoma Theater Center and has lived in Oklahoma since 1976. While raising two daughters, she added to the family coffers through a variety of occupations, including a five-year stint as her husband's secretary in his family law practice. She has had articles printed in the *Ladies Home Journal* and various Christian magazines. Her interest in theater led to joining the O.K. City Chorus of Sweet Adelines in 1997. She wrote many show scripts through the years and was named Sweet Adeline of the Year in 2003. As a member of the Romance Writers of America, she has been a finalist in several contests, taking first place in the 2003 "Gotcha" contest for her entry *Princess Robin.* Echelon Press has published her first two contemporary comedies, *Ain't Love Grand?* and *That Devil Moon.*

You can visit Dana at

www.DanaTaylor.net

Printed in the United States
34793LVS00001B/55-108

9 781590 803448